Choosing

THE AUTHOR

Diana Pullein-Thompson has written numerous children's books for which she is world famous. As Diana Farr she has written two biographical works. Her best-selling memoirs of a country childhood, *Fair Girls and Grey Horses*, written with her two sisters, was published in September 1996. She is married, with two grown-up children, and lives in Surrey.

Choosing

DIANA PULLEIN-THOMPSON

a&b

This edition published in Great Britain in 1997 by
Allison & Busby Ltd
114 New Cavendish Street
London W1M 7FD

First published in Great Britain by The Bodley Head in 1988

Copyright © by Diana Farr 1988

The moral right of the author is asserted

This book is sold subject to the condition that it shall not, by
way of trade or otherwise, be lent, resold, hired out or
otherwise circulated without the publisher's prior written
consent in any form of binding or cover other than that in
which it is published and without a similar condition including
this condition being imposed upon the subsequent purchaser.

A catalogue record for this book is available from the
British Library

ISBN 0 74900 279 4

Printed and bound in Great Britain by
WBC Book Manufacturers Ltd
Bridgend, Mid Glamorgan

*For all my Longborough friends
and in memory of
Betty Arkell*

Chapter One

THE FRIENDLY policeman left and I longed to discuss the nasty incident with someone else, for he had clearly attributed my story to an old lady's inflamed imagination, while taking notes assiduously to make me believe otherwise. I was very frightened, and when I asked that bars be put across my windows he said he would send along a carpenter. He was humouring me. I could see by his fatherly smile that he felt as though he was comforting a little girl who feared ghosts if her bedroom floorboards creaked at night.

Very soon I started to pray with a desperation which had rarely accompanied my petitions to the Almighty since my friend Helen lay dying in the sanatorium. This time, kneeling by my bed, I asked that I should escape from my self-imposed exile, for the terror of the night had shown me that if I continued to shun my fellow humans, apart from poor little Ellen whom I saw regularly, I should become as mad as the policeman imagined me to be. While I prayed, my cat Marco, who is half Siamese and very beautiful, played with my hair and dabbed my face with chocolate-coloured paws.

A convent education had taught me that God sometimes says no and that a sinful life is not conducive to a yes. And yet when I rose at last from my knees I experienced a sense of tranquillity that quietened my fear.

When the grey-headed carpenter came to measure up for the bars, which were to be made by the blacksmith in Moreton-in-Marsh, I thought he might be the God-sent doorway to a new life, for I found myself chatting to him as though he were an old friend. Wanting now to establish myself as a person in my own right, I even showed him several watercolours I had painted when I first came to the village, but, although he made polite comments, I could see that I had left it too late. To him I was a rather pathetic old lady, who invented stories about herself and would soon need help from the social services. In his experience successful artists did not hide away in cottages. My art was another fantasy. Next time he came he thought I would probably claim to be an admiral's daughter.

Neither the policeman nor the carpenter understood that terror can sometimes change lives for the better, that when in the small hours of the morning I had faced death, life had become supremely important to me, that maybe God, if there is a God, had sent the intruder for that very purpose.

The carpenter's heavy footsteps had faded on the winter road and I went to the gilded oval mirror that hangs above my dressing table to study my face. The Anglican nuns who ran the mirrorless orphanage and school in which I had grown up had taught me that vanity is a sin; it is the inner not the outer self that brings a soul closer to God. And after Oliver died, I had, by contracting out of life, returned to that dictum, as people past middle age may return to childhood to remember with wry regrets their parents' homilies.

The mirror showed me a dishevelled, witch-like creature with a small somewhat bony face, a dominant nose and a thatch of thick white hair. But when I smiled I saw that my mouth could still show mirth. And when I waved I noted that my hands were not without a certain style. But it was the brightness of my eyes which held me, for in their piercing blueness I saw the vitality of a much younger woman. Perhaps, I thought, it was my eyes, seen some time, somewhere, that had tempted the intruder. I sat down, found some ancient make-up among a pile of letters in a dressing-table drawer, and tried it on my face. I would not pray again for a while, for even as a child, I had been struck by the thought that God must tire of all the abject apologies, the remorse, the pleadings, the petitions, and the promises of endless love and devotion, that are put to him morning, noon and night. "Ask once, then shut up and wait. Pestering is bad manners," I told myself aloud. Lipstick, a touch of rouge, clever work with an eyebrow pencil miraculously softened my face ... but the wild hair ... I found scissors, and explaining my motives to Marco, who watched me with rapt attention, I started to trim and shape the white locks. "After all," I said, "God helps those who help themselves."

Two weeks of winter passed after the carpenter's visit, while I increased my radio listening to bring me up to date on world affairs and paid attention to my appearance; and then it happened. There was a confident knock on my front door and there stood James Keene with the wind blowing his fair hair into a halo about his head. His blue eyes were darker than mine and his skin was wonderfully new, hardly lined. It was years since I had admired anyone's appearance quite so much.

"Christabelle Lang?" he enquired.

"That's me."

"I'm James Keene," he held out a hand, "I've come to ask a favour."

"A favour?" My voice crackled. But I probably smiled because I have a weakness for pleasant young men.

"It's about Barney Copeland – you knew him I believe?"

"Long since dead. Come in." I opened wide the door. "I'm afraid the place smells of cat. I don't clean it very often. Do you mind?"

"It smells great to me." He stooped to avoid banging his head on the lintel.

"You sound nervous. Don't be intimidated by an old woman. There was a nasty incident here a couple of weeks ago, so please excuse the bars and do take off that coat. Barney's friends are my friends."

"I'm writing a thesis."

Then, forgetting for a moment that he was undoubtedly the answer to a prayer, I said I couldn't help him because I wasn't academic. "I can't remember dates, only conversations. I'm so sorry, but I am afraid you've wasted your time. Have you come far?"

"London," he said with a small deprecatory smile. "I don't need an academic, not a bit. I need flavour not facts. There are not many people of the period left. If you could bear to say just a few words about Barney I should be so grateful. To remember conversations in detail is a great achievement."

No one had flattered me for a long, long time, or needed me, and how could I turn away this polite young man when he had come so far just to see me? Yet I knew Barney would have hated him. "No bloody vices, too bloody sure of himself, bland and soft as a W.I. sponge sandwich," would have been Barney's inevitable verdict. So should I talk to James Keene who would, unlike the policeman and the carpenter, value my words and write them down neatly in the note book which I now saw he clasped in his right hand?

He waited, standing in my hallway, a hopeful expression on his narrow well-bred face.

"My thesis is enormously important to me and, if I get things right, it may make a significant contribution to art history," he continued after a pause, and then I heard my voice say, "Why Barney, always Barney? Why not devote a bit to me? I've never pushed myself before, but once upon a time people thought my work was as good as his. I remember...." My voice trailed off, as an old well-hidden jealousy stirred stickily like a snail after hibernation.

"It's a question of fashion, and taste. Taste is very fickle," the young man said, struggling out of his coat.

"Could things change, as with Augustus and Gwen John?"

"Who can tell?" he gesticulated vaguely with fine well-kept hands. "Judgements are so selective. My tutor feels Barney is a good idea. Not much work has been done on him, you see. But of course any study on him must include an assessment of you and your painting. Your influence was crucial to his development."

I laughed at that, too raucously for the old woman that I was.

"You don't agree?" He hung his top coat neatly on the bannister.

"No, of course not. Barney was always his own man, as obstinate and intractable as a mule."

"It's a fascinating period," said James, missing the chance to push me further.

"Public school?" I asked, suddenly feeling as though I had known him years.

"Sorry, what did you say?"

"Public school are you? Did you go to public school?"

"Well, yes, sort of ... Does it matter?"

"Of course it does. I like to place people, everyone of my

generation does. The fact that I was unplaceable myself doesn't matter a hoot. Sit down, relax. You look like a young man about to promote an insurance policy for the first time!"

And at that moment the sharpness of my retort did not seem to matter, because I could see that we were striking up a rapport, something I had not experienced for years.

"Christ!" said James

"Now, now, mind your words. I was convent reared." I was enjoying myself. "Hang on, while I make coffee, black or white?"

"Would it be an awful bother if I asked for half and half?"

"Khaki."

"Great."

"Great?" I asked. "Like an emperor or a king or a palace?"

"All right, I give in – *delicious*, is that better?"

"Much," I said. "Sugar?" And I thought, we are getting on like a house on fire.

"One spoonful, please." He left his chair to look at one of my pictures. "I like this – the light, and those hills ..."

"Oh, the 'Night Sky' – not quite up to scratch. I've done better. It's a bit insipid, I think, don't you?" I pretended not to care. "Too wishywashy. I never *did* achieve what I wanted in my Night series. The whole enterprise was a vast mistake, but," I said, handing James his coffee, "you've come to talk about Barney not me. Barney's vitality was remarkable and even when he hit the bottle, which he often did, his sureness of hand was incredible."

"Was it drink that broke up your ..."

"Relationship. Isn't that the in word? But I don't want to talk about that. Tell me a bit more about yourself, Mr. Keene."

"I should be flattered if you would call me James," he said, smiling at me as I imagined a grandchild would. "I grew up in South Oxfordshire, near Henley. I went to Tonbridge School where I was bullied mercilessly because I looked effete, and then to the Courtauld Institute of Art."

"Anthony Blunt – *Sir* Anthony Blunt," I said.

"Sorry, I don't quite catch your meaning." James leaned forward eagerly – he possessed an obvious and rather endearing eagerness – and smiled again encouragingly.

"Anthony Blunt was there, I met him you know – the spy.

Cambridge Apostle or something. A bit precious, didn't like women. You could tell that a mile off."

"But a brilliant scholar, despite everything, and a superb teacher," James said. "I'm an art historian, Miss Lang."

"Which means a critic," I said. "Shame on you."

"Oh, isn't that a bit hard? We assess rather than criticise. We place artists in a historical context. We promote too, take the wide view, bring neglected painters' work to the foreground."

"You could fool me," I said.

And so we went on, not getting down to what he really wanted to know, but sparring. I side-stepped every vital question, not to be capricious but because I could not bear to relive the Barney days again. After about an hour James rose, smiling politely although he knew that I had prevaricated disgracefully. (But then why should an old woman cough up the beans just because a well-placed young man comes asking?) His blue eyes looked straight at me, no wavering, as a cat looks when it has been offered tinned fish instead of the fresh salmon in the refrigerator, and he asked whether he might come again. "Or would that be very boring for you? Is it, I mean, too much of an imposition?" After a long pause I said I wasn't sure whether I could help him. "It means raking over the ashes and some of them still smoulder and may scorch my fingers."

"Too painful?"

"You could say that."

Sensing my hesitation, he suggested we might skirt round the tricky bits.

"Even the tiniest morsels of information could be invaluable to me," he said winningly, "and it would be so nice to bring Barney Copeland back into the foreground, and you, too, for that matter."

"Now you are throwing the bait," I said. "Now you are flattering me."

He put on his top coat. "No, not flattering. I should love to see more of your work. I should love to talk to you again if you'll let me come."

"You are so young – dare I say privileged? – that I am not sure you will understand. It was tough," I told him.

"I'm sure it was," he smiled down at me, "and I suppose I do seem very green. I shall quite understand if you say *no*."

But you won't, I thought. You'll go away and curse and wonder whether you should choose another subject and Barney will have to wait a little longer for a new appraisal.

"I'll do my best," I said. "Please come again."

"I'm so glad," he said. "I'm sorry I didn't write first, but people in the know said you would not answer a letter."

And then I heard my voice say, "I'm a bit of a recluse, you see. I don't meet many people these days. I expect I've turned into a self-centred old woman."

"No, not at all," he beamed, like a ten-year-old who has been given his first cricket bat or glass of champagne or whatever he wants most in the world. "In the meantime would you, could you, write down something about yourself? Dig in your memory, make notes. I should love to know how you began, how it all started, at what moment you decided to become a painter. That would be great," he said. "No, not great, *marvellous*. I'll send you a postcard about the next time."

He shook my hand firmly, stepped into an old brown Mini, started the engine and waved before he put her into first gear, and as he drove away, up the village street, I thought: I'm being dragged back into mid-stream on Barney's back. Is it always to be on Barney's back?

And in the evening when the frost came and stayed like splintered plastic on the window panes, when the moon rode a starlit sky like a lone ship on a deserted sea, and Marco, my cat, purred on my knees, I began writing, trying to catch the very moments James wanted.

I was at first a little whimsical.

Think of me, dear James, as you read, I began self-consciously. Small, mouse-haired, shy; think of me, a Cinderella in a grand house with marble staircase and gallery. Think of me in the morning room with its painted ceiling and satinwood furniture and a view across the park where the bare oaks march two abreast like soldiers across the wintry landscape. The First World War has not yet burst upon the Western world; the land is rich; the years stretch ahead, changeless and full of plenty in the eyes of the privileged.

"The girl is a genius, see how she has caught the light," my kind hostess cries, pointing. "And it is the first time she has handled watercolours, the very first!"

The artist stands back, then moves closer; he puffs out his cheeks and blows through his nose. To me waiting, blushing, hands twisting together behind my back, the room seems full of his self-importance. There are rings on two of his fingers which are short and plump. A little sweat beads his forehead.

"Magnificent," he exclaims at last in a German accent. "Remarkable for so young a girl. Who is her teacher?"

"No one," my hostess replies. "She comes from the children's home. Her people..."

There is a pause. No one knows what to say about my people who were clearly unsatisfactory since they abandoned me.

"She has it in the blood," the artist says. "Always it must be in the blood. The lines could be firmer; the execution is here, for example, too loose, but for a child..."

Naive as chicken, the four Randolph children, all girls, gather round me.

"You'll be famous. We'll see your pictures in the Royal Academy. You'll dine with kings and visit Paris and Munich. You'll be rich."

Their materialism appals me, although I could not have named it as such then. This artist who has come in a yellow trap is unlike anyone I have met before; a man who would have shocked the Anglican nuns striving to bring me up as a demure and self-effacing girl. In his blazer's cloth the scent of wine and cigar smoke mingle uneasily with the cloying sweetness of some foreign toilet water. His full, somewhat flamboyant side whiskers suggest to me an unhealthy preoccupation with his own appearance and match almost exactly the grey eyes that bulge like old tennis balls behind steel-rimmed glasses perched precariously on his pugnacious nose. For a brief moment he picks at gold-filled teeth which lean this way and that like terraced houses propping each other after a bomb explosion. At first glance he looks to me seedy beyond measure but his words, spoken with such gusto, such absolute certainty, send my aspirations soaring into unexplored realms of glory and fame. I wouldn't – I couldn't – be like him as a person. But my art....

In this house I am both part of the family and an alien. For years Lady Randolph has charitably taken in a child from the nearby orphanage for a week at Christmas. This is my third visit, extended because of my love of drawing, for she is known as a patron of the arts. In my stocking this year watercolours, a palette and paint brushes have been added to the charcoal, pencils and cartridge paper which have previously mingled with the sweets and chocolates.

In the morning room the praised picture leans against a chair. Painted straight on to paper, it depicts a bare wood; naked trunks, grey as elephants, lead the eye up through the twisting branches to the whirling winter sky. It is a study in grey except for the floor of leaves which glows like burnished copper here, a myriad gold there, for these leaves have been touched but not yet sobered by winter's frost.

"The wind," the German artist says. "Do you not sense the wind? The wind is profoundly felt by the viewer of these trees. See how it moves these boughs, while the trunks remain rigid? This message tells us that even the mighty trees feel sometimes helpless against the merciless force of nature's elements. Nature is supreme, and yet nature herself trembles as the clouds reel across the sky. And what clouds! Fantastic! My child, I forecast a great future for you."

He puts his spectacles back into his breast pocket with a finality which suggests no one will equal the expertise and wisdom of his pronouncement.

Fire-hot the blushes ran across my cheeks, as Katherine, the eldest Randolph child, nudges me into gratitude.

"Thank you, thank you very much." I am suddenly bantam small; like Gulliver I shrink, for seconds ago my head had been sky high, but now I feel an impostor for, encouraged by Katherine, I had merely painted what I saw, and intended no message.

"We are proud of you, Christie." Lady Randolph bends her graceful neck to look into my eyes, so that I catch a whiff of her Parisian scent, and the warmth of her breath is on my cheek. "My dear, I shall take you to the Tate, for I am determined you shall see the Turners in the new Duveen Gallery, and, of course, to the National."

"Show her Bruegel," the artist says. "Let her feel the

strength of his colours, give her time, for she must widen her own palette and, if you're going to the National Gallery, forget the Italians – she has had more than enough religion – and show her the Holbeins. What a master! My God!"

It is strange, I decide watching him, that so educated a man should take Our Lord's name in vain, and speak so dismissively of the faith which has so long been central to my life. Will God strike him down? Do the flames of hell await him? I look anxiously at Lady Randolph, whom I adore from a distance, and see how, smiling, the full lips contradict the delicacy of her other features, like a loophole in a careful statement, suggesting that despite her composed elegance, a loss of self-control is possible.

When the senior girls start their last year at the orphanage and the nuns say, as they always do: "Some of you will marry; some of you will become servants or nurses or teachers; others will answer the highest calling and find their vocation in the service of Our Lord," I shall cry inwardly, "Not me, never me. I shall be an artist." And the fear of being chosen to follow in the steps of Sisters Mary or Thérèse or, worse still, Mother Superior, will recede.

In this mansion I have been corrupted by a heathen, I tell myself excitedly. Now I shall indulge my passion more often and more openly, for since my friend Helen died, drawing has filled every void in life. It has become both my escape and my therapy. The hymn-singing, the prayers, the chapel's stained-glass windows drive me to pencil and paper. Not God. And now I know why. "It is in the blood." Helen had sickness running through her veins; I have art.

And now I have this, I thought, putting down my pen. James's encouragement has been a cerebral release and although the words describe my childhood as seen through adult eyes, they are no less accurate for that; they touch nerve ends present at the time but unrecognised by me.

Chapter Two

JAMES Keene wrote me not a postcard but a thank-you letter, in a small academic hand which suggested an inhibited nature, a complicated character protected by a veneer of good manners. Barney's earthiness would fascinate James because it opened windows on a side of life James would not admit to within himself. He would be a voyeur.

James suggested a date for our next meeting, which I accepted. "I have scribbled a few pages for you," I wrote back. "All rather high-flown, but I think accurate."

When he arrived I was very pleased to see him – the way the old are when they meet the young so long as the young seem to care.

"It is kind of you to put down your thoughts," he said.

"Actually, it did me good. Perhaps I should have gone in for psychoanalysis, perhaps that would have straightened me out," I said.

"I didn't know you were crooked," he retorted as he hung his old brown top coat on the bannister.

"You know what I mean. Don't act silly," I said in a Gloucestershire accent. "I'll make coffee. Here, read these notes."

"Fascinating," he said when I came back with two mugs on a tray. "Absolutely fascinating. But do tell me, who *were* your people?"

"I haven't the faintest," I said, "and I don't care a hoot." But my voice rose just a little so that I knew I was lying. For recently I had begun to care about my roots. Indeed, I often put myself in my mother's shoes, and wondered endlessly about her appearance, circumstances and background.

"But you went to Paris. You must have had a passport, for which you needed a birth certificate."

"How did you know I went to Paris?"

"From Barney's letters; he mentions how it affected your painting."

"You have his letters? Which letters?"

"To June; they're in the Tate Archives."

"How awful!"

"Why? They're for posterity."

"When he wrote to June they were for her and her alone."

"Well, she let him down then," James said.

"Ratted on him, wretched woman."

"There's nothing compromising in them." James spoke soothingly. "But he does mention that your time in Paris was not helpful. I can't remember the exact context."

"Oh forget it," I said. "I refuse to be upset. When you think of the starving in Ethiopia, what does a letter matter?"

"Exactly," agreed James. "But what I was saying is that there must have been some name on the birth certificate."

"Emily Lang – no father. I think she may have been a maid, because one day when the Randolph's children's nurse accused me of putting on airs above my station – sounding my aitches and all that nonsense – she said something about my mother being no better than a scullery maid."

"That doesn't mean she *was* a scullery maid, though, does it? I mean acting is not *being*." James's eyes became very bright again, like the eyes of a perky robin who has caught sight of a worm, and he leaned forward as though he thought he was on to something. "And the nuns, didn't the nuns drop hints?"

"Not the black nuns," I said, "but once in a moment of inebriation – God knows where she laid her hands on drink in that austere place – a grey nun – they did the hard work, the black nuns the spiritual – this grey sister (I refer to the habit) told me I had a fine father. And I said, 'Is he alive?' and she said, yes, 'and kicking', and then, of course, I wondered why he never came to see me, never wrote me a letter. I felt rejected."

"Naturally. Who wouldn't in the circumstances?" said James. "Would you like me to dig around?"

"What do you mean?"

"Go back and find out who Emily's parents were. Get their birth and marriage certificates. Visit the village where you were born. If there was a scandal, some old lady might remember her own mother gossiping. People can cover up so far, but not completely."

"The thought frightens me. But yes, go ahead. Yes, please do. I should like ghosts laid before I die."

"Thanks. I'll report back."

"And," I said, on second thoughts, "I want to know everything, however terrible. I mean if my mother was a murderess, it doesn't matter, not now."

"Fine, that's the spirit."

"But James," I said. "You are researching Barney, not me."

"True," he replied carefully, "but any new material on you will be of interest. I might publish an article."

"In some chi-chi journal like *The Burlington* or *Apollo*?" I asked. "I don't think scandal amuses their readers."

"It wouldn't be scandal, just facts, really, biographical data," said James airily.

"Oh, how cold you make it sound! Blood and tears, passion and sweat! A bastard is created; a baby girl searches for the breasts of her mother, who will give her to the nuns. And it all ends up as data!"

"I was trying to play it down. I thought that was what you wanted. Of course I can include the passion, if I have evidence."

"*I* am the evidence," I shouted. "Me!" I hit my chest. "A hoary old woman with the nose of a witch. Some of the local children think I *am* a witch. Did you know that? It's because I have a besom leaning against my door and I talk to my flowers and to Marco, my cat. You haven't met Marco, have you? He keeps me sane, allows me a monologue."

"Do you draw him?"

"I used to, but I'm not a Gwen John. I've lived more than Gwen John ever did. I've been as good as married, after all."

"And you have a son."

"How did you know that?"

"People remember him. You're not as forgotten as you think. Although some think you're dead now. Tell me about the home, or was it a nunnery?"

"It was both," I said quickly. "It was a convent school with an orphanage attached. Helen, my friend, was an orphan. One of her parents died of TB, the other of typhoid. She had been in the outside world until she was nine. She had known human love whereas I was reared on the spiritual kind. The nuns hated us being fond of one another. They said close friendship between girls kept Our Lord out, but, perhaps, they really feared lesbianism."

"But do tell me," urged James, leaning forward in his chair with the beady look again on his lean, handsome face. "Do tell me, how did you get to St. Stephen's College of Art?"

"Oh, that was Lady Randolph's doing," I told him. "She wouldn't let the nuns find me a position when I was fourteen. They kept me on to teach the little ones until I was sixteen. She took me to the galleries. I think I disappointed her actually, because I was more excited by Millais and Orchardson than Turner, but she persevered. I'm sure she must have contributed handsomely to the orphanage, otherwise the nuns would never have allowed her so much leeway. Mind you, she could out-talk or out-manoeuvre anyone."

"But St. Stephen's?" James persisted, wanting, I suspected, to bring me nearer to Barney, nearer to spilling the beans.

"They liked my pictures, but the interview ... Can you imagine how nervous I was, being quizzed by three men? I wasn't used to being with men, apart from Sir Harold Randolph, who was a literary man, very sensitive but without motivation. Sir Harold treated me like a lady of importance. He opened doors for me. 'You first,' he would say in his high nasal voice, which always surprised me for I expected a deeper tone in a man. Of course it was years before I heard that Lady Randolph entertained lovers on Thursday afternoons. For a long time I thought Sir Harold's gentle courtesy was the normal treatment a man meted out to his beloved wife, and I was deeply flattered by the chivalry he showed me, a mode of behaviour he did not extend to his own children."

"So your inquisitors at St. Stephen's frightened you?"

"My dear, I was tongue-tied, sitting on my hands, leaning forward like a maid being interviewed for a situation. They took me on the strength of a pile of drawings and a couple of watercolours, and Lady Randolph's pressing enthusiasm. Perhaps she gave them money, too, I don't know. She supported all sorts of painters. In Shamely Park there were pictures by Mark Gertler, J.D. Fergusson, Stanley Spencer and Paul Nash, who really were at this time young unknowns trying to make their way."

"So you started at St. Stephen's.... Do tell me more, I'm dying to know."

"Not today, James," I said. "It's all too near the knuckle. I must have paper and pen between us. Those nuns inhibited me. You know what the Jesuits say, 'Give us a child until he's seven etc, etc.' "

"Then you'll edit," James objected. "Add colour."

"A little bit, perhaps, but not much. I swear it will be the truth as I see it."

"*Want* to see it," he said.

"No, no, I shan't turn myself into the success I wanted to be, not for a moment. To a convent girl St. Stephen's was a terrible leap into a cauldron of loose morals and seething ideas. Had I belonged to a different generation I should have suffered a nervous breakdown, but such things weren't really allowed for people like me. You prayed to Our Lord and pulled yourself together and remembered how lucky you were because you had two legs and two arms, a brain and all your senses, *and* a square meal."

"But the other students. There were some interesting people up with you – Courtney Grey, for example."

"Oh Courtney looked like a saluki dog, very aristocratic, very narrow, he reminded me of Sir Harold – the same nasal voice. Oh Courtney was kind," I declared, "with the kindness of a man who is certain of his own place in society. He knew instinctively that I was a nobody."

"Oh surely not," objected James, foolishly interrupting my flow of words. "I can't believe you were ever a nobody. Your character is far too definite."

"I'll write it down. I don't like being interrupted," I said irritably. "Let me introduce you to Marco. He's half Siamese and quite remarkable, and let me tell you about this village, where I have never quite fitted in ... "

"Don't forget your promise then," James said. "Please, and I'll let you know the result of my researches."

"I've got so used to *not* knowing that any information may be a shock, so let me down gently," I said.

He asked for photographs, and I said I would think about that, not meaning to disappoint but overcome by a fear of my own reaction in returning to a past I had so purposely jettisoned when I came to my stone hideout. Here I had hoped to forget and to hibernate until death mowed me down. I had indeed run away and now this young man with the fresh complexion and the wonderfully clear eyes was trying to drag me back to face my failures.

"You are raising matters," I said, "which I expected to meet only at the pearly gates with St. Peter at my side."

"Please think of posterity," he said. "You have a great contribution to make to learning."

"Nonsense," I cried, handing him his coat. "Now you *are* flattering me."

"Oh can't you see, Miss Lang," he exclaimed. "Can't you see that you are a living link with so much that has gone before?"

"Then," I said, "my writing will be of greater importance than anything I can tell you, because it will be straight from the horse's mouth and in my own hand. And now I suppose it may be published after I'm dead, whatever my wishes – in the interest," I added with a touch of good-natured mockery in my voice, "of learning and posterity, along with any letters which may turn up on the market, and I shall be assessed by art historians as a minor artist who is only important because her writings now throw fresh light on the major ones. All right, all right, don't cringe, James. I'll co-operate, but in my own way and my own time, and I'll edit as I see fit. Now that is the Riot Act. I'm not bitter at all, only realistic, and happy to have you to talk to and rail at now and then. Please come to see me again. I should like that, very much, and forgive an old lady her tart tongue."

He smiled, held out a hand. "I understand," he said. "Of course I understand. Please write something about St. Stephen's for me. Anything you put down will be invaluable. May I come to see you in ten days' time?"

"Yes," I said. I would write the date on a card and stick it on the dresser. "Now take care how you drive. There's ice on the road."

I watched him go, felt lonely as his car turned the corner and disappeared out of sight, and was suddenly angry with myself for having disappeared from the London art world. Johnson was right: tired of London, tired of life. But now suddenly I wasn't tired any more. At eighty-two I was reaching out towards the mainstream, my long, long convalescence over. Tomorrow I would catch a bus as I did once a fortnight and go to the market in Moreton-in-Marsh and stock up with vegetables and fruit, soap powder, indigestion pills and loo-paper – everything I needed for the house, and a packet of chocolate wholemeal biscuits for James's next visit. I would take my basket trolley and join all the other old women jostling for a place in the queues at the stalls. But now all the world would be new for me again, as it must be for an artist whose vision must never age or ossify.

I scrambled myself eggs, ate two apples, fed Marco and reached for my pen, for I was determined to write while the adrenalin remained in my system. St. Stephen's College of Art was in the Fulham Road; red brick, with frowning Victorian windows, a cobbled courtyard. Very austere it was with simple minton tiles for the entrance hall, and elsewhere naked, dark-varnished boards whose risen nails tore your flesh if you walked barefoot. The walls were cream washed, the doors brown, the ceilings high and white. For me, accustomed to frugality, the building was unremarkable, and for those boys who came from big houses it was merely an extension of the bareness and discomfort they had endured at England's public schools, a far cry from home. Its very ugliness was perhaps a spur to our work; beauty was absent so we must create it. At that time we all knew that beauty was truth, and truth beauty.

Like Dora Carrington, whom Mark Gertler loved, I cut my hair short: unlike her I bought my clothes from second-hand shops, for I had come on a scholarship which hardly met my needs. But the old order was dying, the war gripped the nation, and one by one our younger teachers left to fight and probably die for their country.

Men frightened me. At first I did not fit in; female nudes bored me. I painted feverishly, turned out too much and was termed slapdash. I didn't care. Landscape was my *métier*, so why waste time on figures? Some innate arrogance drove me to make statements I later regretted but was too shy to withdraw. I quarrelled, flew into senseless rages which I could not understand, suffering I expect a delayed adolescence without parents to bear the brunt of my disgust.

James, it is impossible for me to write sensibly about that time without considering the class consciousness of the day. To be a true lady or gentleman was a matter of great importance both to those who were born with silver spoons in their mouths and those who strove to climb the social ladder. Few of the climbers passed beyond the first rungs because the nuances, the shibboleths, the special significance attached to certain aspects of dress and speech, were not something which could easily be learned; they had to be absorbed from an early age. You had to be born or adopted into the upper middle or upper classes to be accepted as a member and perhaps one of the worst names to be attached to anyone was that of social climber or careerist. The best people were always amateurs, so well endowed in social graces that they did not need to compete in any way to prove their worth.

Genuine scholars were among the few exceptions. True learning was always respected. Poor boys who had won scholarships to Oxford or Cambridge were taken up by kind dons and learned, sometimes painfully, to be gentlemen. It was normally essential to know who your *people* were, even if you despised them and spoke of them with mockery.

People like me might talk with the right accent, yet use the wrong words: "pardon" instead of "what" or "toilet" instead of "lavatory". The coarse was usually preferred to the refined. A spade must be called a spade and not a bloody shovel. You could give yourself away by describing a huntsman's coat as red instead of pink, or talking of dogs instead of hounds, or by putting your gloves on in the street instead of in the house you were about to leave.

I had quickly learned to speak with two tongues, one for the Randolphs, the other for the orphanage. Despite warnings from servants at the Park I considered myself middle class. At St. Stephen's however Art was supposed to be everything and many students were trying to react against social distinctions while still unable to rid themselves of class consciousness. They would talk of revolution, mix deliberately with working or tradespeople and then shudder inwardly at "plebeian attitudes" or "common habits". In theory my lack of parents did not matter, since my colleagues, especially those from the most privileged backgrounds, made fun of their parents or claimed to despise them. But in fact the lack worried me incessantly. In addition, my newfound freedom was a burden; decisions irksome. I was like a battery hen let out of its cage, lost, bemused. Each plunge into a new experience was followed by swift retirement; each burst of conversation by shyness and retreat. Socially inept, I was ridiculously grateful for the smallest act of friendship, exaggerating its significance, looking for reasons. A man had only to talk kindly to me for two days running and I thought in moments of optimism that he was falling in love with me and then was plunged into despair and self-analysis because he wandered off with other friends on the third day. I missed Helen, the closest friend of my childhood, and in morbid moments I forgot all past happiness and relived her death, stood again at the grave. Then I wished God would speak to me, bring understanding. But He only spoke in moments of happiness, when beauty of landscape or roofscape or skies caught me by the throat, or someone I admired was very kind, or for a few moments I loved the work I was doing and every stroke of pen or brush came right. He only spoke when I didn't need Him.

But my loneliness was of my own making; no one actually rejected me. There was indeed a group of three students who often invited me to join them; but I always had to be *asked*. I could not take their liking for granted for fear of rebuff. Sometimes I thought they asked me only out of charity. You see, not one of these three was like anybody I had met before. They were all arrogant, dismissive of convention, poorly educated and outwardly extrovert, although I am sure each one of them had a sensitive inner core of which I was totally unaware. The boys both had medical conditions which prevented them from being called up, for which they were grateful since they were determined to ignore the war as far as possible and get on with their painting. Art, they said, had no national boundaries. It rose above war. It was international. Only through art could world peace finally be obtained. Courtney, the eldest, was almost obsessional about this particular theory, and when he saw me blundering conversationally, he would tell me it did not matter, not one iota; what mattered was my work, which he said was far more important than me. "It is what you *produce* that matters not what you *are* or say." Courtney was fair, with the sort of upper-class fineness about his face which I have described. He was normally laconic and chivalrous to women, but when he was excited he peppered his talk with expletives which I do not think were part of Harold Randolph's vocabulary. The second man, David, was Jewish with black eyes and a beautiful, very expressive face, strong and bony, yet not without elegance. I loved him for being exotic and foreign. He lived at home in Spitalfields and seemed to smell differently from the rest of us, of spices and unfamiliar herbs, I suppose, but he wasn't an orthodox Jew; he was an atheist. The third member of our quartet was Georgina, daughter of an actress and a scenic designer; a big bosomy girl, with a long chin which she thrust forward as though it were a weapon, a high complexion and large, very brilliant brown eyes. Georgina seemed to exude energy; she was impatient of compromise, full of plans, sociable and argumentative; she seemed to carry an umbrella of kindness which gave me protection. Looking back now, I see that she more than anyone else was aware that I suffered from having no *people*, and a background which was unacceptable to the majority of the population. She mothered me in a brusque way which made thanks seem out of place, and in private almost certainly talked about me as a poor little devil.

Our teachers were old men, steeped in earlier traditions and suspicious of innovations. They were tired men, too, dispirited by the war and critical of our generation, and they wanted to get on with their own work rather than teach us. We treated them politely, but without deference, and agreed among ourselves that they were inflexible and bigoted. In trying to ignore the war as totally irrelevant, some act of madness that could only be damaging to art, we did not care what others thought of us. We were, although we would never have used the words, in our own minds, the élite. That was the collective us, the quartet. Individually we were more vulnerable. Alone I was hypersensitive to criticism, thin-skinned and defenceless. Words always failed me. And perhaps this is what Georgina, with a stroke of intuition, realised when she took me under that umbrella and allowed me the strength of her presence.

Reared primarily on fairy stories, the Bible and religious tracts, I was in my tamer fantasies a Cinderella figure who must, if there was any justice in the world, find a modern version of the fairy prince, and if there was not, I would of course invent one. I chose for this role Paul Bellows, a gentle fellow student with spaniel eyes and retroussé nose, whose amused affection aroused in me a teenage infatuation. He was a twenty-year-old homosexual, given to good works and kind thoughts, who befriended me generously because he had heard from Georgina, who, it transpired later, had connections with the Randolphs, that I had been dumped in an orphanage. Every time we met he smiled encouragingly; sometimes he put an arm round my shoulders saying "Cheer up. Everything will come right in the end." Other times he spent precious moments appraising my pictures, or invited me to join him for a cup of tea. And that was all. But it was enough to stir an unnourished heart. All my reading had suggested to me that friendship between man and woman led to love. I believed he spoke to me because I attracted him, for I was ignorant of homosexuality and never saw myself as a pitiful figure; brusque, yes, inept, unlovable at times, but not pitiful. And in suffering I struggled with my own unrecognised sexuality, not his which would have been more relevant. I wonder now whether he suspected how I hung on his words, how he had at first, like some ancient god, the ability to lift me up or cast me down. Realising at last that he would not rise to the role I had allotted him, I became resentful and sharp, snubbing him for his kindnesses, because I wanted not patient concern but action. Was he not aware that each morning I dressed for *him*, powdered my nose, divided my hair, curved it in gentle loops either side of my brow, shivering before a spotted mirror in an unheated room in Hammersmith? I suppose any unattached man with warm eyes which smiled at me would have done, and for people of my temperament and upbringing such idiocy was all part of growing up. I suppose too that I wanted the warmth of someone's arms around me, to be pressed against a manly bosom, like the heroines in the novels I now borrowed from the penny-a-week library, to feel that I had come home at last. And yet perhaps I chose Paul because some primitive, subconscious, female instinct told me that he was safe. I probably yearned for sentimental love, not sex, which would have appalled me. And so I bit my nails and painted in darker colours, turning hills claret red and houses night blue, and then I turned to black as one depressed turns to whisky and solitude behind drawn curtains.

Do you know, James, how many shades of black there are? How you can paint a whole picture in black and yet differentiate between light and dark? On some landscapes I put gibbets from which lifeless figures hung – not Christ-like – unholy figures like scarecrows, society's throw-outs. No doubt any psychiatrist could tell what that meant and, if ever I became famous, a significant link between more talented painters, someone, no doubt, will analyse them.

Looking back, though, I think Georgina was the person who meant most to me in my student days. She was so gorgeous, so full of life, a girl ready to burst out one day like a crimson peony out-classing all the smaller neater flowers in a border; the one who would always catch the eye. She was precious, of course, we were all a bit precious, but while I envied her looks, she envied my art.

"I am an imitator; you are an original," she would say. "You paint from the soul!" For, in our arrogance, we believed that creativity was an activity of the soul. Academics, politicians, businessmen and generals had no souls. (Even David, the atheist, believed this.) True artists, authors, musicians were the cream, because they possessed an inner passion and conviction that could not be corrupted by convention or worldly considerations. True artists were above war, above all pettiness. They were soldiers and revolutionaries only in the name of art and humanity. I do not think other members of our quartet realised that for me at this stage, and perhaps all through my life, the struggle with paint and form, the art of creation, was also connected with my struggle to be *somebody*, to find an acceptable identity. And yet at the same time my artistic gift was a burden from which I could not escape. Painting was an addiction, a need outside and beyond myself; it was as necessary to me as the air I breathed. But while we painted, the war raged and, in different ways, touched us all. Georgina lost a brother and David a first cousin and Paul a balloonist uncle, and when we saw the soldiers marching off to war or tired nurses creeping home in the cold hours of the early morning after a night's duty we denied a sense of guilt which was really a thorn in our flesh.

In those days we ate when somebody, usually Courtney, could afford to pay, at the Café Royal where sometimes we saw people we knew by repute: Mark Gertler with his dark curly hair, blue eyes, Dora Carrington, melancholy Gilbert Cannan who had cuckolded James Barrie, Alix Strachey, all were there celebrating the day war ended, when, because we had stood aside, we turned our conversation not to peace but to Vorticism. By then our course was over. Lady Randolph had moved out of my life, caught, I was told later, in a love affair from which she could not extricate herself. Those colleagues who had claimed to dislike their relations now did not hesitate to live with them while they sorted out their futures and, as though protecting themselves from unpleasant thoughts, my colleagues changed the subject when I wondered aloud where to go and what to do.

It was one of the elderly teachers we despised who came to my rescue when he recommended me for a teaching job at a private school in Kensington and took me home to dinner three nights in a row. Clare, his wife, a small, eccentric, broad-hipped woman with a weakness for wide straw hats, long skirts and bleached cotton was my first buyer. She hung her purchase, a dark picture of warehouses on the Thames, in a passageway at the back of her house and declared it "brilliant in both concept and technique".

I rented a room with a skylight and a wide window looking into tree tops for a few shillings a week, and Clare gave me a rush-seated Van Gogh chair, which inspired me to paint my walls yellow. I bought coarse brown matting for the floor and red cushions for the bed which my landlady provided, and hung my clothes on a hook at the back of the door, and started reading books about artists whose work I admired, identifying with their struggles and loneliness, glad that I was not crippled like Toulouse-Lautrec or mad like Van Gogh or sick, like Gauguin, with an illness I could not identify.

At school I found my well-groomed and privileged pupils inhibited but, at first, respectful. Deprived of paints, I had to fall back on charcoal and eventually, in despair, bought poster paints out of my own wages. A young teacher with aspirations, Stevie Durrell, commiserated with me. An inveterate talker, she had met Katherine Mansfield and Middleton Murry after sending a poem to the magazine *Rhythm*. She subscribed to *Blast*, admired D. H. Lawrence's writing and championed the Futurists. We saved our wages and went together to plays by Galsworthy, John Drinkwater and Granville Barker, and afterwards talked far into the night about art, religion, philosophy, anything but ourselves or men in general. Sex was still a terrifying half-understood fact of life for me, and marriage an ideal which we scoffed at, although Courtney and David were to wed within three years of leaving St. Stephen's.

Chapter Three

"FASCINATING," said James when he had read my piece about St. Stephen's, "but nothing about Copeland yet."

"As an art historian you surely know that all artists are egocentric." I spoke more sharply than I intended. "He will appear soon, when the time is ripe."

"Tell me more about Stevie Durrell, especially about her father, if that's not too painful." Unperturbed, James stirred his coffee. "By the way, do you mind the tape recorder?"

"I'm rather frightened of that machine." I started to walk around the room.

"It's so much more reliable than my note-taking," said James, helping himself to a biscuit.

"But I can't say *off the record*."

"You can."

"But I can see your pen stop. I know when you're not *writing*."

"I'll simply turn off the tape when you speak confidentially," he promised. "All right? You'll see then."

"I write better than I talk."

"I don't agree. Your writing is self-conscious; you leave out the tart bits, the spontaneous comments."

I looked hard at the youthful face, which I wanted to please, hoping to see again the delighted smile which lit up his expression when I gave way.

"You're very persuasive," I said. "All right, here goes. Where were we – Stevie, Stevie's father was very remote, a teacher of the old school, pedantic to the point of madness. He kept qualifying words. That didn't matter when they were his own, but when they were mine it grated. He suspected Stevie of immorality and asked embarrassing questions. His pale blue eyes were pebble hard behind thick glasses. His snub nose twitched like the nose of a frustrated pug who has picked up a scent he is not allowed to follow."

"You painted him," said James, leaning forward, a triumphant look on his face again.

"How did you know?"

"It turned up at Christie's."

"Oh God! How much did it fetch?"

"Two hundred pounds."

"Not much." My voice dropped, because for a mad moment I had imagined ten times that figure.

"Quite a respectable sum for a small portrait of a singularly ugly and little-known man."

"By a little-known artist."

"I shouldn't bank on that."

"Who bought it? That's important." Now it was my turn to lean forward in my chair.

"I did. Three days ago. Now you know why I'm asking questions about Stevie Durrell."

"But you don't even like it," I said, after a long pause.

"I don't like *him*, but I think you bring out his nastiness brilliantly. It is a very good likeness."

"How do you know?"

"I went to the school where he taught and the bloke who looks after the archives found some marvellous end of term photographs for comparison. It's amazing how long schools keep records."

"I admire you, Mr. Detective," I said. "But your thoroughness frightens me. And what of Stevie? Was it she who sent my picture to Christie's?"

"Stevie's dead."

"Oh no!" There was a tremble in my voice. "I didn't know. Such a sad life."

"Was she pretty?"

"Handsome," I said, remembering the fine bone structure, the strong nose, the fine straight brows, the fringe that aped Katherine Mansfield's. "Her mother was a librarian, bespectacled, silent. Stevie never thought she was her father's child. 'That's why he picks on me,' she used to say. I think my doubtful origins, as she called them, were part of my attraction for her. When the holidays came Stevie wanted to be with me all the time, but I wanted to be alone, painting warehouses. I wanted to catch the play of light and shadow between the dark buildings, the shafts of sunlight and sometimes the mist coming up the river, not still as people see mist, but moving in coils, alive. In the evenings I found there a strange murky world unlike anywhere else I knew, which fascinated me because it combined grandeur with poverty, beauty with ugliness. My pictures became studies in greys and blacks with brown tones, occasionally touched by the rare brilliance of a setting sun. Yet I could never quite catch the atmosphere, the feeling of the great dark forms, the warehouses, against the London sky, the solidness of the man-made against the subtle ever-changing world of nature. Sometimes I would stay out too long, wanting to catch and convey the twilight; the air would turn cold; the dampness and the smell of the river would catch me by the throat and I would find that my feet were half frozen and my fingers stiff, exposed as they were beyond the mittens I had knitted for myself.

"After a time I noticed that there was often a young man watching me, hands in pockets, cap pushed back, head just a little on one side. I might have been frightened had his face not been so wide and open, lacking any trace of furtiveness or menace. Eventually he summoned the courage to offer to carry my easel for me. 'How do you manage it day after day?' he asked. 'It's not a nice place for a girl to be all on her own.' "

"Was that Sam?" asked James, all agog.

"Don't interrupt," I said. "Don't stop the flow. I am normally a very inhibited person."

He apologised at once, effusively. "I'll sit as quiet as a mouse, but all ears." He huddled his long body together, wrapping his arms round his chest, trying to seem contrite.

"A cliché," I told him. "I'm surprised to find a Courtauld student sinking so low."

"I don't follow you," he said, brow creased.

"*Quiet as a mouse*? Terrible! Stevie taught me about mixed metaphors and clichés."

"Listen," said James taken aback, "I'm being an awful imposition. Do you want me to go?"

"No, I like your company. Don't take me too seriously," I

advised. "Actually I never thought I would *ever* care for an art historian. *All parasites*, I used to say, *feeding on the true creators*. But you seem different." And what old woman, I wondered, could resist talking to a young man who so charmingly sought her life history? "Would you like me to talk about Sam?" I asked. "That's all new. You'll be the first in the field, and, if long after my death, I become a little famous..."

"I should love that," he said.

"Son of a carter," I began, "left school at thirteen to work on a farm, where he stayed four years handling the shire horses, ploughing and all that. Then his boss died and the poor boy was thrown out of work. He lied about his age and joined the Ox and Bucks Light Infantry, but never saw service abroad, as the war was already ending. He came out jobless and finally landed up in London, driving a milk float. He was dark-haired with a wild forelock which sometimes fell across his face and half obscured his eyes which were hazel or green depending on the light. He had a sort of straight nose with a good bone in it, a strong squarish face with the tough skin of a countryman, and a wide smile which showed healthy white teeth. He had a cleft in his chin."

"I've seen a picture of him, by you. Tremendous, unbelievably good."

"I told you not to interrupt, James. You promised. Where? Tell me where? For heaven's sake."

"In the house of a professor of art history. Bought it for a song, he said, but he didn't say where. When he heard I was interested in Barney he invited me round. I appreciated that very much."

"Another parasite," I said.

"Well, at least he bought your picture."

"But I didn't get a penny from it, did I? Someone else made the money, and no doubt when the professor dies his heirs will reap a bit more. Not because of me, of course, but because of my connection with Barney," I added moodily.

"I shouldn't be so sure about that," James said. "And what did Stevie think of Sam?"

"Not much," I said. "She used to come sometimes to be with me and write in an exercise book while I drew or painted, but she often became impatient because I was so totally absorbed in my work. When I was inspired – no, inspired is too pretentious, too grand – when I was obsessed with a visual problem, when every fibre of my being longed to transform my vision on to canvas, or whatever, she felt shut out. Her writer's drive came and went, and when it went and I was still working like a demon, she was enraged."

"And Sam?"

"Why is Sam so important?"

"A major influence on your life?"

"A rung, I suppose, up the ladder to maturity. Is that a clever phrase, James? Overdone? Oh well, never mind. I am after all a garrulous old woman when I'm in the right company. Sam, I must tell you, looked at me that first day with a mixture of wry amusement and disbelief. Ladies, he knew, dabbled in watercolours, I was the first ordinary girl he had seen with what he later considered to be a crazy addiction to painting. He spoke with a broad Gloucestershire accent, a very comforting accent, which reminded me of the villagers where Lady Randolph lived – not the Shamely staff because she employed only servants from London, to protect herself from gossip. Gradually I came to look for Sam when I went to the warehouses."

"But what did he say when you first met? How did you come to know each other?" asked James. "I want the romantic bit. You're rushing on too much."

"Oh, I can't remember. *That's a pretty drawing*, or some such nonsense. I shouldn't have answered, of course, but I must have replied and then, with the arrogance of people who know nothing about painting, he probably made a few suggestions and I turned and saw his kind face, and liked what I saw. I was at times very lonely, James. It's easy to be good and careful with men when you have many friends and a reliable confidante, but Stevie was the only person close to me at that time and although she swore she cared for me, I was well aware that she found me unsatisfactory. Let's stop now, James," I suggested. "My voice is tired. I'll make you an omelette if you can spare the time to stay a little longer, I've a dozen free-range eggs I bought from the post office."

"Oh, great, I should love that, but can I help?" He stood up, a very clean, well-mannered young man in conventional clothes of good cloth.

"Come shabby next time," I said, suddenly sharp because I had given away too much. "You make me feel a derelict. Do me a favour and dress less formally. I'm not accustomed to discussing my life with people in suits."

He reddened and his eyes evaded mine, so that I knew that dress was very important to him and that I had struck at his own self-image, diminishing him.

"Oh, I'm sorry," I said at once. "That was rude, personal. You look very nice. There was a very dear friend of mine who dressed like you, and I wished he wouldn't, and now he's dead and I wish I had never complained. Don't take any notice, do as you please. I can be a very stupid old woman."

"No, no," said James. "You're absolutely right. My girlfriend likes me best in a huge, hand-knitted turtle-necked sweater. I'll wear that next time."

"Your girlfriend? That's good. Look, I've become a bit of a health crank and given up alcohol, but if you dig in that cupboard you'll find an ancient bottle of sherry. Help yourself, while I whisk up the eggs."

After we'd eaten, I couldn't go on.

"Sorry," I said, "I've dried up. I'll write it down. You know in some ways I'm very old-fashioned and what I want to say is too personal for the tape recorder." Then James wiped his mouth delicately with the yellow napkin I had unearthed, and smiled beguilingly. "You don't feel you could talk about Barney instead?" he hazarded.

"Oh dear me, no," I cried. "Not yet. You'll have to put up with me for a little longer. I have to be chronological; otherwise I shall lose my way. I'm not being capricious, I do promise you, James, and perhaps one day when I'm long since dead that tape will be worth something. Who knows?"

"Oh please," he said. "Don't imagine for a moment that I do not enjoy listening to you. It's just that my tutor keeps asking how the thesis is going. It's for my Ph.D. you see."

I was moved by his anxiety (I have nearly always been moved by male anxiety so long as the sufferer was attractive). And so after a pause while my mind threw up ideas, I said, "Listen, James, I'll give you some names next time you come.

There's June, for example, one of Barney's long-term friends, she could help. He never slept with her so her view will be unbiased."

"Unless she wanted him to."

"True," I said. "How perceptive you are. But I don't think she did. I don't think there was that sort of chemistry going between them."

"You are so kind," James told me, carrying the plates and glasses through to the small scullery where Marco was mewing plaintively for attention. "I'm looking at every Copeland picture I can find, but you are giving the background of so much that went before. Haven't you drawn this cat? I can't believe you wouldn't, he's so drawable."

"A few in red chalk," I said. "When I came to this cottage I vowed never to draw or paint again, but you're right, I couldn't resist Marco – the way he moves."

I opened a drawer. "See, dozens." I threw James a handful. "But they lack originality."

He sat down, examined them one by one, a critic to his fingertips.

"Very interesting," he murmured.

"*Interesting*," I snapped "is the kiss of death." I snatched them back.

"Please don't be angry," he pleaded, "they're very beautifully executed, but just not quite up to your highest standards."

"That's why I stopped painting twenty years ago. My work was deteriorating," I said, becoming emotional, as the pain of the painting block, the dead sense of failure came back to me. "I think I came here to die, but nature wouldn't let me go – I have a strong heart – I hated everybody and everything. I was bitter as crab apples. I was like a spoilt child who has been refused a toy she hankers after, only my tantrum lasted two decades. I shouted at the boys and girls who played ball against the wall opposite, because I couldn't stand the sound of their happiness – discipline allowed us so little fun at the orphanage. I snubbed the vicar because he generalised about art and spoke as though all artists were bohemians. My nerves were as raw as scorched flesh. I wasn't liked because I was unlikeable. Gradually people stopped talking to me, and, because I told them nothing about my life, the villagers invented a past for me. I was to them a frustrated spinster, who had never known what it was to love a man. Me a spinster! And when that man came" – glancing at the window bars, I laughed harshly – "no one believed me, not even the police accepted my story, they thought everything was an old maid's fantasy, a compensatory dream! I had got off on the wrong foot. Once you have done that in a village it is hard ever to get on the right one."

"I don't follow you," James said, looking alarmed at my outburst. "I don't understand – what man?"

"No, why should you? I'm rambling on, getting worked up. Now you go back," I patted his shoulder, "go back to your charming girlfriend and I'll write you a nice piece about Sam, which you'll be able to sell for a tidy sum when you're an old man, when almost anything written about events in 1920 by a participant will have become valuable as social history."

"You won't over-dramatise, will you? I mean the nice thing about this tape," he tucked the recorder under his arm, "is that it's so wonderfully spontaneous and when you get going you're so superbly articulate. It has the ring of truth and some of the pain and passion of life."

"High falutin' words," I said. "When I write I stop and think, *is this right*? I refuse to allow my memory to play tricks on me, and I analyse, I'm better about my own character when I have time to think, and, as I sit, whole conversations flood my memory, as though I have pressed the right button on the computer. Perhaps this is because I have been so much alone."

"Yes, you may be right," James said, in so conciliatory a tone that I suspected he was humouring me. But never mind, I thought; it is good that the young should humour the old so long as they don't patronise.

"You are very well brought up," I remarked, calming down. "I congratulate your mother. I wish you were my grandson; then I would be proud of you."

At that he leaned down – he was around six foot tall and I have shrunk to a mere five feet three – and kissed my cheek, and I said, "Even more so after that."

A few moments later when his brown Mini turned the corner and disappeared from sight, the cottage seemed unbearably empty and I felt totally alone. And as night came the air filled with all the might-have-beens which normally only haunt me in the early hours before the birds proclaim the dawn and the bantam cock, that lives in a little hut on an allotment, crows.

Chapter Four

THE NEXT day I relived my interview with James over and over again until I felt I was back there by the misty river with Sam carrying my easel, and then I started to write again, and I did not stop to think at all, not once. I have never talked about my time with Sam to anyone, so perhaps all the emotions had until then remained pent up inside me, and that is why the words flowed, why even the dialogue seemed to flow on to the page with astonishing accuracy. I tried at first to work soberly, to keep everything in perspective. I wanted to tell the truth; to be cool.

Gradually I came to look for Sam when I went to the warehouses. I began to listen for the tunes he whistled, to wait for him to come up behind me when his work was done, a warm human presence on those damp December days, but I did not admit to myself that I cared for him until the day he took me to see the horses at the milk depot. Then standing with Sam in that warm stable, listening to the munching mouths, smelling the unforgettable mixture of hay, horse and freshly cleaned harness, I felt a sort of peace creep over me, a calmness which quietened my nerves and stripped the tenseness from my body. They were in stalls; their tails facing me; their haunches rounded like apples. As Sam went to them in turn, they turned their heads and looked at him with soft welcoming eyes; one or two whinnied. He ran his hands down their necks, talking to them very gently, caressingly, in his quiet Gloucestershire voice. Their names belonged to the country: Blossom, Meadowsweet, Bilberry, Bluebell and Damson; grey, cream, dark bay, blue roan and black, they stood in their stalls, resting hind legs, tired and patient after their long day's work. And Sam, I saw, cared for them. For a country-bred boy they must have been like an oasis in the urban desert.

"I do like a good horse," he remarked simply. "I always have and always shall. There's no altering that."

Bilberry, the bay, ran his lips down Sam's coat, then tweaked his cap, holding it for a moment in his mouth.

"Hi, none of that," he said laughing. "Mind your manners now or the young lady in the doorway won't be visiting us again. Come and touch them," he urged me. "Come on now, don't be scared." I went. "Which do you drive?" I asked.

I wasn't afraid of Sam as I had been of other men because he seemed so full of kindness and warm comfort; suddenly I wanted him to stroke me as he stroked the horses; I wanted to lean my head against him and steep myself in what I saw as his simple country ways, to feel again the rustic peacefulness which had sometimes enveloped me at Shamely, ironing out anxieties and – Georgina would have said – touching the soul.

"Bluebell," he said, "this one, the roan. Now if you could paint her, that would be something, wouldn't it, seeing you are a lady artist."

"There's no such thing, Sam. I'm just a painter," I said. "A lady is grand, and I'm too small to be grand, and I haven't the right clothes or temperament."

"No," he said. "I grant that your dress is not silk or satin, but your face, I thought that was the face of a lady."

"Then you're a gentleman," I countered.

"Never that," he said simply. "My guvnor was a carter, up at five every morning of his life, wash under the pump, bit of porridge and off to work."

"And I don't know about my father," I said, with a sudden rush of confidence, "because I grew up in an orphanage and my mother ..." I paused, looking at Sam, handsome now in the dim light of the stable. What had I said? How was he taking it? In the flattering light of dusk his eyes were soft.

"I would never have guessed," he said. "Who's the girl who comes sometimes, then? The one writing the book."

"A friend."

I turned away, for suddenly I felt weak, and I didn't want him to see in my eyes any evidence of the physical feelings he had suddenly and unexpectedly aroused in me. I was nineteen, stupidly innocent, immature for my years, impressionable, sentimental and alone. All at once that warm stable seemed like a haven and that man like the father, brother and lover I had never known.

"I must go," I said. "Now! Where's my easel?"

He looked surprised at my abruptness. "Come again, any time. I'm always here at half past three after the others have gone. I stay till last, not having anywhere special to go."

He handed me my folded easel which had been leaning against the wall.

"Will you be all right now, go carefully. Catch your tram, will you? I'm sorry to have kept you so long."

"I loved seeing the horses, and thank you."

I went. I was trembling, aware suddenly of a weakness and a longing which were to remain with me half the night.

Since I wrote those lines it has snowed and the village is very still under its white blanket.. A few birds flutter from tree to shrub. The sky is grey like smoke and the east wind cuts the cheek and yet moves nothing. Sam would have known the snow was coming. The long stable where the milk-float horses lived had a weathercock, which he watched with all the diligence of the country-born. The state of weather, he explained to me, had once meant the difference between having a plain dumpling for dinner or a bit of meat or bread and cheese, because when he was small, snow or constant rain could deprive his father of work.

"We near starved then," he said. "And my old mother used to cry, wiping away the tears on her apron. I shall never forget that."

In the spring he started to think of the fruit, for too much wind could ruin the crop and leave pickers unemployed. Too little rain, on the other hand, might lead to a shortage of hay. Later, his thoughts turned to sunshine to ripen the corn. When the weathercock pointed to the south-west he would say, "Ah, in for a mild spell, I reckon, we won't be needing our gloves for a while yet." When it moved to the north-east he would be gloomy, although he admitted that frost killed off "the vermin".

I wanted quite desperately to paint a beautiful picture of Bluebell to repay Sam for watching over me when I worked by the warehouses, which he felt were no place for a girl, and for carrying my easel and wondering whether I had caught my tram. He could not understand why I was obsessed with ugly old buildings when there was so much that he saw as beautiful for me to paint. He was like a tone-deaf person, only it was his vision which was limited, not his ears.

I looked at the work of artists who had painted or drawn horses: Wootton, Wright of Derby, Stubbs, Munnings, Degas, Toulouse-Lautrec, even Cecil Aldin, whom I thought of then as an everyday illustrator rather than an artist of note.

I wasted paper and paint I could not afford and many times wiped clean canvases of various sizes. Then I took to charcoal, catching the mare's outline in a few strokes. But Sam wanted colour, the charm of her blueness overlaid with grey, the darkness of that muzzle and upper lip which would find its way into any pocket in search for titbits. He shared my frustration; together we struggled, and all the time I wanted to get back to my warehouses, to capture at last that special play of light and dark, of form and space which always seemed in the end to elude me. I drew Sam in charcoal – ten sketches – five with his cap pushed back on his head in a characteristic pose, five hatless. I revelled in the thickness of his straight jet-black hair. His face was cheerful in expression, almost cocky yet strong in bone structure, cut in clean, well-defined lines, without flabbiness. The greenness of his eyes under thick dark brows never ceased to surprise me, for there was something glittering about them, a sort of intensity that did not fit in with a nature which seemed comparatively phlegmatic.

Sam sent three of my sketches to his mother who thanked me on lavender-coloured paper in a neat, looped hand. I have lost the letter, but I remember she mentioned my "clever likeness", and my "gift". I remember too that she mixed up *as* and *has*, not being sure where and when to put an "h".

"A wonderful woman, my old mother," Sam said. "She worked her fingers to the bone for us kids, and always managed a welcome when we came back from school or work, and something hot, even if it were only a few boiled spuds with a bit of gravy poured over."

When I showed Stevie my sketches, she said, "Oh, that's the man who watches us. You haven't been talking to him?"

"Why not?" I asked, on my guard, but at the same time ready to defend Sam against any attack.

"Well, you don't know anything about him, do you? He could be anyone. You haven't been introduced. He might be a murderer for all you know."

"He drives a milk cart," I countered. "And feeds me on bars of chocolate."

"Well, that's no recommendation. What I mean is, it's all right to draw him. I mean you're an artist, so you're sure to be attracted to unusual faces, but don't get too friendly. The lower classes have different rules than we do. You could get yourself into deep water, just by being kind and interested."

"I think I know as much about the working class as you do," I said. "He's just a nice young man, who takes an interest in my work. He's never met a painter before, and I've promised him a picture of his horse, and now all the other drivers want pictures too."

"You're not talking to them as well, are you? You're not becoming the pearly queen of the milkmen? Christabelle, to use my father's outworn phrase, you are putting yourself in moral danger. You are naive."

"Oh, Sam will protect me from the rest," I said. "His role is purely protective. Look, I've mixed with all sorts of people in my life. I know what I'm doing."

"But he's *common*," objected Stevie. "Surely you don't want to get involved with *common* people. You're far too good for that."

I said nothing then, for I was thinking how strange it was that Stevie should speak in this way. Everything she claimed to have revolted against now seemed an innate part of her. For a moment I felt embarrassed by the intensity of her glance, by her shocked expression. Perhaps sensing my astonishment, she said, "Well, I mean the commonness wouldn't matter if he were intelligent. I mean there are plenty of authors and writers from humble backgrounds."

"How do you know he's not intelligent? You haven't spoken to him."

"Intelligent men don't drive milk floats, and they don't gape at young girls sketching."

"You don't know because you have never spoken to a milkman, except about milk," I retorted.

"Well, why don't you draw me? Isn't my face interesting enough?" asked Stevie, her eyes suddenly vulnerable under the dark fringe of hair.

"I didn't know you wanted to be drawn. I didn't know that you liked my sketches. I think they are terrible," I said. "I don't like to inflict them on people without invitation."

"Oh, now we turn into Uriah Heep," said Stevie, with her half-affectionate laugh. "The little unloved orphanage girl! Oh cheer up, Christo, you're going to be a great and famous artist, so long as you don't allow yourself to become some illiterate man's slave."

We were in my small room, sunless because of its north window. I opened a drawer, pulled out charcoal, a piece of paper.

"Sit still, I'll start now," I said, "but I'm not a portrait painter. You'll be disappointed."

I was right, of course; Stevie accused me of making her face too silly. "I have a strong face," she declared, "and you've made it all soft and feminine; you've knocked the force out of it."

I tore the sketch in half, chucked it in the wastepaper basket, knowing it to be false for I had wanted to temper the slightly harsher lines which her face had taken on over the last six months. I had tried to recapture the expression she had worn so often when I had first started teaching at the school. Sketching her as she now was I would have been admitting to myself how much she had changed; and preferring the earlier less aggressive Stevie, I felt baffled.

"Let's go for a walk," I suggested.

"But you keep stopping to look at things."

"Well, why not?"

"I don't feel like stopping."

In the end we made cocoa in the manner of our generation, crouching over the gas fire as the rawness of the April day seeped into the room through a cracked window pane.

"If you care for me, don't go on seeing Sam," Stevie said. "Forget your obsession with warehouses and paint something light and cheerful. The Thames at Richmond. That's an idea, isn't it? Come to lunch – you haven't been for ages – come to lunch and then we'll go out on the tow path and you can set up your easel and I'll get on with my novel."

The quartet had broken up. They had, I felt, gone on while I stood still. They looked down on me, for they had no intention of becoming teachers. David had won a scholarship to the Royal College of Art; Courtney, who had private means, planned to study in Paris; Georgina had fallen in love with an Italian count and was soon to join him in Florence. She had blossomed and her blossoming made me feel like one of those shrivelled frost-bitten buds which never matures. I went back to the warehouses, back to the tranquilising, bucolic calm of the stables, back to Sam with his ready smile, his strong hands and green eyes which now seemed only to glitter for me.

My one real friend in the art world at this time was the lady of the bleached cotton and sandals, wife of Edmund, the college teacher who had taken an interest in me. One April day I took her a folio of my paintings and drawings, and we sat drinking lemon tea and talking far into the night. Half Austrian, she possessed one of those wide placid faces that encourage confidences. She designed and made jewellery, was a feminist of much conviction and little militancy; and, unknown to me until that conversation, she had taken numerous lovers besides her husband. Admiring my sketches, she tried to help me clarify my feelings about Sam; she mentioned birth control in passing, in a matter-of-fact manner; she advised against early marriage for me. "You're an artist first," she said, "and a woman second. You must not commit yourself." She fetched her husband to look at my warehouses, and he offered to speak to members of a new group who were planning an exhibition of the work of young modern artists. He asked about the school where I taught and clicked his tongue disapprovingly when I mentioned the shortage of materials. His own work was, in my view, too staid and traditional to be of contemporary interest, but he was a fine draughtsman. Much later I realised that he was also a brilliant technician and wished then that I had studied his methods more carefully and listened with greater respect to his advice. Clare, his wife, was more open. She showed me her jewellery. I showed her my work. She must have been fifty, but the gap between our generations closed. We were like colleagues.

No account of our friendship would be complete without admitting how Clare became my surrogate mother; although at the time I thought that she was just a friend, a sort of sister. Her fair, expertly dyed hair was wound into two coils either side of her ears, and parted in the middle above the brow which at first glance was deceptively demure. Her mouth was fairly wide and pleasant. There was nothing in her expression or the outline of her features to jolt or jar. The face was, I think, memorable in its wholeness and balance. At the same time there was nothing weak about it; the darkish blue eyes gave an impression of depth, not the sort of emptiness some blue eyes throw back at you as though any communication will bounce off them without the kindness of a genuine response. Once a nurse, she seemed to possess the wisdom of those who have seen birth and death many times, and have developed a personal philosophy of life. She was an antidote to the intolerant morality of the children's home, whose staff had mentioned sex only as a dark and sinister activity to be repressed; a game for men, a burden to be borne by respectable women so that babies might be made. Marriage, she said, was a useful institution for most people since it offered security for children and a background for mutual aid and comfort, but one had to remember that when the Bible was written, the majority of the human race lived for around forty years, whereas now many people reached seventy or even eighty. Forty years with one person, she said, could be monotonous, even exasperating, especially if one partner cooled before the other. This veiled suggestion that women might enjoy sex for its own sake came to me as a revelation, which is astonishing when you consider that I had known both Lady Randolph and Georgina.

"One must recognise and beware of one's own sexuality," Clare said. "Always try to go into a love affair with the eyes open."

"Literally?" I asked, putting down my tea cup, trying to appear blasé.

"No, not literally, of course not. Some close the eyes when making love. For them it is part of the enjoyment. Metaphorically."

It is hard now to say how much Clare altered the course of my life. Certainly she turned many of my preconceived ideas upside down without shocking or irritating me, probably because we do not anticipate in foreigners the reticence we have come to expect from the English, scandalous views and comments being more acceptable when expressed with a foreign accent, however slight. Clare's fluent English was charmingly overlaid by a touch of Austrian, excusing her from the normal rules of respectable British behaviour, and men especially were amused and sometimes captivated by her verbal deviations. She might pronounce, but she did not ultimately judge.

I returned after that first evening of tea drinking and discussion exhilarated by the feeling that I had found a true friend for I was looking rather naively for *real* people, as opposed to the sham: people without that social veneer of politeness which camouflages private likes and dislikes; people who could say "You look awful" or "I feel that painting is brilliant except...." without causing offence because you know that their concern for art and for you is genuine, that they actually care.

Clare had advised me to stop painting warehouses.

"You have exhausted that theme," she said, "drained yourself. The weariness shows in these later pictures. Why not turn to something different, street markets, for example? You have occupied yourself with a dead world, stillness. Now give us life, bubbling and exuberant. You can be cynical if you wish, think of Gertler's 'Merry-Go-Round' – what life is there, and yet comment too. He takes us beyond ordinary vision. He shows us something we had not seen before."

I thought I knew what she meant, but I also knew that at that stage I was not capable of social comment, that there could be no literary interpretation of my pictures. I was more interested in the play of light, the juxtaposition of form against void, solidity against emptiness, than in the question of life and death and man's place in the universe or his role in society.

In addition I could not bring myself to disappoint Sam, who would be waiting for me in the early evenings or on Wednesday afternoons when school broke up at midday. His eyes, I knew, lit up for me alone, glittered as I struggled with my easel or despaired when the work of my brush did not conform with my notion of the world I wanted to depict.

So I pushed Clare's advice aside, and returned to the warehouses on a Wednesday afternoon even though the mist was coming up from the river and the whole of London smelt of coal, smoke and the oil and steam from the boats on the river. I set up my portable easel, found my brush and started work at the top of a street. Few pedestrians were about, but, now and then, carts passed me pulled by great horses with feathered legs and wide blinkered faces, splashed with white as though someone had thrown milk at them. I thought then that Sam's father must handle giants like these, with jingling brasses and clinking polished harness. Was he like Sam? Was he dark too, with hazel eyes which turned green for those he loved? I stopped then at the word I had chosen, turning it over in my mind, fearful and exhilarated.

"I love Sam."

I felt like painting it on a wall for all to see, and then I felt ashamed of myself, thinking, in the other half of me, the part Stevie liked, that I should only love respectable men to whom I had been introduced or artists, who were striving to give the world something new, wonderful and different through their work. People of aspirations and ideals, real people. I put my brush down and stood very still seeing nothing but Sam's face, the cleft chin, the eyes below the dark brows and the forelock of ebony hair. The mist came down; boats hooted eerily; the buildings looked through the greenness like mountains. It was spring, but raw dampness was everywhere: in my eyes, my throat, my joints. It wetted my hair, touched my cheeks and made my nose run. I started to pack up. A wagon rumbled by, and then I saw the round, yellow blobs of a lorry's lights and heard the throbbing of its engine. I turned away, started to walk back; the fog was now what Londoners called a real pea-souper. It was thick, almost glutinous; it cut my vision down to a few feet. Its smell clung to my clothes like bonfire smoke. I found the footpath with my left foot. I held one hand before me like a blind man; the other carried my easel and case of paints and brushes. The fog moved; yet each wave of it was followed by another equally thick. I started to cough. I wished that I had a muffler with which to cover my mouth and nose. I felt as though smoke was entering my lungs, seeping down my throat like poisonous gas – a thought conjured up by a sudden memory of Sargent's picture 'Gassed', with its pathetic column of blinded vomiting soldiers. The next moment I told myself not to be melodramatic; this was no more than a common London fog which killed only the old and the bronchial. I coughed, cleared my throat and pushed on, feeling my way from lamp post to lamp post. I had not eaten since lunch at twelve thirty. It was now five and suddenly I felt cold with hunger. I was afraid that I might be walking in a circle; normally I crossed a stretch of wasteland – the main cause of Sam's anxiety – but this time I had not reached it. I tried to remember all the streets in detail, to know when I came to the next crossroads which way to turn, then I tripped over an old saucepan and fell. Where was Sam? Why wasn't he looking for me? I had come only for him and he wasn't here. I called his name. A voice answered.

"Yes, dear. Where are you? Can I help?"

It was not Sam's voice. There was a leer in it, a mocking note. Perhaps it belonged to one of his mates, Ricky, Will or Arthur. They were all right individually but collectively they were boors. They egged each other on, showed off and made fools of themselves. Sam was better than all the others put together. There was something honest and down to earth about Sam. He never larked around. He was more adult. Oh Sam, where are you? the inner me cried.

"Here I am."

A figure loomed through the grey murkiness, tall as a tree he looked and wide as a table. "Go away!" My voice carried a note of despair where I wanted anger and dismissal.

"Lost, are you?"

"Show me the way to the tram, please show me the way to the tram."

"In exchange for a kiss and a cuddle."

"No." I lunged at him with my easel, and then my case. His arms were very long, gorilla's arms; he smelt faintly of beer overlaid with tripe and onions. His eyes gleamed like wet pebbles, his breath mingling with the fog. As his head bent down towards me, I hit it violently with my case, summoning all my might. There was a cry and a thud as the body collapsed. I wanted to run then, run and run like a scared rabbit, but I would not let myself go. I clenched my left hand so hard that the nails drove into the palm and left little marks.

"Are you all right?"

There was a strain of hysteria in my voice, which I recognised with alarm. A little blood dripped on to the pavement. I thought: This is the end. I've murdered someone. I shall hang. I shall never see Sam again. I shall never produce a perfect picture. I shall have a rope around my neck. I made myself look at the bulk lying like a heap of old clothes on the pavement. I knelt down beside him. I was shivering all over. I could feel my lower lip trembling and my teeth chattering. I was very frightened.

"I never meant to hurt you badly. I never meant to kill you."

The body moved. It wasn't dead; there was breathing within the thick brown coat, life. "You're not going to die, are you? Speak, please speak."

A cold, work-reddened hand moved. Colour was coming back into the face; the blue eyes focused; the blood dripped very slowly like spilled claret.

"I only wanted a kiss. I wasn't going to hurt you, to interfere with you. I'm a decent man." He put out a hand.

"No, no thank you."

I hated his nose, a red-veined blob in a face too coarse; his dirty hair was half covered by a greasy cap. Most of all, I hated his smell.

I started to run. My legs were like cotton wool, heavy, sodden, without energy. My head swam and my lungs rebelled. I stopped to cough, and thought of Helen struggling for breath before she died. I had been very happy in the morning. I had been singing under my breath as I came to the warehouses, and now in a matter of hours I had turned to morbidity and fear. I had faced the thought of murder and death.

"Sam, where are you?" I dared not call again. The cry came out as a silent prayer. I strained my eyes, and then through the vaporous coils, the yellow greenness of the fog, I saw the back of a familiar building and realised that some instinct had driven me to the stables. No sailor was ever more glad to see land than I was at that moment to see those red walls and smell the scent of hay and horse. I crept inside, feeling suddenly very small, a vulnerable animal finding familiar shelter after escaping from a predator. My stomach rumbled. I sat down in a pile of straw. I wanted to cry but my eyes were as dry as sapless sticks and my throat was tense with a lump in it.

He might die, after all, I thought. People can speak minutes before death. His reaching hand might have been his last movement. I wondered whether there was blood on the corner of my case, where the point had driven into his head, but the stable was in semi-darkness so I could not see. A little light would probably have raised my spirits, driven out the morbidity, for its lack always depressed me, just as fog had bred in me a strange and claustrophobic terror.

Gradually the munching of the horses calmed me. I went back to the straw, curled up. I slept fitfully, dreaming of the man I had left bleeding on the ground. Then a light came swinging through the fog, a hurricane lantern glowing yellow, footsteps sounded on the gravel. A figure stood in the door way, quite small but wiry, with a perplexed look on his face. It was Sam.

"Well I never!"

"Have you been looking for me?"

My voice was a whisper; somehow I had left its strength somewhere else, perhaps by the wasteland I could not find, by the injured man.

"Christabelle, what is it?"

"I'm cold. I was lost, that's all."

He rubbed my hands, took off my shoes and rubbed my feet.

"Better?" he asked. "I've been searching for you in case you came."

I looked at him, deep into his face which was caught in a shaft of light from the lantern. His eyes were very bright, like jewels, his cap lay on the ground and his hair smelt of soap and hay and Sam. I put out a hand to touch it. I couldn't speak; instead I began to tremble.

He put his arms round me.

"I'll warm you," he said. "I'll put some life into you."

I do not think he meant to go any further than that; it was simply our bodies that took us on, into another world of the senses, so that we clung together and then suddenly I melted, melted and floated away on a tide and then he couldn't turn back. He had to rise on the tide after me; then we had to unbutton together, to go on and up together, fuse and become one. Afterwards he said he was sorry and then he said something which hurt, but I didn't tell him how much. He said, "There's a full moon tonight, only we can't see her. The last time I had a girl the moon was full. Funny that, isn't it? Does it make me a moon case?"

I had been very hot, but then I began to cool. As I dressed I thought of the man lying there in the dark, cold and damp, perhaps dying or dead. I thought of his big face and the red-veined blob that was a nose, and the dark blood dripping.

"How long does it take someone to bleed to death?" I asked. But the remark caused confusion. And, when I had explained about the man, Sam picked up the lantern and said he would go and look. He returned about half an hour later with two packages of fish and chips. The man, he said, had gone; he had found the blood stains, but there wasn't a pool, so the wound couldn't have been that bad. The fog was lifting, Sam said; the lights had been lit. Soon he would take me to my tram, but first we should talk a little about what had happened. Perhaps he should find a decent couple of rooms somewhere so that we could be married. If I went on working until a baby came, we wouldn't be short of money, not with my salary and his wage put together. I sat very still then as though to move was to give an answer, and I did not know what to say. I took his hand and held it. I liked his hands. I can see them now all these years later. They were rather square, but each finger was beautifully formed, with the nails neatly cut. I knew that he washed them in the harness room at the end of the day's work, heating a kettle of hot water on the Valor stove, scrubbing them with a brush. I was glad now that his hands had warmed me.

"You're not eating your fish and chips," he said, starting to hold pieces out to me, from the newspaper in which they were wrapped, coaxing me softly as though I were a dog, so kind that, had he not made that remark about the last girl he had taken, I might have agreed to marry him. But now I saw in him a flaw, like a bad piece of brushwork in a picture which is otherwise remarkable. I thought it might nag in the back of my mind as the faulty brushwork would irritate the eye and in the end force one to take the picture from the wall, even though the rest of it was exceptional, even a great work. I wanted more time to get used to the idea of the other girl. I was too immature to accept that any young man of twenty-two was almost certain to have tried his luck before. Jealousy lurked at the back of my mind like some snake ready to strike at the very heart of the affair, to kill the easy friendship, the coming together which had seemed to hold out so much.

"Another, another, sweetheart?" He held a long chip out for me to take in my teeth. "Now smile," he said. "I love to see you smile. Come on, Belle my darling, it will all turn out all right in the end. You'll see. I'll find somewhere."

"Do you think we could have made a baby?" I asked. "Because I don't want one just yet."

"No, of course not, they don't come as easy as that. There, my little darling, don't fret, don't take on. I'll get the old Valor going and make a nice little pot of tea."

"You talk to me as though I were one of your horses," I said.

"No," he replied. "No, I don't. Girls and horses are different."

"I know that," I said, beginning to laugh a little at last. "Oh Sam, you're ridiculous."

I looked at him, and thought, That man is my lover, my man, and I liked the lines I saw. He was beautiful. He was mine.

I did not understand then how strongly physical the attraction was or realise that I possessed a weakness for handsome young men. Not accepting that women could be as frail in this respect as I somehow knew men to be, I saw everything through a romantic haze which left no room for serious consideration. The exception was that brief moment's apprehension about the other girl, the utter rejection, the tastelessness and timing of that remark about the full moon, which had struck cold a nerve of sensibility in me.

When at last I reached home, Stevie was sitting on the stairs outside the door to my room.

"Christo, where have you been? I've waited an hour on these damned stairs! You smell of horse."

"I saw Sam." I dug in my coat pocket for a key.

"Oh, not him *again*! Look, people make jokes about women pursuing milkmen, not people like us of course but maids and lower-class wives."

"I'm lower class," I said. "So the cap fits."

"You look utterly tired, done-in. Let me make you some cocoa, come on! Where are the matches? Heavens, there's no gas. Have you sixpence for the meter? You stink of the manure heap!"

I put down my easel and case. I climbed on the bed, lay my head back against the cushions and stared up at the cracks on the white ceiling which I had painted with such loving care.

"Half a mo," said Stevie. "Cocoa coming up."

"You are very kind," I said.

"What happened? Come on, tell auntie."

She was pouring hot milk into a cup, a sturdy figure with square shoulders.

"I might even use your experiences for a novel. The Bloomsbury Group all use each other, you know; it's all frightfully in-bred."

"You would be shocked," I said with a sudden smile, as the warm drink slid down my throat. "Even though you once said you believed in free love."

"You haven't! You haven't let him ... Christo, I don't believe it!"

"You know Georgina once told me that your heroine Katherine Mansfield had a baby that died," I said.

"But she was married," countered Stevie. "That's different, isn't it?"

"And she went chasing off to Paris after an artist – Carco, I think his name was – and she lived in sin with Middleton Murry. Artists and authors don't abide by the usual rules. We are a race apart." I stared across the room, surprised by my own arrogance, yet determined to excuse myself, to find myself a code of behaviour which would allow me to see Sam again without necessarily marrying him. "Free love is an accepted fact now."

"If you have ... with a milkman you are no better than a common whore."

I threw the cocoa at her then, and watched it run down her woollen blouse, a frothy pale brown trickle, lighter, sweeter than the blood on the pavement. The cup lay in pieces on the floor. There was a moment's silence. It was my second act of violence that day, but I didn't care.

"Perhaps your mother was a whore," remarked Stevie, cool in her sudden hatred. "Perhaps you have inherited a bad streak. Perhaps my father is right after all. Bad blood will out."

"Why are you trying to hurt me?" I asked more calmly, because this argument seemed all at once of little significance in contrast with the events of the afternoon and evening. Suddenly Stevie did not matter to me very much any more.

"Because you will destroy yourself," she announced dramatically. "Your reputation, your self-respect and your soul."

"Well, I suppose that's my affair," I said. "So long as I put art first, nothing else matters."

"I will go now," said Stevie haughtily. "See you at school tomorrow."

"Yes, that's right. I'm sorry we quarrelled. You see you have a stereotype milkman in your mind. You are prejudiced."

"I suppose you are going to turn Sam into a sort of A. E. Housman character," said Stevie, at the doorway. "Or Piers Plowman."

"Listen, on the surface, to the prejudiced eye, everything looks awful, but it isn't. There's no hypocrisy. Can't you see that – no hypocrisy in Sam. He's a real person, genuine."

"A man of the soil you'll be saying next," said Stevie slipping on her coat. "Ugh. Clichés are sliding off your tongue."

I listened to her feet going down the stairs, heard the door close, then sleep came, bearing down on me, moulding my body to the bed, to the dip in the horsehair mattress, turning the light to darkness and conscious thought to dreams and then to nothing, nothing at all.

Chapter Five

WHEN James finished that piece, while I paced about the room like a dog waiting for a promised walk, he told me I should take up writing.

"But artists can't write. Do you know *one* who can?" I objected.

"Paul Nash," he replied instantly. "His autobiography is marvellous."

"But I can only write about myself," I said. "These pages," I added, taking the manuscript from him, "are an exercise in self-indulgence."

"I suspect the same could be said of lots of books. But honestly, Mrs. Lang, I think you should write your life story. I think you have something to contribute to the sum of human knowledge."

"That sounds very high falutin'," I said. "I think writing is perhaps a therapy I should have taken up earlier – all those wasted years! But it doesn't mean I'm any good at it. And by the way, James, I am not and never have been Mrs. Lang. Please call me Christabelle, or Christa or Belle – take your choice. I answer to them all."

"Yes, yes, of course you have never been Mrs. Lang." He sounded angry with himself. "I do apologise. But do you know, I think I could find a publisher for your autobiography, especially if you can bring in a bit about Barney. He's becoming a cult figure. I have a friend, an editor...."

"I would be baring my soul to the world."

"Why not? It's a good soul," said James. "Do you want me to help you? I mean I have the tapes, I could help you put it all together."

"But why should you? Why should you bother with an old

lady like me, a has-been? Do you know, there used to be stories about Victor Gollancz, sitting in the Ivy with his favourite author and pointing out all the has-beens? Publishers and art dealers can be very cruel. They could assassinate me."

"But journalists most of all," said James. "Anyway, can we carry on where you left off?"

I looked at the pages. "Oh yes, Stevie's jealousy," I said. "I think I have written the truth, but perhaps I haven't been fair to Sam."

I haven't conveyed the charm of his Gloucestershire accent. I have forgotten to indicate that he dropped his aitches, I haven't mentioned that he was later on in the main a patient and tender lover, that after that first time he led me on slowly. He wanted to believe I was very delicate, very feminine. To work me in gently as he would work a young horse. He had in some respect an ability to put himself in a woman's place when it came to making love. Like Mellors in *Lady Chatterley's Lover*, he could be very tender with animals, and he was good with kettles and fires. He could manage the simple homely things of life with a quiet competence that I admired. He loved chicks and brown eggs and wild birds. He was very close to the earth. But, of course, he wasn't a super-human lover, like Lawrence's Mellors was. He had his ups and downs like everyone else, which he associated with the moon and the stars, as he associated my moods with the weather.

"Get a bit of sunshine and things will come right, you'll see," he would say. "Wet weather never did encourage genius."

After the night of the fog, James, I was horrified to find Sam waiting for me at the school entrance, still wearing his breeches and gaiters, but not, thank heaven, his milkman's coat or cap. I had to dodge out another way and then explain to him that the headmistress was very stuffy.

"She doesn't like the children to see their mistresses with men."

"Aren't they human, then?" he asked. He bent to kiss me, and I had to say, "Not in the street, Sam."

Then he wanted to come home with me and I had to explain

that my landlady did not allow her tenants to entertain male visitors – it was after all, 1920!

"The sooner we get married, the better," he said, assuming that I was not the sort of girl who would wish a man to make love to her more than once unless she wanted matrimony.

Within a week he had found two rooms with a kitchen in a seedy terrace of ill-kept Victorian houses. "We can start there and move on to something better later," he said.

I told him I needed a studio. "I don't want to paint out of doors all my life."

"There's a yard out back," he said, "with a privy and a shed. I could put a skylight in the shed."

"Oh Sam, you're a genius." I spoke gaily, but inside I felt guilty and unsure of myself.

"There's a couple of borders, too," he went on, "where I could plant out a few cabbages, and sow a bit of spinach, and maybe a little horse radish. Next year we'll have sweet peas for the front room. I do like a fine bowl of them: they smell so nice and look a treat. Time you started to save for your bottom drawer, Belle," he said. "We shall need furniture and bed linen, but I'll buy the bed. And seeing you're on your own, like, we can get married from my 'ome – we've got a dinky little village church, pretty as a picture."

Then my stomach contracted, for I wanted my life to remain open and unpredictable. I didn't want a long grey road with a baby every two years and sweet peas in the front garden and roast beef every Sunday with horse radish.

"I need more time," I said, deeply ashamed that my senses had led me into such a predicament, that I could get carried away and risk pregnancy, and yet want more love without strings.

"But it's only right we get married now, seeing what's happened," insisted Sam. "It's only proper."

And he didn't make love to me again; he waited, and I could sense how the waiting tormented him, and sometimes at night my own frustrated needs kept me awake.

I went to see Clare. Red-faced, I confessed to the loss of my virginity.

"Don't marry him," she said. "Don't tie yourself down.

Live with him if you can't do without him. See how it works out."

"I feel so guilty," I said. "Split half and half. I don't know my own feelings."

"Typical convent girl, do you want a husband in Christ? Are you Roman Catholic, Belle?"

I told her I was Anglican. "Jesus loves me, yes I know, Bible, Bible tells me so – we sang that most mornings when we were in the nursery."

"I do not understand," said Clare.

"Christian indoctrination," I said.

The next night I told Sam I would not marry him.

"I never thought you were that sort of girl," he said. "But then I suppose artists are different," and now his eyes didn't glitter any more; they looked browner like half-ripe hazel nuts, and his mouth drooped at the corners, so, feeling sad too, I squeezed his arm and said, "Don't take on."

"You didn't like it in the stable then?" he suggested. "I went too quick, and you seemed so keen like, as though you couldn't wait. I shouldn't have done it, I knows that."

"I liked it, Sam," I said, "truly I did."

"We'd better not see each other any more then," he said. "We had better finish," and then I put my arms round him and said, "Couldn't we live together, but not as man and wife?"

"I couldn't do that. I should want you, see," he said.

"You could have me. We would, I mean we could, I shouldn't mind," I said.

"Don't you want a husband then? Doesn't marriage come into your way of things then?" he asked. "It don't seem right. And you such a nice little thing."

"Not right now," I replied. "But love does, love has no rules."

"I'm thinking of your reputation," he insisted doggedly.

"Artists don't have reputations," I replied. "They only have their art. We all agreed about that at college. The importance of art is absolute."

"It's college that's put all these daft ideas into your head then. Them places are not suitable for nice girls. But there's something about you, something that's different. I can't put my finger on it. You're such a lonely little mite ... You catch at my 'eart, Belle."

When I touched his arm, he went on to tell me that he had paid a deposit on the rooms. "I reckon I'll lose that now," he said, and I was so moved by the despondent look on his normally cheerful face that I rushed into words.

"Let's give it a try," I suggested. "Let's be unconventional, dare-devils, Sam."

I leaned against him as we walked and felt his body wanting mine, and the wanting became mutual until we were both weak with desire.

The next day we moved into the rooms and soon put a skylight in the shed and Sam helped me sort out my paints and canvases, and, although there were occasional moments of anger and reproach, we were at first ridiculously happy, and God did not strike us as I thought He might. We remained healthy, cheerful and passionately in love.

Almost at once I started to work as if my life depended on it. I drew Sam washing, shaving, tending the fire. I drew him bare-headed and with his cap pushed to the back of his head ("My cocky look," he called it). I painted him sitting at table with a knife and fork in his hands. I drew our bedroom with its plain Victorian window, its simple wooden bed, which we had picked up second-hand, its basin and jug and my yellow Van Gogh chair. I painted, in watercolours, the deserted front room with its bowl of flowers for the passers-by to see, and the bookcase of stained wood which I had bought for three shillings and sixpence. I drew the packing cases on which we sat before we could afford chairs and the small kitchen with its cold-water tap above the stone sink, and the black range with a kettle boiling on top.

Then an invitation came to a private and press view of an exhibition of work by ex-pupils of St. Stephen's for which two of my 'Warehouses' had been selected.

"It 'ain't my cup of tea. I should feel like a fish out of water," Sam said when I showed him the card. So I went alone. And Clare introduced me to Professor Tonks of the Slade, and Paul Nash and a dealer called Simon Hardcastle who looked over my head in the hope that someone more famous might come his way. Although only represented by one drawing Georgina arrived with her Italian count in tow.

"My dear," she cried, "you look wonderful. Quite apple cheeked."

"In Italy," the count explained, "our women do not have the rosy complexions for which the English are notable."

But I could not be as friendly, as warm, as I should have been to anyone, because I was deeply disappointed with my own work. In most of the exhibits you could perceive a link with a movement: the Futurists, the Cubists or the Vorticists. Mine alone were dark and different. And looking at my pictures in the bright light of the gallery, I thought I had laid on the paint too thickly where the buildings stood in terrible brooding splendour and too thinly for the shafts of light which lacked the dramatic effect I had intended. Everyone seemed to pass my paintings by or stand with their backs to them. And at that private view, where the rich mingled with the artists, my work seemed to matter more to me than anything else in the world. So, as often happens, I left what I had anticipated would be one of the great glories in my life with a sense of disappointment.

"And the critics?" James asked, replacing a tape. "Did you get a mention?"

"Of course not. They had nothing to link me with. I provided them with no opportunity to coin a clever phrase, to show off their own knowledge, to make a telling point."

"You sound bitter," he said.

"I am bitter. Of course I'm bitter. Unsuccessful artists always are; the lines of disappointment deepen around the mouth. The wise boys at the private or press view concentrated on the work of those who were being methodically billed for stardom by art dealers and critics."

"And what did Sam say?"

"If I remember rightly he made me a cup of tea, patted me on the shoulder, told me not to mind too much, I would get there in the end. He was always comforting, because he was kind, but I don't think he actually believed my work was first-rate. He cared more about his own welfare, always wanting meals or a cup of something. He would make tea, but otherwise he sat and waited for me to provide the nourishment or he pestered me, even when I was painting. 'Time for a spot of dinner, love,' that sort of thing. I could never make him understand or accept the supreme importance of art.

"We lived cheaply in a poor area and with our two wages we were not badly off, but Sam, who bought food on his way home from work or at a discount from the dairy, saved for our eventual marriage and the babies he wanted. For he felt that one day I would change my mind."

"And did you?" asked James.

"Did I what?"

"Change your mind?"

"You're rushing ahead. You are asking me to skip, as children do when you read them stories and they want to know the end without plugging on."

"Not any more. Fashions have changed."

"Anyway, enough for today," I declared. "Will you hand me that little packet over there – I need a throat lozenge."

"I've got to go away for six weeks, to Malibu," James said. "With Belinda."

"Your girl?"

"That's right, for the spring vacation and a bit more."

"But it's only March now," I objected.

"Look, what I'm trying to say is that I can't come over again until May."

"Oh, what a shame!" My cry was spontaneous, for James was becoming an important part of my life. "And we haven't even got to Barney."

"Yes, you are spinning it out rather. But it's all been tremendously interesting – I mean exciting – and I am wondering whether you could just keep on writing while I'm away and then when I get back, we'll see if it will make a book, and I'll pick out the pieces, if I may, which relate to Barney. Do you think that's a good idea? I mean, would you mind?"

He sounded sycophantic, so I said, "You are not trying to indulge an old woman's vanity, James, are you? I should hate that. I don't like flattery, not a bit."

Then he crouched down in front of me, took my hands in his and said, "Christa, don't you believe me? Please go on writing."

I thought he was overdoing things a bit, down there in front of me as though I were a child or a cat, but I still felt moved, and inside myself, acknowledged only by me, was the hope that he was right; that I was about to make a comeback, not as a painter, after all, but as a writer.

"Of course I will," I said. "And don't forget to send me a picture postcard. Lucky you and love to Malibu."

Chapter Six

ASHAMED of our unmarried state, Sam would not take me to meet his parents nor out in the evenings with his friends from whom, I subsequently learned, he had to face many jibes about living sinfully. Yet I loved those rooms especially in the evenings with the range glowing, the curtains drawn, the snug, sheltered world just for the two of us. One day Sam brought back a cross-bred collie dog which he had found lying bleeding by the river. The animal was soaked, a chain embedded in the flesh around his neck and a deep gash searing his left shoulder.

"He needs a veterinary surgeon," I said. "Soon, or he'll bleed to death."

"Fetch me a needle and thread," ordered Sam, kneeling beside the dog. "That's right. Now boil them. Good. Hurry now."

He held a hand over the wound as he spoke, trying to slow the bleeding. "Some fool put this chain round the poor devil's neck when he was young and forgot that he would grow."

Presently I threaded the needle and Sam sewed the two flaps of the wound together, while I held down the dog's head.

"Now you stay with him, while I go for a hacksaw. Comfort him, talk. He's too weak to move."

"Poor dog," I crooned. "Poor, poor fellow. We'll nurse you back to health." He was tri-coloured with a wide forehead, large eyes and young-looking teeth, and, because his body was emaciated, his head looked over-large, even grotesque. Knowing little about dogs I found him ugly and ill-proportioned. A forsaken ugly duckling, I thought. He'll take up too much room, get under our feet.

Gently Sam sawed through the chain, then tried vainly to

ease it from around the neck of the dog, who bared his teeth and growled.

"If only I had a swab of chloroform," said Sam. "Then I could do the job in a jiffy. We'll let him rest till after work tomorrow and then I'll take him to an old man I know, a grand farrier, retired now but as good as any veterinary surgeon."

The dog recovered, stayed with us and became our most devoted friend. Sam named him Skipper.

"We only need a baby and then the house will be complete," he said, looking at me from the corner of his eye, unable to make me out, thinking it was natural for a girl to want to marry, settle down and raise a family. Why was I holding back, insisting on birth control? But he was a patient man. "The best things are worth waiting for," he said one Sunday morning, kissing me. "One day you'll be ready." And I knew then that he was again breaking me in gently, biding his time in the hope that I would mature and grow steady with age. In his country way he was very well brought up: he never swore in front of women or expected them to carry coal or dig the garden or even light the fire. He always brought me a cup of tea when he left at four in the morning and washed up his own breakfast things. But the roles of male and female were well defined in his mind. A wife should be queen of the home, mistress of the kitchen. Apart from in the early morning, he lifted no hand to help with the washing up, make the bed or cook. He would sit reading the newspaper while I prepared meals or washed up, but he was king of the yard and the two borders of garden. When the cabbages were ready for cutting he laid them in front of me as proudly and diligently as a fox lays out the corpses from a night's hunting for his vixen and cubs.

One Wednesday afternoon there was a knock on the front door and, opening it, I found Georgina on the doorstep.

"My dear," she said. "What a job I've had finding you. I say, what a bohemian you are, living in this working-class quarter with a groom!"

"Not a groom," I said. "Come in. No, not the front room. Come into the kitchen."

"Where do you paint?"

"There, in the shed. Have some tea."

"You've nothing stronger?"

"No, we live very humbly."

"I like your dog."

I told her Skipper's history.

"Marriage suits you. My, you look happy as you talk," she said.

"Not marriage," I said.

"Well, you know what I mean. What difference does a piece of paper make?"

"The ever and ever bit," I said.

"And you, wise girl, are not prepared to do that?"

"This seems a step," I said. "A wonderful idyll, a tranquil pause before the next torrent. I can't explain it. But I can't see myself here for ever." I had not put my feelings into words before; I don't think I had known that I felt exactly like that. "I love Sam," I added, "but sometimes I feel I'm playing a part, as wife, that the whole of me is not engaged."

Georgina said she thought an awful lot of wives were doing the same. "But do you remember when we four used to talk about free love far into the night. None of us had tried it. We were all virgins. And the talk made us feel we were not. We were somehow very modern, even avant-garde. How sophisticated we felt."

"Oh yes," I said, pouring tea. "I was quite bewildered at first."

"I know. You looked at us with your big eyes like some horrified bird. You were visibly shocked. And not for one minute did any of us suppose that within a few years you would be actually living with a man in a back street, as so many of the great painters have lived with working-class women. Do you realise you have reversed the roles, Christa?"

"I don't care. It's not like that. It just came naturally, like the next move in snakes and ladders or something," I said. "At any moment I may have to take six steps backwards. This is a breathing space, half way up a ladder, that's all."

"The pictures?" asked Georgina. "I came to buy some to take back to Italy, not just for the sake of old times, but because I've always admired your work."

I said there was a terrible muddle in the shed. "It drives Sam mad – he likes order you see – but there's lots to show, only I'm not sure about the quality. I think I've used the palette knife too much in some of the oils. And the subjects are so everyday. Perhaps you'll find them boring. I'm rather cut off from other painters these days." I started to pour out my troubles, to talk rather fast as though I wanted to fit in a lot of conversation before she left, surprised to find myself so pleased to see her. Once I had felt a little in awe of Georgina, but now I faced her as an equal, despite the fact that she was beautifully dressed in the sleek, well-cut Italian style, while I wore a simple cotton skirt and broderie anglaise blouse – a dowdy hen beside a silver pheasant.

I brought out my pictures sheepishly at first and then more boldly, as I was infected by her enthusiasm.

"Oh, how interesting. Oh, I like that! Now isn't that beautiful? I like the way you've caught the light!" She was the perfect audience: generous with exclamation marks; and when I showed her my sketches of Sam, she said, "Ah yes, I understand. But a man like that shouldn't be just a milkman. Look at that face. He can't act, I suppose?"

"He has a beautiful, incurable Gloucestershire accent," I said, "as rustic as the trees and hedgerows. No, he's no mimic, he's too honest to act."

"There must be something else he can do," suggested Georgina.

"He's happy with the horses," I said. "He more or less manages the stables now. He's the best man there."

"Ah, there's my cab. I hear it."

"What about the pictures?" I asked.

"Oh yes, let's see." She thrust her chin forward in the gesture I remembered so well. "Let's have this interior. It's so wonderfully back-street England. The Italians will love it. And the sketch of that adorable dog. How much?"

"Oh, a present, with my love, take them."

"No, no," she said. "Here, take this." She pressed two five-pound notes in my hand. "Promise to spend some of it at the Café Royal in remembrance of the old days, and take Sam. Begin his education. Let him see himself in the gilded mirrors, stand him a glass of champagne on me, and introduce him to that rogue Augustus John, if he still holds court there. My dear, I do admire you. Somehow you are very D. H. Lawrence, you know. I *couldn't* do it."

She kissed me fleetingly on the cheek, then hastened through the yard to where her taxi waited. To me at that moment she was wonderful, a figure from another world, a world from which I had retreated. When she had gone I slipped back into the house, poured myself a second cup of tea and tried to readjust to the quietness and smallness of the house. Skipper looked anxiously into my face, then put a paw on my knee.

"Yes, I know, you're there," I said. "And I love you and I love Sam, but suddenly I feel rather lonely, moored on my own, Skipper, like a little boat that no longer goes out to sea."

The headmistress looked up from the letter she had been reading.

"Take a seat please, Miss Lang," she said.

Her grey eyes seemed expressionless behind gold-rimmed glasses, but one finger and thumb rolled a pencil up and down her leather-topped table. She wore a tight blouse, long-sleeved and buttoned sternly from neck to waist, and a long skirt, and button boots. Miss Skindle had not moved with the times. Even her face seemed Victorian, perhaps because of the grey bun that rested so neatly on the top of her head, and the straightness of her back which seemed to suggest rectitude of the highest order.

"It has come to my notice," she began, "that you have moved house, and that you are now living in a quarter which is not wholly desirable for a teacher of this establishment. I must remind you that all our pupils come from very respectable homes, many from the highest echelons of society."

I felt a cold hand of terror on my back, a tightening in my throat.

"Yes," I said. "Yes, I have moved. That is true."

"And why was your move considered necessary?"

"For personal reasons."

"I have heard a rumour, Miss Lang, and it is my sincerest hope that my informant is incorrect." Her eyes expressed a question mark. Sweating, I took a big gulp, held on to the sides of my chair. I wanted to be very calm, to stand firm on the philosophy of life which I imagined I was developing.

"No," I said. "I am sure that your informant is right. I am living with a man at an address among the working classes. Perhaps you are not aware that I came from an orphanage and am therefore classless. I am not ashamed."

"You shock me into silence by your impudence," said the headmistress and indeed a faint flush spread across her cheeks which were starting to pucker and yellow with age. "Living sinfully with a common man? Words fail me."

"You must understand that birth control has brought in a new era," I said, beginning to harangue. "Women are no longer shackled to men for the purpose of producing babies. We do not have to sign a life sentence to live with the man we love." I stopped. These were Clare's words not mine, coming out pat as though I had learned them by heart. Where was the real me?

"You have come under a bad influence. I can sense it, Miss Lang, and I am deeply sorry," Miss Skindle said astutely. "Have you a local church in your parts?"

"I don't know. Yes, I'm sure we have. Yes, certainly."

"You have turned away from Our Lord too? In the circumstances I can do nothing but regretfully terminate your employment here. You must understand that this is a Christian school and if your behaviour or way of life came to the notice of any of my girls' parents, we would have many children withdrawn. Such a scandal would rock our beautiful Kensington. In view, however, of your good work and regular attendance and your difficult circumstances, I propose to give you a month's salary, but I must ask you to leave today, forthwith. I cannot tolerate so evil an influence under this roof for a moment longer than is necessary. If you had shown one iota of remorse or shame I might have felt a little sympathy."

"Oh Miss Skindle," I answered rising, arrogant in my youthful advantage. "Please understand that we will never agree because you are Victorian in your outlook and I belong to the new post-war era. This is nineteen twenty. I am one of the young Georgians. England will die if she cannot rid herself of her old snobberies and class divisions. My Sam is as fine a man as any Guards' officer, as any over-fed aristocrat." I paused, searched for words, then continued. "I have lived among all classes you see, unburdened by class prejudice, unblinded by an upbringing that teaches a child to judge a person not by his virtues but by his class. To be well born does not automatically turn a man into a virtuous and God-loving person with a generous heart and honest nature."

The headmistress now rose too, like a statue rising from the sea. "Miss Lang," she said. "It is not fitting that you should harangue a person of my standing. Please do not add arrogance to impudence. Please leave now. You have said enough. Seek counsel." She gave me an envelope, made a gesture of dismissal; behind the gold-rimmed glasses her eyes were passionless. Had she rehearsed the interview in advance, knowing what the outcome would be? Had my patronising little lecture been both ill-timed and unnecessary?

"Thank you," I said, pausing in the doorway, taking one last look at that spacious room with its moulded ceilings and rows of books. "Thank you for employing me in the first place. You gave me a start."

"For what, Miss Lang, for what? Ponder that."

For a second there was a light, not of dislike but of despair, in the pale eyes. "England needs fine, clean, virtuous young women as never before," she added, as though it was a line she had forgotten to recite earlier.

I shut the door, pocketed the envelope, collected my few belongings and, feeling now more shattered than my words had implied, crept out into the bright sunlight into a stuccoed world of great white houses, magnolias, clematis, the first roses and the last forsythia. At least I had gone down fighting. For the first time in my life I had stood up to authority and given as good as I got. But was there any point in arguing with someone so entrenched in prejudice? And what would Sam say? I should have to concentrate on selling pictures which was both a pleasing and a frightening prospect.

I broached the matter carefully after we had both eaten. "That settles it," Sam said. "I'll look around for a better paid job, we'll get married and start a baby. It's time we made ourselves decent. Don't you notice how folks in the street look askance at you? Doesn't it make you feel bad? I know it does me. You haven't a friend to turn to, have you? They've cut us off. We're a blot in a respectable street, Belle. T'aint fair to other folk, us carrying on like this." He put his arms around me. "What's the matter? Aren't I good enough for you?"

"I may not be good enough for you," I said. "I may not be cut out for rearing babies, for housework."

"Well I must admit you don't keep the front door step as white as what our neighbours do, and that range could do with a blacking right enough, and there's a fine cobweb up in the corner to the left of the bed, since you've brought the matter up. No offence meant, sweetheart."

"There, you see," I cried, looking up into his weather-tanned face with its hard lines. "I'm not any good. It's best we just go on loving each other a little longer without ties, please Sam, please. Let's wait and see."

I only had to say please in this special way and he melted; his eyes softened and the hardness went out of his face.

"I love you," I added, "every bit of you."

"And me you," he said.

That night in bed I ran my hands all over his body. It was beautiful, without a spare bit of flesh anywhere.

"I'm you and you're me. We are as one," I said. "We don't need a bit of paper, or a priest's mumbo jumbo."

But Sam stiffened. "Don't speak of the clergy like that," he said. "It's wicked; it's wrong. They are men of God. We may not go to church, but we must give them the respect they deserve. It's only right and proper."

On the chimney piece stood a photograph of Sam's brother who had been killed on the Somme; a taller, more flamboyant version of Sam, with a bushy moustache that drooped a little at the ends – an unnecessary decoration, I thought, to a face already beautifully proportioned. Joe, the firstborn and family favourite, had been engaged to a farmer's daughter, and Sam's mother had hoped for lusty grandchildren. For what else is there for a countrywoman of her sort to look forward to? Her whole life had been given up to rearing her four daughters and two sons. Babies and children were her profession. Joe, her greatest hope, was dead, Sam was now left to carry on the name, to bring into the world a son who might show the flair and genius she had anticipated from Joe's union with the girl he loved. Meanwhile the daughters' chances of marriage had been lessened by the unparalleled slaughter of the recent war. At the time I did not understand how great these pressures were on Sam, how reluctant he was to visit his mother without news of an engagement. I thought I loved him, but was keeping back a part of myself. I was using him to protect me and satisfy desire. Perhaps in a way I patronised him.

When June came I went off by train every day with Skipper to the Kentish countryside to paint or draw the women working in the fields: the strawberry pickers and, later, hop pickers, potato lifters, the gleaners and the harvesters. Sometimes when I was very late back, Sam would be waiting for his meal.

"Thought you were never coming. I'm that hungry," he would say.

"Why didn't you help yourself?"

"There's not much in the cupboard, is there?"

Now that I no longer taught he expected greater efficiency. But at twenty, I did not know how to housekeep. I wrote lists, left them at home and frequently returned with only half the items I meant to buy.

"I must earn money," I said. "I must go on and on until I get it right. Look at this and that, here see, is that better?" I would begin to show him my work. "Are her buttocks all right this time?"

"I want to eat," Sam would say. "Get the meal first, then let's talk."

He left the milk business and took a job as a van driver for a higher weekly wage, quickly becoming proficient at the wheel. On Saturday afternoons he went to a garage to learn about motor mechanics and returned smelling of oil. From time to time I refused his marriage proposals.

One day a week I would pack a portfolio and visit the smaller dealers, peddling my work, but although they might praise my efforts, pat my shoulder or fondle my cheek and express sympathy with struggling artists or a wish to know me better, none offered to promote my pictures. The few sales which continued to come through Edmund and Clare amounted to so little that I was virtually supported by Sam. And since I would not provide him with marriage and the baby he so ardently desired, I felt both guilty and selfish. Occasionally I caught him trying to make love to me without having taken precautions, and then, after a bitter row, we would sleep or lie awake back to back for the rest of the night.

Then one wet Sunday matters came to a head, when I was painting in the shed, working, from memory, on a Kentish barn, trying to catch the pattern of brick against flint, red against grey in the light of a dying sun. Suddenly the doorway darkened. Sam stood there, a frown above his brows, one hand raised in a gesture of impatience. Quietly he suggested that it was time I put the joint in the oven.

"Otherwise we won't sit down to dinner till three o'clock, like last week," he said.

"I can't," I shouted. "Can't you see that the flints are too dark, the blueness isn't there? Move away from that doorway. You're spoiling the light. Move!"

"Don't speak to me like that, Belle," he said. "That's no way for a woman to speak to a man."

"I *can't* leave at this moment. Who cares about food anyway?"

"Well, I'm getting hungry," replied Sam still standing obstinately in the doorway. "You're the woman of the household even though we are not wed, and it's your duty to look after the wage earner."

I stared at the flints I had painted; the grey in them was the colour of cast iron. It was a dead colour, not bluish and ash grey, not full of the subtle variations that make flints so exciting. It was totally wrong and, feeling utterly impotent to put it right, I was beside myself with frustration.

"Oh, for God's sake," I shouted. "Go away and cook the joint yourself, feed your stomach and leave me to finish this. Go on, go!"

He did. He went to the pub and predictably came back drunk at three o'clock, just as the lunch I had belatedly cooked was ready for eating.

"I'm sorry, Sam," I said. "Please understand how difficult painting is. Look, look at this pie I've made. I bought the gooseberries yesterday in Swanley. Isn't the pastry perfect this time?"

The kitchen was now deliciously warm with the smell of

roast beef and parsnips; a Yorkshire pudding, rather biscuity but still a pudding, was golden in the oven. The beef spat and crackled. But Sam was past any food. Looking at me from the corner of a glazed eye he made his way to the bedroom, lay down on the bed and in seconds was snoring loudly.

While Skipper and I shared the lunch, I tried to come to terms with my feelings. Was I wrecking Sam or was he wrecking me? Our bodies searched each other out while our minds quarrelled. Wasn't that the answer? No, not quite. It was more, I told myself, a question of attitudes to life. We were both in love with love; we melted each other; we were addicted to each other, but underneath it all there was a small worm nibbling at the foundations of this love, saying *you are not right for each other; you are too fundamentally different*. I am convinced now that loneliness was at the root of our love, loneliness and sexual need, and propinquity at the exact moment when we both were desperate. And even more strongly Nature's craze to propagate the species, and in me the addictive personality of the artist, for when one drug fails, the addict will go for another, so that when the brush cannot capture the images in the mind, the painter must turn to illness, to sex, alcohol or heroin, or put a bullet through his head like Currie, or gas himself like Gertler. Is that the answer? I did not know then on that darkish Sunday and I do not know it now as an old lady of eighty-two. That problem must go to the grave with me, a question mark carved on my heart.

Then a loophole came, the chance of a break, in which to look at ourselves from the outside. Clare wrote that Edmund had secured a three-month scholarship for me in Paris to study French painting and work in a more conducive atmosphere – whatever that may mean.

Sam was against the idea; adamant and immovable. Absence would break our love, he said. Absence, I argued, would strengthen it. We would both come together again rejuvenated.

"And who's to look after me? Am I to go into lodgings?"

"Sam," I replied. "You are quite capable of looking after yourself."

"And what about Skipper? I thought you loved that dog."

"He can go in the van with you."

"Mr. Saunders won't like it."

"I'll talk to him if you like."

"No, thank you. He doesn't like his drivers not being married. He thinks we *are* married. I told a lie. You make me lie. If you went to see the guvnor you would let out the truth, 'cos you 'ave no shame."

"But think of the great opportunity for me," I pleaded. "Every artist needs to go to Paris. All the great people go: Katherine Mansfield, Gertler, Nash, everyone. Why, Whistler worked there for many years. Besides I must see French pictures – Courbet, Lautrec, Gauguin. Oh, there are oceans of pictures to see."

"I forbid it," said Sam, like a Victorian husband.

"Oh, don't be ridiculous," I said.

"I know about the French," Sam went on belligerently. "My brother used to write home. I know the muck they talk. Their minds are like cesspits when it comes to women. If you go you won't come back."

"Oh now you're being ridiculous," I said, kneeling at his feet, taking his hands in mine. "Sam, I love you, there's no one else, but I want to make a living from my pictures. I want to grow."

"You'll grow all right. You'll grow big inside with some froggy child."

"Oh Sam, don't be coarse, don't be *stupid*, narrow."

"Well, you're not a virgin and you're not married. You're fair game, my girl."

"You insult me," I said, reacting to his Victorianism in the obvious way, as though we were characters from the last century, as though we had not lived through the licence of the Edwardian age, nor witnessed the beginning of the liberating twenties.

The quarrels increased. Between them lay long silences like the muffled calm after a snowfall before the next blizzard. Animosity stirred Sam's eyes to a new glittering green. He glowered. No decent girl, in his opinion, went to Paris. Such a visit would be the final undoing of me. His first loving had been unpremeditated, driven by a sudden overflowing need, but anyone who subsequently took advantage of me would bring moral damnation, mark me out in Sam's eyes as well as the world's, as a loose woman. Sometimes in the night we came together again, embraced in a sort of hopeless, passionate love, desperately wanting our minds to meet on common ground as our bodies did; each trying to force the other to accept his point of view.

For me these rooms were home, but also a base from which to venture out into the world. I wanted to leave and come back. Sam wanted both of us to stay. He saw a permanency in the arrangement; in a way, Sam was for me father and mother as well as lover. He wanted me to remain the same, the pathetic, pretty girl he had found painting all alone, day after day, the small figure staggering with the easel. He wanted to keep my childlike vulnerability to himself. He wanted me to stand still, to need him utterly, and provide the comforts a practised wife could bring to marriage.

But like a daughter I was going to find my own feet; I would not give in. And behind my resolution there was Clare with her suffragette views, a personality which dwarfed that of my lover, a force that was articulate, composed, taking the straight white road to liberation. "Your art must come first. Your art will live on. He is selfish, blinded by the intensely conventional upbringing of the respectable British working class. He is like a railway truck moving on lines, stopping at signals, unable to swerve off the rails and see life as it really is."

How ridiculous all this seems now. An old woman, I look back on my life as a worthless struggle, provoked by an exaggerated sense of my own self-importance. And yet if I lived it again, I am convinced I would make the same mistakes. Perhaps I was the one on the railway line, rushing faster and faster towards disaster, my wheels chanting "Art comes first, art comes first," meaning with supreme conceit: "*My* art comes first."

I went of course, early in the morning to catch a bus to Victoria and then the ferry train. Sam stood at the gate, not offering to carry my suitcase or my easel; his handsome face drained of expression, his eyes pale in the light of an early sun. I ran back and kissed him.

"Oh, Sam, don't take on. Three months will pass in a flash

and I shall come back full of ideas. We shall grow rich on my success. Sam, please, smile!"

He gave me a rough pat on the shoulder. "Be off with you," he said.

I leaned down and kissed Skipper between the eyes. "You know I shall come back. I couldn't leave you. You know that."

"I should have given you a child," said Sam with sudden ruefulness. "Forced it on you. That would have put paid to this trip. I've been too kind." He turned away. "You'll miss your train. That'll never do, better hurry," he called over his shoulder. I set off down the rough road, picking my way round the puddles, so that I should not spoil my new shoes.

Chapter Seven

PARIS was for me a minor disaster. I was too young and immature, too limited in experience, to take advantage of my scholarship. Life in a structured environment had not prepared me for complete freedom and without the need to be anywhere at any given time, I became despondent. I did not know then that isolation would always breed in me a terrible inertia.

I went to the galleries of course, knelt metaphorically at the feet of the Impressionists, drank in the genius of Degas, Lautrec, Rodin, Utrillo and many more. I wandered dreamily by the Seine, set up my easel, painted in oils, drew in charcoal and graphite and destroyed everything before it was finished. I think I suffered from too sharp an awakening. I saw too much and developed visual indigestion and so overwhelming a sense of my own inferiority that I could hardly bear to communicate with anyone. Suddenly I realised that my technique was limited, my use of colour hackneyed and my whole approach to painting too tame and traditional.

And all around me were couples, accentuating my loneliness, fingers entwined, arms round each other's waists, laughing, whispering, kissing in public. Wanting to observe the literary scene, for Stevie had earlier steered me to Balzac and Flaubert, I went to the Deux Magots and ordered a liqueur. Gauche and ill-dressed I sat alone at a table, but almost at once a Frenchman joined me, his eyes appraising my young skin and brilliant eyes. He smiled at me charmingly, but unable to speak more than a few words of French, I fled. Someone had told me once that all loose Frenchmen suffered from syphilis. At that moment I longed for Georgina who would have made a joke of the encounter or flirted, or at least shown me how to behave.

I wrote home daily, although in the beginning the posting of my letters was delayed because I had not realised that stamps could be bought from newsagents and restaurants. But Sam's replies, which gave no indication of his feelings, were few and brief. Some bore a Gloucestershire postmark so I presumed he was visiting his mother. The last one, signed simply *Sam* with no endearments, said, "There's got to be a change. I'm warning you, Belle, things can't go on as they are. It won't be the same when you get back." The envelope was crumpled, the date illegible, so that I suspected it had been kept a long time in his pocket before being posted.

"What things? Have you lost your job, love? Please tell me in detail," I wrote back. "I long to see you with all my heart and soul. And how is Skipper? Has he missed me? Have you both missed me? I shall return early. All my love – Belle."

Sam's handwriting was excellent for a man of his limited education, and although his vocabulary was sparse and his prose often stilted, he knew how to spell. So now, alone in a shabby hotel room at the back of Montmartre, I told myself that he might go far with help and encouragement. Now at last I wanted marriage. Humbled by my lack of sophistication and talent, I had decided to settle down and have children. We would move to the countryside, I told myself, somewhere near his mother, and perhaps we could rent a little land and grow fruit, run a smallholding, as well as a shop, and keep hens. I would paint as a hobby when there was time to spare, but Sam and the babies would come first. We would turn the boys into the sort of men Sam might have been had he been given a better start in life, and the girls – I could not decide about the girls, for somehow the thought of growing daughters caught me on the raw – perhaps I would only produce males.

Suddenly, even in my condescension, Sam became vital to my happiness. I longed to feel his arms around me again and chastised myself for my cruelty to him. I began to lie awake at night full of unfulfilled desires, forgetting how little we had had to say to one another, how long the silences sometimes lay between us like a No Man's Land waiting for a flare to light up the darkness and bring us to life. I saw only the good side of our love affair, grabbing on to it as the only hope against my loneliness, building it into an idyll which had never quite existed. I decided to leave before the time allowed by my scholarship ran out.

Two days after receiving his last letter, I set out for home. Too excited to eat I felt drained when I left the ferry at Dover. The train for London waited puffing steam, and as it bore me through the Kentish countryside, nothing had ever sounded sweeter in my ears. At Victoria I caught a taxi and directed the driver to take me to our rooms.

It was autumn; the smell of burning rubbish hung on the air, boats hooted in the gathering dusk. I felt very old, worn like a broken-down shoe that has walked miles and miles and lost its shape. I wanted Sam's mouth on mine, to feel loved again. I would make a cup of tea, sit down at the table and tell Sam that my mind was made up. We would make real plans at last, and at night we would try to make a baby, our baby, proof of our love.

As I came to our front door, I was stopped by a neighbour who had always disapproved of me and the "goings on". "He's gone," she said in a voice of approbation as the taxi drove off. "Gone away. A decent young couple live there now with a baby boy. Decent people."

I put down my suitcase, because suddenly my arms felt like sodden rags and my legs weak. I saw now that there were different curtains at the windows.

"Have you an address?" I asked at last.

The woman turned back. She wore a tatty black hat and summer gloves, in her world the hallmark of respectability; her iron-grey hair was dragged back into a bun; glistening with triumph, her faded blue eyes looked up into my face, their whites streaked with yellow; her hairy jaw trembled, probably through old age as well as excitement. "They say his father died. He went back to the country. He never did belong here, not really. He weren't no cockney."

"No," I said, "he was Gloucestershire through and through." I turned away, the tears were spouting embarrassingly from my eyes. "Cruel," I said, stumbling back up the half-made road. "How could he be so cruel?" Now suddenly my body seemed to scream for his; the longing was so sharp that I wanted to throw myself down in a spasm of unearned ecstasy, biting the dust, kicking my legs, beating the hard stones like a small child in a tantrum. My pictures, I thought a moment later. My pictures, where are they? I ran back; the gate was ajar; I unlatched the shed door, looked inside and saw only a few garden tools, a pram and six or seven plant pots. Everything we owned had gone. And Skipper? I thought then that if Sam had destroyed my pictures I should want to kill him. I would catch a train tomorrow. I knew where his mother lived. It was only nine miles from Shamely, I had not used all my grant and I had changed several hundred francs into pounds at the port, so I had plenty of money. I spent the night lying awake in a flea-ridden bed in a cheap lodging house. It was the first time I had wanted to die for several years. This time I wanted a gun. I could see myself pulling the trigger, feel the spring of it, the cold steel against my temple. "Bang," I kept saying to myself, "Bang." It would be a brave way to go, better than sneaking out with a few whiffs of gas or a drug overdose. "Go out with a bang, a big bang," I said aloud. And I thought of a man I had seen shooting a horse at Shamely, the blood and the breaking of wind had been awful; the scene had become part of me, a horror like Helen's death, locked away in those files marked SECRET, whose contents come up only in moments of solitude and silence when a masochistic mood takes over and the heart seems to bleed.

Sam's mother came to the door, a short thin woman with hollow cheeks and thinning grey hair piled into a neat bun on top of her head. She must have been barely fifty but child-bearing, poor diet and hard work had taken their toll; she looked ten years older, she wore spectacles and her false teeth showed too much artificial gum. But her features were Sam's features, only older and thinner, and her voice was Sam's voice, yet higher. But her hands were long and slender, a lady's, only worn, as Sam had said, almost to the bone.

"Come in," she invited. "Would you like a cup of tea?"

A little wire-haired terrier scuttled at her heels.

"It's quite a pickle, you coming back after all," she added, putting a black kettle on the fire. "It won't be a moment. It was on the boil a minute ago."

"I don't want to be a trouble," I said.

"You won't be. But you're one of the new modern girls, aren't you? An artist and all that. I liked your pictures of Sam. I still have them. You have a gift. God has been good to you. We never thought you would drag yourself back from the gaieties of Paris."

The kettle began to sing; the little dog sat in front of the fire like a cat gazing into the flames; a few drops of rain spattered the window panes. "We'll be having a storm soon, I shouldn't wonder. Wind's gone round to the north-west."

So this was where Sam grew up, in a little semi-detached cottage built of honey-coloured stone, too small for six children, but with a sense of peacefulness about it, a sense of eternal values and grace which must have helped, and were created by the woman not the man.

"My husband died. It was a pickle, but Sam's tidied everything up a treat. Sam was my prop and stay. I don't know what I would have done without him." She poured me a cup of tea. "Sugar?"

"No, thank you."

She had a sort of ageless grace which I envied. "It takes time to get over a death," she said. "But I have a daughter at home now – the other three are in service – and my little dog's a great companion. And Sam's only fifteen minutes' walk."

I wanted to ask where, but I felt suddenly paralysed; my tongue seemed glued to my palette. I had left for an unfulfilled dream the only being I loved in the world.

"My pictures?" I asked, picking up my tea. "Do you know where they are?"

The cup slipped out of my hand and crashed on the floor. It was white porcelain decorated with little roses, perhaps one of a treasured service.

"Don't worry," she said. "You're all upset. Just a minute while I sweep up the pieces and get you another."

"There now. The pictures. I don't know. I don't think Sam brought any with him."

"Did he burn them?" I asked in sudden terror.

"No, no. My Sam would never do a thing like that. They are bound to be safe. You have no cause for worry. I'll find out and write to you. You must leave me your address."

"I thought of going over to see him."

"I shouldn't do that."

"Why not?"

"Well, he's married now, my dear. He's married his childhood sweetheart. He's a chauffeur now, up at the big house." I gripped the tea cup hard. "He's got the dog with him. It was very sudden of course, people wanted to gossip about the suddenness but the banns were called in church; it was all proper like. Been married a week this Saturday. It had to be quiet like, being so soon after my husband's death."

"So, I was just too late by three days," I said.

"Too late, too late? He said you wouldn't have him. You refused. He thought you would never come back. He was that hurt. He would have made a decent woman of you any day. Our Sam's like that, never been capable of a mean trick in his life. Would you care for a biscuit?"

"No, I'll go now, thank you, thank you very much."

I stumbled out across the fields to the big house and found Sam's cottage which adjoined the stables. A young girl opened the door and I looked this time into a wide smiling face with one front tooth missing and a pair of pimples on a nose which was short but well shaped. Sam's wife's eyes were blue like mine, but bubbling over with friendliness. She wore a flowered overall, stretched tight across large breasts. She was big, comfortable and, I thought, kind. Her legs were very fat; her hands large and rather coarse, but her smile had a welcome and simplicity that I recognised as genuine. She was in my own words a *real* person.

"I'm Christabelle," I said.

"Never!"

She looked me up and down, as a dog may sum up another while deciding whether to welcome or attack.

"You look very tired. Are you just back from Paris? You know that Sam and me are married, don't you? Last Saturday it was." She turned the thin gold wedding ring.

"Yes." My voice was a whisper, supernatural, outside myself. It spoke automatically, remembering manners, while my mind was a tangle of emotion, hate and admiration.

"Come in, sit down and would you like a cup of tea?"

I gulped. Suddenly Skipper bounded up, licked my hands,

splashed my face with his tongue, enjoying the taste of the tears, then sat down beside his new owner.

"He's a great one, our Skip," she said. "I'll just put on the kettle. I expect you want to know a few things."

"My pictures?" the voice whispered.

"Oh, don't you go worrying about them. Sam's been and taken them to those friends of yours, the art teacher and his wife. Sam said you would be broken-hearted without your pictures. Said they was your world."

"I'm sorry," she said later, handing me a cup of tea. "I can see you're all upset, but Sam couldn't go on the way you wanted. 'E's been brought up decent, and 'is mother wanted grandchildren that badly, and 'e wanted to be near 'er, now that she's alone. I've known Sam since we were little kids, see. There's been no one else for me. Of course 'e had Lily Perkins, that I do know, but all the boys 'ad 'er – learnin' you see. Well, men aren't like us, are they? Like children really."

"He's happy?" the voice asked.

"Well, yes. 'E worried a bit about you, of course, being on your own in Paris, but 'e said art would always come first with you. 'E couldn't see any way round. 'E's 'onest, you see. 'E said 'e thought 'e could grow to love me again. We would begin again where we left off. I would have taken 'im anyway, I wanted 'im that bad. I cried when 'e quarrelled with 'is father and left for London. I thought my 'eart would break. We were at school together, see. 'E used to make me daisy chains, really romantic 'e was, as a little boy, and then 'is brother was killed, that upset 'im terrible, and 'e 'ad to try to take 'is place, but 'e wasn't the same sort as Joe. 'E was quieter."

I looked around the room. "There was a chair," I began.

"The rush-seated one? Yes, 'e knew that was kind of special like, something you 'ad bought for yourself and put in your pictures. So 'e took it with the other stuff to the art teacher. 'E's not kept anything which belonged to you, except one picture of our Skip and one of the mare. 'E said you gave them to 'im."

My hands were twisting each other, as the future stretched ahead like a great desert, going on and on into nothing, dry as dust.

"I must go," I said. "And I do thank you."

"Yes," she replied. "I think it would be wise. We don't want to upset 'im."

As I left the cottage there was suddenly no focal point to my life; yet I knew that I should be glad for Sam, and beneath my despair was the certain knowledge that I did not want to be a chauffeur's wife, kowtowing to the people at the big house, minding my manners. I would not want my husband to be at any rich man's beck and call. It would eventually diminish him in my eyes and in the end diminish me too. His wife, I saw, could give him everything he wanted – a loving comfortable home, children, peace of mind – everything that I had failed to provide.

Chapter Eight

I WENT TO see Clare, told almost all that had happened, my words coming out too fast.

"Honestly, Paris was a fiasco," I finished. "I was suddenly frightfully shy. I felt quite alone, divorced from everyone else and when that happens all my self-confidence goes. I never followed up any of your introductions. I was quite stupidly miserable and ridiculously homesick. Clare, to tell the truth, I am disgusted with myself."

"But you saw pictures. You feasted your eyes," she said in her calm voice. "You absorbed great art and the benefits will turn up in your own paintings. People don't matter so much. It is vision not talk that counts."

"I feel such a failure," I went on, unconvinced. "I should never have taken up with Sam in the way I did. Perhaps my mother behaved in the same sort of way, and that's why I'm here. I'm not an orphan, Clare, I'm illegitimate. One of the grey nuns told me that my parents were still alive, that they had to dump me to avoid a scandal. I've got their blood, and I don't know what it is: and sometimes that frightens me. I treated Sam so badly."

"You've been alone too much," Clare said. "Would you like to come here to stay for a bit? I should like that. I've always wanted a daughter and it never happened, you see."

I said I could manage all right, thank you very much. In the orphanage I had learned to be alone with God, because close friendships were discouraged. Only the trouble was I wasn't sure that I believed in God any more, not the nuns' version of God, anyway.

Then Clare said I was being very selfish. "I need you and alone you'll moulder and get TB like Helen."

I said I wouldn't. I had a hard core. "Two's company, three's none. You have a happy marriage and you won't want me tagging on."

"Who said it was happy?" she retorted, with unexpected sharpness. "You underestimate yourself. Tell me, what will you drink?"

When I suggested gin and lime she said I was very modern, then handing me a glass she told me that Edmund had only a few months to live. "Cancer of the stomach, poor darling, so it's going to be pretty horrific. I don't want to be alone. I think your hard core will help us both, Christa."

So of course I said I would stay. I said I was terribly, terribly sorry, although in my heart I was simply sad, because Edmund seemed to me so old that I thought his time had run out, and I was sure that I would want to die if I had become as fossil-like as he.

So I moved into Clare's house, which was in one of those leafy Hampstead roads that run down to the Heath, where people dropped in to stay a while, drink a while, and then move on. I had a new status as Clare's right hand and protégée, and, at every opportunity, she promoted my work with very un-British enthusiasm which both pleased and embarrassed me. Facing death together, sharing secrets, we became close.

Meanwhile Edmund continued to paint in a desultory way, driven by habit rather than inspiration, but the vigour had gone from his work and often we found him sitting in his studio, staring into space. And now Clare and he played out a terrible charade, pretending that he was going to recover while both knew he was about to die. Disturbingly, Clare sometimes talked of him to me in the past tense.

She told me that despite being so old-fashioned he believed in free love. "He gave me so much leeway, because, you see, the gentler he became as a man the less passionate he was as a lover. He never did an ugly thing. He believed beauty was truth and truth beauty. Oh, poor Edmund, how hard he tried always to be generous and good."

And although it now seemed to me that truth could be very ugly, I saw no point in arguing with my mentor.

"I think a little hate might have improved his art, but you

cannot create beauty unless you are true to yourself," Clare continued as she arranged in a pottery jar grasses she had dried in the airing cupboard.

"It is hard to be true to a self you do not understand," I said.

"Ah, but," Clare replied, "understanding and genius only come through acute suffering. God always extracts a payment for genius – think of Van Gogh, Swinburne, Coleridge, Lautrec, Milton and, of course, Oscar Wilde – what a dramatist!"

I said I was sure she was right, but at the same moment I was thinking, not me, not yet, for even in my darkest moments, there had always been a little hope stirring like a chick pecking its way out of an egg, and fantasies with a pistol at my head had been brief and dramatic rather than serious.

While Edmund's cheeks hollowed, I met in that house many notable painters and some critics. When a picture dealer turned up, too, he was invariably shown my work, but, although polite noises might be made, none offered to act for me.

"Such fools!" Clare would exclaim afterwards. "They call themselves experts, but they don't lead fashion. They follow it."

During those weeks in Hampstead, my interlude with Sam sank into perspective: an experience rather than a lost idyll. Now only Edmund's approaching death, Clare's friendship and my art mattered. And yet paradoxically, although I cried when I saw Edmund writhing in pain and the proximity of death filled me with sorrow, I remember that time as happy and rewarding. Unable through some contrariness of spirit to model myself on any nun I had lacked a female figure to emulate until Clare filled that gap. In Hampstead I felt for the first time a loving admiration for another female, for in my friendship with Georgina there had been reservations on my part, and Stevie had asked for more than I could give, so arousing my guilt. Most important perhaps, I found my art developing under Clare's encouraging eye and Edmund's kind comments.

Soon I joined a small group experimenting with tempera,

which produced the translucent, pale shades I needed to capture the peculiar charm of Clare's dried grasses and flowers, the semi-transparent beauty of honesty's autumnal discs, the freshness of Clare's bleached cottons and her own face with its pearly whiteness enhanced with the touches of rouge she applied so expertly. The shades of the house, the shades of herself were predominantly yellow, gold and cream, soft and clean but warm too, as ornamental pampas is warm to the eye in winter and cool in summer. Her furniture was modern even by today's standards. She recognised the pleasing simplicity of stripped pine and had a passion for graceful, unadorned pottery, and pale wickerwork in moderation. Dark colours were now no longer part of my painter's vocabulary; everything for me had to be light, airy and lucent. I studied Utrillo's work but did not like the way he applied his paint. I went back to Whistler, was vaguely influenced by Japanese art, tried my own symphonies in honey-gold and cream, attempted to reduce my work to basic lines without losing charm and grace. My life seemed calm now but my art was full of change and experiment. For a time I became a listener rather than a talker at parties.

Meanwhile Edmund grew weaker; the veins on his hand stood out like ropes, he shrank so that his clothes became too big and he took on the image of a scarecrow. And although everyone could see that he was mortally ill, no one dared to mention to Clare that the end was near. The unspoken law that forbade anyone, including me, to speak of his dying, to spare embarrassment at all costs, remained unbroken.

He had never looked well as long as I had known him, but now he looked so close to the grave that people stepped back when he came near as though they feared contamination. Clare began to specialise in soups for him: together, we sieved and chopped, ground and whisked. We flavoured with herbs and when spring came collected dandelions from the Heath for wine.

In May I exhibited with other tempera painters in a small Hampstead gallery run by one of Clare's friends. Not many people now worked in this medium, apart from a small group in Birmingham, but although the practice was in decline, we received a good deal of notice in the local papers and a passing mention in some of the national press. Friends bought my picture of Clare in her parlour arranging dried grasses and flowers, and strangers bought a pale imaginary street in spring sunshine and a still life of bread, cheese and fruit. By May Edmund was on the strongest painkillers, by June he was failing to keep down even the blandest of Clare's soups, by July he was dead, slipping away. One moment he had been within our grasp, haggard beyond belief, but alive, conscious, and the next he had gone; his face a mask, his eyes like glass, his hands useless as the stalks of dying flowers.

Yet, stunned though I was, I knew that this was a moment which I must record. Here like Wallis's 'Death of Chatterton' was the subject for a picture. Colour drained, the moon-white face attained the magnificence of a statue, the hands unspeakable pathos; the brows a sudden sternness they had not shown in life. Through Edmund death attained an unexpected nobility that would be filed in my memory for future use.

"Come away," said Clare "It is all over. Mrs. Kirkwood will lay him out. Wasn't it a peaceful death? I'm so glad he didn't suffer at the end."

Her courage shamed me, yet in that instant I had recognised that for the artist no less than the author all experience is grist to the mill. While others suffer, there is always at the back of their minds an eye for the visual or an ear for the spoken word; the collector instinct ensuring that they fill the store cupboard with a terrible single-mindedness that in a way isolates them from other people. I would not rest until I had transmitted on to paper or canvas that figure on the iron bedstead. At the precise moment when I should have been burdened with a great sorrow, I was excited by a new awakening.

"I'll make a cup of tea," said Clare.

"No, sit down, let me."

"I'm not an invalid. At these times one must be busy. I am so glad, so very glad, he just glided away like an old ship slipping off on the tide. And I was there. I was so afraid it might happen when I was out, when there was nobody to hold his hand. When I was young I was a nurse and held many hands."

"A nurse? I never knew. A biscuit?" I said, reaching for the tin. "Have a biscuit?" I wanted to help, but was unable to make the right gesture, to touch. At the orphanage no one touched. To touch was to tempt unclean thoughts. Instead I treated Clare as though she was a disappointed child rather than a wife bereaved after twenty years of marriage. I hated myself for my awkwardness.

"He was so brave," I said at last.

"Most people are," said Clare. "Perhaps your nuns were right and there *is* an Almighty who gives them strength at the end."

For me a way of life was ending: things were being wound up. Clare decided to return to Austria.

"What will you do?" Clare put a hand on my arm. "You need to move on, too."

"I don't know. Find lodgings."

The future was suddenly frightening, a stage without actors. There would be doors of course, but who would come through them? Had my script been written years ago, acted and rehearsed a thousand times? Or was it being written now? Or was I about to write it? Did we write our own scripts or were we tossed by fate like a character from a Hardy novel? In those days my head was full of verse, hymn tunes and religious incantations and now one of Stevie's favourite quotes came to me.

> It matters not how strait the gate,
> How charged with punishments the scroll,
> I am the master of my fate:
> I am the captain of my soul.

Could I not also be the master of my fate and captain of my soul?

"I'll be all right," I said. "Something will turn up. I shall make it turn up."

"You sound like Mr. Micawber. I want to see you settled before I leave. I feel somehow responsible, but conflict is good for creativity. Oh, yes, it is comfort that is bad. You were sinking into a comfortable trough with me; your work was suffering from pernicious anaemia."

For a moment I was offended, for, although I had outgrown

my pale pictures, I did not want to hear their faults; then I realised that Clare had to convince herself that I needed to go, in order to destroy any guilty feelings in herself. She needed to think she was turning me out for my own good.

She said, "You cry out for a man, to be an equal, to understand. If only we could settle you with someone suitable, someone who would provide just enough conflict to keep your art going, but, at the same time, a stable background."

After the funeral Clare put the house up for sale and started to ask friends round again. "What are we going to do with Christabelle?" was one of her constant cries. Many suggestions were made, while I said I would go into lodgings. Then a big rumbustious artist, Barnabas Copeland, said, "Let her live with me. Would you live with me, my darling? I should love that. Think of waking every morning to see those forget-me-not blue eyes."

"They're not forget-me-not, they are violet, you old rogue," cried Clare. "Ignore him, Christo. He's a womaniser, a seducer of charming, well brought up young women, a bad influence."

I looked at the man, whom I had met on earlier occasions. He was large and warm, with wild, curly fair hair, a blob of a nose but fine quick-moving grey-blue eyes that teased and a face that was warm and welcoming. He looked at me and I turned away.

"She's shy," he laughed. "A shy forget-me-not. Now doesn't that sound winsome and awful? You're not winsome, are you, Christo? I couldn't bear that."

"You don't have to," I replied stoutly, "because I'm not coming to live with you."

"Well said," shouted a red-haired young artist called Arthur, who looked as though he had come straight from Rossetti's brush. "Someone's got to put him in his place."

I found an attic, high in a Victorian house on the borders of Finchley. It looked across gardens; there were eaves, an iron bedstead, brown patterned linoleum on the floor, a gas ring in one corner, a square table in another, two chairs and a commode with a tin pot of the kind known by the women at the orphanage as an "article". It was a cold bare place, which I quickly gave the appearance of a junk room by moving in pictures, pieces of pottery given to me by Clare, clothes and books, much of which had to be put on the floor as there were no shelves. I hung my coat and dresses on the back of the door.

It was autumn and up from the street came the sound of horse and motor traffic, the rustle of leaves, the last songs of the birds, and, faintly, the scent of the roses that lingered still on gates and walls waiting for the first frost to turn their petals and subdue them. Life had a melancholy about it, which I refused to accept. Clare had generously bought three of my pictures before she left and, with some of the money from this, I threw a house-warming party, so that people should know where I was. Barnabas came, and Arthur, and a quiet young potter called June, and half a dozen other people whose names I have forgotten. Barnabas said the room was awful, the most uninspiring place that he had ever entered. Didn't the brown paint drive me mad? He opened the commode door and found the "article" and went into peals of laughter. He became rather drunk on the punch I had made and later wore the "article" as a hat, pretending to be a commercial traveller. After a time we played charades, using my few clothes as props. When all the visitors had gone at one o'clock in the morning I carried the dirty glasses down to the pantry on the second floor to wash them up, and was met by a furious landlady in dressing gown and curlers, gabbling with rage. Her false teeth moved up and down as she talked; yellow as pus, her wrinkled time-pocked face twisted in fury and disgust. I was indecent, she screamed, a disgrace to a respectable house – having male guests at that time of night. People would accuse her of prostitution. Tomorrow I must go, first thing. She would turn my belongings out into the street. She would call a policeman if I objected. Hers was a decent house. "Nothing happened," I said, "but just a few games." "Games," she screamed; she knew all about games. "Don't talk to me about games. And you looked such a decent little thing."

"I am a decent little thing," I told her. "It's all in your mind."

"Don't you speak to me like that. I'll have the police after you, you filthy, dirty girl!"

A thought had planted itself in her head as firmly as an oak sapling; nothing, no amount of argument would move it. I was everything that was bad. She was everything that was good. There was no room for argument or negotiation.

Doors were beginning to open along the passage and on the floor above, as curious lodgers looked out to see who had caused the commotion. I stood there in my twenties gown, shoulders bare, a long string of ambers around my neck, feeling very little and quite dreadfully alone.

"I'll go," I said. "Don't worry."

"I should think you will," the landlady screamed quite unable to accept my capitulation gracefully. "You've kept the whole household awake with your goings-on."

"Just let me wash up the glasses. I only bought them today, specially. I was in a celebratory mood having moved in." But the woman had turned and was retreating now to her own quarters, puffed up with righteous indignation.

I was putting my clothes back into my suitcase the next morning when Barnabas arrived carrying a great bunch of chrysanthemums.

"Rather funereal I'm afraid, but I did want to make up for behaving rather badly last night. It's the punch. It was so extraordinarily potent. Was I really awful? Absolutely bloody? What did you put in it, you little witch?" I realised then that he could not remember the party at all, that he was afraid he had peed in public or something, so I reassured him.

"Why are you packing? You're not going away? Shall I make us a cup of tea on that gas ring?"

I told him about the landlady. "Oh my poor Christo, my poor Christo. What a B.I.T.C.H. Where's the tap? You'll need some tea afterwards to revive you." He picked up my kettle. "Cheer up." He ruffled my hair. "We'll think of something. If the worst comes to the worst I can let you have a corner, the opposite corner to me, of course, in my studio. It's very cosy with a wood stove and not a shred of hateful lino to be seen."

"On the next floor."

"What?"

"The tap."

"Oh yes, the tap – tea."

While he was seeing to the water, I put the books back into their cardboard boxes.

"I say, penny dreadfuls – I thought better of you than that," said Barnabas on his return. "Wicked girl reading about the seduction of maid servants by young lords."

"You're thinking of *Red Star Weekly*," I said; then later, "Actually I'm through with that phase. It was just an aberration to counteract the excessive moral atmosphere of school."

"Oh, you're wonderful. I do love you," cried Barnabas, pouring tea. "Sugar? Where will you go?"

"I don't know."

"Well, bring your belongings to me, anyway. I mean you can't exactly leave your pictures out in the street."

"Yes, thank you. I'll get a taxi."

"No, you relax, I'll get it for you. Not now, silly, when the time comes, when we've had our tea and carried everything downstairs. Clare said you came from nowhere. Is that right? I mean it sounds far-fetched."

"Sort of," I said.

"But you are not a second immaculate conception? That would be too awful. I mean the next one, after Jesus."

"Now *you're* being silly," I said, shocked by his blasphemy.

"Come and be my concubine, please."

"Now I shall have to ask you to go," I countered, taking his hands off my knees.

"No, I promise I'll behave. I'll help you. You need me. You can't carry all that down by yourself."

"I carried it up."

"Well, you shouldn't have done so. It's wicked. Someone should have done it for you. Let me be your slave, just for today. I can't bear to think of you struggling all alone."

As we went down, the landlady peeped through a door.

"Good, you've seen sense, then," she said. "This is a respectable house."

"Oh shut your trap, you silly bitch," shouted Barnabas. "You've got a dirty mind. There were no goings-on last night, simply a few childish games. Women like you should be taken to court for malicious slander against innocent, unprotected young girls."

The door slammed. "Is that what you were secretly longing to say? Was I your mouthpiece? I wanted to be," he grinned.

"More or less. Take care of that bowl – it's one June made for me as a present."

"A sad girl, don't you think, a sad girl?" asked Barnabas. "A bit dried up, bitter lines round the mouth, hair too tightly curled, stocking seams always straight – that sort of person. Do you know what I mean? I'm sure her suspenders *never* break."

"Should they?"

"Should they what?"

"Should girls' suspenders break?"

"Well, it's so much more enticing if they do. It does brighten up life. I mean, think of a world peopled only by Junes. It would be a bit dreary wouldn't it? No fun. I mean she is dreadfully earnest about her A.R.T. isn't she, and her enthusiasm is so misplaced because pottery is a craft rather than art, isn't it?"

Barnabas was always good at attracting taxis and very soon we were bouncing back to Hampstead. A pale sun touched the rooftops, bringing the redness out of the brightest leaves that lay so thick on the pavements, despite the efforts of street sweepers.

"*Season of mists and mellow fruitfulness*," quoted Barnabas. "Did you learn poetry at school? Diabolical, wasn't it, and quite useless? All that Shakespeare. Well, Shakespeare can be rather grand, but Shelley and Keats. Ugh! I suppose Housman was all right. Why don't you try reading something really modern, Gilbert Cannan or H. G. Wells or what about that man Onions? Compton Mackenzie is for vicars' daughters."

He talked so much without waiting for answers that the journey to his place seemed only to take minutes. The studio was, as he said, warm with a great cast-iron stove burning wood and a huge sofa as well as two divans. There were three tables covered with paints, paper and palettes, brushes and charcoal. Many canvases leaned against the walls; a few, turned outwards, showed that his main influence at the moment was Gauguin, but he was becoming more abstract, trying, he explained, to fine things down to a few basic shapes.

He put a pot on to cook, a stew, which he said had been going all the week. He opened a bottle of wine. "To us," he said pouring two glasses. "Long may we both prosper." His hands were short and wide, a workman's hands; his eyes prominent but very expressive. He was a bear of a man, a yellowy bear, warm-blooded, a little too fat, but kindly-looking with that wonderful capacity to make me laugh, to make fun of everything but the most serious matters.

"I'm so glad you've given up all that tempera stuff," he said. "I always think it's all a bit too fussy, too calculated. Do you know what I mean? I prefer splashes of colour. Such meticulous work loses spontaneity. Spontaneity is so important in painting. I believe absolutely in inspiration, the gods, do you?"

He looked deep into my face, as though trying to understand me, to read my soul. "Do you like men? Or are you frightened?" he asked.

"Some men. Look, I must go. I've got to find another room."

"Oh no, not till you've had lunch. The pot is on now. You can't cheat me out of lunch," he said, grinning.

"I can," I said, "easily."

"But you won't," he argued. "You won't because you are a nice polite girl, who doesn't turn a man down when the meal's cooking and he's helped her with her luggage and offered her storage space."

"That is a sort of moral blackmail," I said.

"Yes, and why not?" he asked. "A desperate man uses every weapon that comes to hand."

"You're not desperate."

"How do you know? How do you know what thoughts are bubbling up inside me like fizz in a bottle waiting for the top to be lifted?"

"I don't."

"Exactly. Now then: you are my new little friend who's come from nowhere and we are going to help each other. Tell me, how did you find Clare?"

"I liked her."

"That goes without saying, but her brooches, her jewellery-making? Just a little ornery, I thought, and poor Edmund, a bit of a dogsbody. Yes?"

"No, no, I don't think so."

"He wasn't quite up to her. She was too quick for him. I think he was wrung dry by her. So much compressed vitality, so much energy to spare within that small frame, so bland she looked, and yet underneath it all wasn't there something a little calculating?"

"Oh no," I said, stoutly. "I was with her when he died. She was heartbroken. She confided in me."

"Oh do tell, all about the lovers."

"No." I started to get up.

"The pot," he cried, "hear it singing? You can't *not* eat my stew."

I resisted all Barnabas's blandishments to "stay for ever" and found a room in Earl's Court in an Edwardian lodging house.

"It's not suitable," Barnabas commented as he helped me move in my luggage and my rush-seated chair. "It's too small, and your neighbours will complain if you have a party. The place smells of respectability, of elderly unmarried ladies with fur tippets, potted plants and antimacassars. An artist to them is a person of great moral turpitude. You won't be happy. You had much better stay with me. You can have the divan nearest the stove, and I promise not to touch you, despite the slightly murky past. I have an iron self-control when it comes to not imposing myself on other people. It's the Yorkshire blood in me, the good honest side."

"If you can keep my canvases for a while I shall be very grateful," I said. "You have been very kind, Barnabas."

"You sound like someone's maiden aunt, and why don't you relax just enough to call me Barney like everyone else? And for heaven's sake stop running your hands through your hair." He looked into my face. "Funny? Aren't you going to laugh?"

"You're impossible," I said, a smile splitting my face, almost against my will.

"Do you know that Clare called you her 'sad little orphan'?"

"No, I don't see myself as an object of pity."

"All hoity-toity," he said. "Gone stiff again, but eyes bright, blazing a little."

"Oh, shut up," I said.

"That's better, that's the spirit. Well, I'll take myself off. Come and see me when you like. This room won't be much good with a window facing south, so please use my studio whenever you like. I'll give you a key and be your big fat Daddy for the time being."

He puffed out his cheeks and twirled an imaginary moustache. "Well, my dear, be seeing you soon," he crooned. "So long."

His footsteps were loud on the uncarpeted stair. The room seemed smaller and colder now that he had gone. The clay pipes of the gas fire, broken here and there, reminded me of damaged false teeth staring at me angrily, as though somehow I had cheated them of life. My room looked out on rooftops, blue-grey as wet seals, and chimneys from which blackish smoke curled into a sullen sky. The sun had gone; the moon had not yet come. Dusk was like a hand of caution on the shoulder, the negative word whispered in the frightened ear. I would paint the roofs. I would paint the chimney pots with their square stacks, and all the little attic windows that were beginning to light up now telling me that I was not alone, that all over London were single girls like me in small shabby rooms, wanting men, wanting money, wanting fame and, above all, at this moment wanting companionship.

"Your work is so fantastically promising," said Barney, a glass of wine in his hand, "but so dead. The colours you use are dead. Why?"

"Perhaps I'm dead," I said. "A zombie in a shell, a dried-up stick, a stone."

"Well, you would think so from these," said Barney, looking at a few of the paintings from my days with Clare.

"We were waiting for death, you see. Could that be the reason?"

"Well, now you're waiting for life, for the sap to rise, for love to warm the cockles of your heart and set the blood racing again, so turn to colour, no more black, no more sludge, putty or beige – reds and blues and yellows – and put it on more thickly, watch me."

I had come to fetch three canvases to show June and I ended up having a lesson in the freer use of paint.

"Cast away your inhibitions," cried Barney, pausing to pour me a glass of wine. "Let the subconscious take over." A cigarette hung from his mouth; deftly and quickly his brush flew. A letter box appeared, a street, corner shop, a lady in Victorian clothes leading a blue dog.

"But dogs aren't blue," I objected.

"Oh you poor little philistine! Have you never heard of the kerry blue and, anyway, must our pictures be factual, like a boring little lecture from an overblown academic? We make pictures; we don't copy. We don't need footnotes. We don't qualify. Art for art's sake, my dear Christ-*a*-belle. So long as the result is beautiful, so long as it is alive and quickens the pulse, who cares about accuracy? Accuracy is for people like poor dear Edmund, the timid and everyday. Not for us, not for the post-war world. No, you and I are different."

"I can only paint what is inside me," I said rather naively.

"You mean if there was a baby you would paint that, or will you concentrate on your intestines, or what about tripe? They could provide another opportunity for those dead colours."

"You're mocking me," I said.

"Well someone had got to get rid of the hang-dog look," he said.

"I must go," I said on another occasion, picking up my shopping bag. "I have to stock up with food."

I was always going, always leaving Barney; that seemed for a time to be part of the pattern of my life. I visited him and then ran away, back to lonely virtue in my little room, to boiled potatoes and Oxo prepared on a gas ring. And it kept on raining; the skies were as grey as the water-streaked pavements; yet the dawns were beautiful, pink and frail as a cinnabar's wings then darkening to gold, to be overwhelmed by nine o'clock by the whirling clouds, so that I remembered Sam's overworked remark, *Red morning, shepherd's warning*. My life with him now seemed ages away, although sometimes I would see a face, in the Tube perhaps or the street, sharp and strong, that brought back his presence like a stab at the heart; for a moment I would catch my breath, then breathe deeply again, and push back that memory like an unwelcome guest I no longer wanted on my doorstep; a reminder of all that might have been.

For weeks I struggled to paint the newly dead Edmund, to catch the majesty and pathos. I depicted him close up and from a distance of about five yards. I worked over his face again and again, using gouache to try to bring out the extraordinary almost alabaster whiteness which seemed to come so soon after death; to describe in paint the strange emptiness of the eyes and the mouth's last grimace, the lips drawn back. Perhaps this was a kind of exorcism, but I think of it more as a voyage of discovery; that somehow through death we can also discover life. And yet sometimes as I painted the tears ran down my cheeks as though it was for myself and the whole of mankind that I was crying. And when I stopped I would find that I was quite cold. Catching a glimpse of my face in the chipped mirror that hung by my bed, I would see that my face was ash-white and that under my eyes were two shadows like ochre, and that my lips were the colour of dead leaves. And then I would run for a lipstick and make them red again, and I would pat Coty's powder under my eyes, and make myself a cup of tea. If Barney called at such times I would cover my work, these pictures of Edmund being my most private possessions, and he would say, "Christabelle, you look awful, you need a drink. You will kill yourself. Come out at once. Where's your coat and hat, or whatever you wear? Come on, we're going to a café to fill you up!" And, when I was ready, he would take my hand and run me down the stairs, and when we reached the bottom, he would say, "There, that's put some colour in your cheeks."

But sometimes Barney would become angry. "Do you want to destroy yourself?" he would shout. "Why don't you eat, you silly child? Are you a masochist? You look like death warmed up. Your bones are sticking out. You're a toast rack. Why don't you let me give you some money? Why are you so damned proud?"

But although I was poor I was not penniless. Various friends of Clare bought my work from time to time and now, looking back, I suspect that before leaving for Austria she had asked them to support me. When spring came again I went to the Embankment and, leaning my work up against a wall, I tried to win trade from passers-by, charging a pound a picture; then I found I could make a few shillings offering to sketch people in charcoal, especially young couples walking arm in arm, who wanted me to record in a few lines a moment of happiness or new-found love. All at once I became interested in street corners, street life. I visited the East End to paint the poor children playing hop scotch or Tom Tiddler's Ground, and the laundrywomen carrying baskets of freshly washed clothes, and then I went back to the river, to the Thames, and became obsessed with boatmen and the steamers crowded with people on Saturday afternoons. Suddenly, after struggling so long with a corpse I needed movement and life, the magic of sun on water.

Barney, who was moving all the time toward abstract art, declared my work old-fashioned. "Girls are never adventurous enough. At heart the female is a conservative, a traditionalist. New movements are formed by men." He lit a cigarette and surveyed my latest street scenes. "There's too much Edmund in your pictures and Wilson Steer, even Sargent and Stanhope Forbes and, my God, this is pure Fred Brown. Surely you don't want to ape the Professor? He's such old hat."

"I paint what I see," I said stoutly. "What I feel. I can't do otherwise. It's the only way I know."

"Oh, for heaven's sake," he exploded. "Don't be so conventional. Every amateur claims to paint what he sees! Experiment Christ-*a*-belle. Step out into the great world of the unknown. Take your courage into both hands and explore. Look to Gauguin, Matisse, Monet and think what doors they opened."

"But perhaps I'm not a great artist, perhaps I'm run of the mill," I answered quietly. "You cannot compare me with geniuses and then complain that you find me wanting."

"But you've got to aim for the highest. Don't you see?" yelled Barney in despair. "You've got to move forward all the time, not look back. Onward into battle, hear our trumpets blow. Oh, Christ-*a*-belle, you have so much talent and you're letting it go to seed." He threw himself down on my bed. "Are you going to make something to eat? I'm exhausted. I've been struggling with those bloody trees all morning. Trees are not my *métier*. Nor is light. God, how I hate sunsets. Form is what I'm after, shapes. I'm sick and tired of the surface of objects. I want to get deeper. Somehow I've got to paint the whole, all dimensions, and yet reach beyond Cubism, which is now as dead as a bloody doornail. Perhaps Constructivism is what I'm after, perhaps that is what I mean."

"Why do you have to give a name to your type of painting? Why do you have to belong to any movement? It's all too cerebral for me," I complained, lighting the gas ring.

"I know. That's because you are female. The feminine mind is intuitive; it works on feel, preconceived ideas and emotion rather than logical thought. That's why you won't live with me. Somewhere deep down you have some little moral reserve, some prejudice, some middle-class streak of respectability which whispers no, even though your emotions and mind say yes. Now if you looked at the idea logically, like a man, you would see how well it would work at both practical and emotional levels: (A) living would be cheaper, because it always costs less to feed two than one; (B) you would have no rent to pay; (C) you would have company on tap whenever you wanted it; (D) you would eat more and therefore look better, because somehow one's always hungrier when one isn't alone; (E) we should be able to help each other more with our respective work if we actually lived together; (F) you would escape from this appalling, cramped, horrible little room in a seedy area quite unsuitable for the expansion of the soul of a beautiful young girl who has come from nowhere."

I went to the window and looked out across the rooftops. What a patchwork of mixed surfaces of varying density there was before my eyes and how individual in character was every attic window. I knew them by heart now as though they were faces, for when you are alone, windows and clocks can take on personalities of their own. They seem to grow eyes that look back at you, features that light up or die down. They become the companions of solitude.

"I like it here," I said. "I'm like an animal. I've filled it with my smell, my emotions and thoughts. The room has become me."

"What nonsense," shouted Barney, bouncing up and down on the bed until I thought the springs would break. "What ridiculous talk. It's nowhere near you. You are young and beautiful with sharp, bright, beautiful blue eyes and a nose that twitches a little at the end, rather parroty, but delightful because it is so expressive. You're alive, your hands gesticulate; sometimes your body wriggles deliciously as you talk. Sometimes you are like a little child, other times like an old old woman with that dreadful knowing look in your eye when you think I've said something silly. How could this sterile room be you or even an expression of you, with its awful gas ring, and that mantelpiece and that looking-glass, and that dreadful stained bamboo table?"

"Here's your tea," I said, "and I've splashed out today on some chocolate digestive biscuits. Come on, have one and calm down. You look like an overheated boiler that is about to burst."

"Oh really, Christabelle, how can you be so ridiculous? Of all the inept similes I've heard that takes the ticket."

He started to gulp the tea – he always gulped hot drinks.

A few minutes later I showed him my pictures of Edmund. He was silent for a few minutes and then he said, "Christabelle, one day you might show genius." It was the highest praise I had received from anyone since my days at Shamely.

"Don't let Barney have you," advised June, kneading clay as though it were dough. "You won't be his first. He's an awful old seducer."

"No, I'll be firm," I said.

"Your much flaunted belief in free love and all that rot makes me feel doubtful. For me, it's marriage all the way." June moved towards her wheel. She was slim, almost skinny, with long legs and a small high bust. "He knows you're alone. Men are artful."

"So cynical! Doesn't love enter in?" I asked.

"Not for long. And Christabelle, he isn't even self-sufficient. Some old aunt gives him an allowance and pays his rent."

"Money's not relevant. Love is and a woman's freedom of choice," I said. "Have you seen St John Hankin's *The Last of the de Mullins*? If not, you must, June, you really must. It's so stimulating and modern. I went with a haggard girl who lives on the bottom floor of my rooming house. Lillah McCarthy was magnificent, totally dedicated. And the theme was so apt to us all. It was suggested that every woman is entitled to have a baby if she wants whether she's married or not. The fact that the war has decimated the males available for procreation should not deny a female her basic right to reproduce."

"Babies need fathers," said June with absolute conviction. "And don't forget that Barney's immature, a spoilt child, who pushes everyone aside who gets in his way."

"Some people call that determination," I said.

"I call it selfishness," retorted June. "Don't act on impulse. I know Barney thinks I'm a prig, but you see, Christo, my parents lived good simple lives in India. They were servants of the Crown and that has rubbed off on me."

I showed recent examples of my work to a dealer whose gallery was just off Bond Street.

"Humph," he said, "quite pleasing, but a little lacking in conviction and, if I may say so, a trifle insipid. No power."

"Surely this is better?" I handed him a charcoal study of Sam washing at the basin. "Isn't there strength here, those muscles...?"

"I'm afraid there's not much interest in male nudes, especially if they are drawn by ladies. There's a sort of convention," he explained. "I know this will sound narrow and perhaps old hat to a young painter like yourself, but I have a very respectable clientele who don't really want to hang that sort of thing in their drawing rooms; they want pictures that gladden the heart, lend charm. Now a pleasing landscape..."

"Well then," I said, "what about this?"

I produced two oils of Kentish hop and potato pickers.

"Yes, I recognise a certain rustic attraction, but, to be frank my dear, who wants to look at a pair of bucolic buttocks?" The dealer smiled as he spoke as though he had been clever and I saw that he was in his own estimation a superior being both in looks and temperament. His eyes were a bold uncompromising blue, his teeth even; his fair hair, parted neatly on one side, was scrupulously clean, pink nails neatly filed. He wore cufflinks, in his pale blue silk shirt and, incongruously, an old school tie. I felt sure he lived in an exquisite Mayfair flat full of pleasing *objets d'art*. He made me feel poor and grubby.

"It's very working class. All your pictures are and on the whole the rich don't care to grace their walls with portraits of common people."

"Constable," I suggested, "Gainsborough, not that I can compare with them of course."

"Ah, but *their* peasants are delightfully romanticised; they are unforgettable pastoral figures. Yours are uncomfortable, frightfully matter of fact. These buttocks ... why, you can almost smell the perspiration. Do you care," he asked, "for a gasper?"

"No, I don't," I said.

"I thought you were one of the modern girls – with your shingled hair and your long beads. Are you sure?" He opened his silver cigarette case. "Do take one."

"No, no thank you." I was irritated by his persistence. The pictures were important, not my shingled hair and his blasted cigarettes. "I have a sad picture. Perhaps you would like that. Here. This is just the study for a larger version which I left at home."

"But it is Professor Edmund Santbury!" he said. "What a terrible picture. It is deliberately morbid. Oh, I don't think you can show that."

"Does it shock you?" I asked.

"I suppose it does," the dealer said, taking a long draw at his black cigarette holder, then blowing spirals of thin smoke through his delicate nostrils. "No one wants to hang this sort of thing in drawing room or boudoir. Why it's uncomfortable, even upsetting."

"It's death," I said. "Death is shocking, uncomfortable and upsetting. How can I paint death as something it isn't?"

"Why do you have to paint death at all? Why not choose more pleasing subjects? A girl of your age should not be concerned with such matters."

"Why not? Nurses are. What about Florence Nightingale?"

"It's obscene to offer Professor Santbury, or rather his corpse, for sale like this. Does his wife know?"

"No, all right I'll keep them for myself," I said quickly. "I think he has a special beauty like this, a statuesque quality that he did not quite achieve in life."

"Are there more, then?"

"About twenty. I became a bit obsessed with the memory," I said.

"Good heavens, you're very strange. Look, my dear, I don't think we're going to be able to do any business together. I don't think your work has quite the charm my clients look for in a picture."

"Wait a minute. Here, what about this?"

I brought out two paintings of Skipper.

"Not quite a Landseer," the dealer said with a faint smile. "And there's a young man called Cecil Aldin specialising in horses and dogs. I am afraid your animal work falls between two stools. Gun dogs – a shoot, pheasants flying – I can always sell those sort of studies. But a portrait of a mongrel dog has to be very special – a work of art in its own right – to find a buyer. You see, my dear, my business is to sell pictures. I must know what is marketable, or go bankrupt."

"Perhaps I should find someone who wishes to promote art then," I replied, stung and crestfallen.

"I think you should destroy those pictures of Professor Santbury," the dealer said, looking at me with his sea-blue eyes. "It is not right that he should be recorded at such an unfortunate moment. It is unfeeling of you, if I may say so."

"But death masks," I said. "What about death masks?"

"They are executed at the relatives' request. Did you, did you work from life – I mean death?"

"No, memory. That moment is etched for ever on my memory." I paused. My brain's filing system threw up June's voice. It said, "Don't over dramatise, don't be emotive."

"I'm sorry the picture has upset you," I said. "I was trying to show the beauty as well as the finality, the awfulness of death."

"I don't want to talk about it," the dealer said, stubbing out his half-smoked cigarette in an elegant ash tray. "I'll ask my secretary to ring for a taxi for you. Half a mo'." While he went I thought of the two pound notes I had left at home and the ten shillings in my skirt pocket, of my shoes which needed repairing, and the canvases and paper I wanted.

"Thank you, thank you very much. It was awfully kind of you to see me," I said, when he had returned, and somewhere inside me a voice was singing "Christabelle is a hypocrite, a hypocrite. Christabelle licks the dealers' boots."

"Of course he's a pansy," said Barney.

"I don't know what you mean," I said.

"Oh, never mind. I mean he doesn't like women."

"He called me 'my dear'," I argued.

"That doesn't mean a thing. I call you my dear and you don't take a blind bit of notice. *I* mean it. I *do* think you are a dear, even in a way *my* dear, but he doesn't. For him it's just a veneer, a social nicety. Don't burn those pictures of Edmund. They are *awful* in the truest sense. I mean they inspire awe; they are the most powerful things you've done, Christabelle, far better than all the delicate tempera things. Those studies of death are a cry from the soul, a sudden awakening to the enormity of man's microscopic place in the universe."

"But that's how I see it!" I cried. "You have used my very own words! We are as one."

"I'm so glad," replied Barney with his most rueful smile. "How about giving big fat Daddy a kiss then."

"Don't call yourself that. I can't bear it! You're not a paternal sort of person as far as I am concerned; you are, you are a ..."

"What?" asked Barney, leaning forward, turning a little red, his rather prominent eyes filled with a sudden hope.

"A brother."

"Oh, blast and damn," he cried. "I would rather be a big fat Daddy. At least girls sit on the knees of Daddies. Come and sit on my knee, Christabelle, just for once."

I went. I went out of gratitude for the words he had spoken which had made us seem suddenly in tune. And I went because, after my trying time with the elegant art dealer, I needed the comfort of arms around me, the feeling that someone understood my disappointment.

"Stay the night. Do please stay the night, Christabelle," said Barney after a while, holding me tight.

"No," I said. "Let me get down now, please."

"You are the hardest nut to crack," Barney said.

"Now you are being vulgar. I shall go home."

"But are you tempted? That's the important thing."

"Oh yes, I'm tempted," I said, from across the room.

"What are you living on now? Have you any money left? Can I lend you some, Christabelle?"

"No, I won't borrow from you, thank you," I answered, after a pause, while I had considered yet again the possible consequences of being in debt to Barney.

"Why won't you let me help you? Why won't you live with me for that matter? You say you believe in free love; yet you reject me."

"Perhaps ..." I began.

"No, you want me. Don't say you don't want me. I can feel that you want me. I know from your eyes that you want me. And it's not the first time. If it were the first time I would understand. Your wanting comes across this room like a sort of scent, a secret message. I know, you see. So why hold back? We could be so happy together helping one another."

"You are so undisciplined," I said.

"You've been listening to June."

"But it's true," I said.

"So you want me to go on whistling for you, keeping away from other women, till Kingdom come?"

"Who said I wanted you to keep away from other women?"

"But the other night, when I was talking to Poppy – pretty little Poppy with that fantastic hair and those peridot eyes – I saw the look you gave us. I saw jealousy like a knife glinting, and then I saw your face cloud as though you had suddenly remembered another jealousy, another moment when some equally powerful emotion had stabbed you by the heart, had filled those blue eyes with a sudden piercing hatred."

"Now you are over-dramatising. You are being melodramatic," I countered unsteadily.

"But it's true, isn't it? Even though my imagery is a bit overdone?"

"There's some truth in it," I said after a pause.

"Be careful," he said. "Don't be too enthusiastic, it might kill you."

"Would you marry me?" I asked.

"I don't know. I should have to try living with you first. But as we both believe in free love, the matter doesn't arise. We are not provincial ladies and gentlemen who care about what the neighbours think and whether the tablecloth is straight."

"I just wondered," I said rather lamely, "that's all."

"If we are still together and happy after three years, I'll marry you if you want, how's that? Now come back and sit on my knee."

"No, I'm going home."

"Back to that miserable little room."

"It's not. It's my little hole and I'm used to it."

"But the light's wrong."

"Yes, I know, that's why I come here so much."

"You don't come to see me then?"

"There's a bit of that, too," I said. "You're a good friend, but Barney, I don't think I could live with you. I don't think it would work. I'm trying to be sensible and self-controlled. Don't you see? I can't afford to do anything silly, I've nothing to fall back on."

"But then you could fall back on me. I'm big enough to support you, God knows. Look at your shoes. Why don't you have them repaired? What can that pansy have thought of those shoes?"

"He didn't disapprove of me, only of my work."

"How do you know?"

"I could feel he liked me."

"Oh you feel, you feel." He jumped up and started to pace about the room. "Listen, I could pay for your shoes. Let me pay. Please. Come and live with me and I shall pay for everything."

"Then I should be a kept woman. And I shall never be a kept woman. I refuse to be a kept woman."

"All right. Don't get excited."

"If I live with any man I shall live as his equal. That's what free love is all about. I won't be your vassal."

"All right. Don't get het up, calm down. I love you when your eyes blaze but it isn't good for you. You'll wear yourself out. Keep your anger for your art."

"I'll go now. But thank you for the tea and the encouragement. You always help me so much." I backed towards the door. "You do, I mean it."

"Stay and have one more cup of tea. Do, go on, be a devil."

"No, really, thank you all the same."

"When shall I see you again?"

"I don't know," I said. "Life is so difficult."

"Come tomorrow," he said, with a sudden brightening of his eyes, as though some encouraging thought had crossed his mind. "And then on Saturday when I'm going to throw a little party, just for a few of us, June and Arthur and a few more mutual friends. I'll make a champion stew. A sort of Lancashire Hot Pot Supreme, all peppered up and we'll open some *vin ordinaire*."

"Can you afford it?" I asked, one hand on the latch.

"Oh yes, Aunt Daphne coughed up again yesterday. I'm in funds for the next month. That's why I was so anxious to pay for your shoes. I wanted to share my good fortune with you. After all, you have been sharing your misfortunes with me."

"Only metaphorically," I said. "Just telling you."

"Ah, but a trouble shared is a trouble halved," said Barney, mimicking the voice of a prissy middle-aged woman, possibly my landlady. "Would you not say so, my dear?"

"Well, I'm grateful," I said.

"I wish you would show it in a more positive way. Never mind. See you tomorrow. Farewell, dear chronicler of death." He blew a kiss, pursing his rather thick lips into a sort of ball; his eyes suddenly amused, but kind, too, so that for a moment I longed to run back and throw my arms around his neck and say, "I relent. I'll stay, I'll stay for ever and ever, if you want."

It's my mother's blood, I thought, going down the stairs. It must be my mother's blood.

There were candles in bottles for the party, cushions on the floor, a huge cast-iron cauldron full of stew and gramophone records of *The Chocolate Soldier*, *La Bohème*, *Madame Butterfly* and Gigli singing various arias from Italian opera. For me the atmosphere was highly charged; Barney was flirting outrageously with Poppy who had had her eye on him for over a year. Now and then he gave me a sideways glance to see how I was reacting. I despised him for trying to win me in this way and yet within me, do as I would, an insidious strain of jealousy stirred like a latent virus gathering strength as its victim weakens from some other illness. I looked around, hoping that there was a man who could be my counterpart for Poppy, but not one was without a girl of his own. I was alone, unpaired. The invitations had been cunningly given so that this should be so. And, although little groups gathered together, I always seemed outside some circle, the single figure trying to break in, the misfit on the wrong side of the wall. Meanwhile Poppy sat on Barney's knee stroking his face, crooning, drawing him to her, openly for all to see. Her face was very white; her thick hair a wild golden yellow, her eyes cat-like, hedged with fair lashes heavily mascara'd. She had a little face, weak as a rabbit's but for the charm of her colouring, and a high piping voice, and a laugh that escaped from her like water from a tap when an air lock has been released.

"Your tiny hand is frozen," rumbled Barney. "You are Mimi. I know that you are Mimi. Oh Mimi, my love, let me clasp you in my arms."

Poppy wriggled. She pressed herself against him, twisting herself into the most suggestive positions; his eyes glowed; his hands ran down her body. It was obvious. It was obscene. It brought out all that was brash and awful in Barney, and I told myself that I did not care. Let him make a fool of himself if that was how he wanted it. But inside the virus struck, the hatred that Barney had wanted to arouse welled up. I longed to pick up a bottle and hurl it at his head, to run across the studio and drag Poppy to the floor. I wanted to bump her head on the boards until her eyes bulged and the blood ran. I knew suddenly what it was like to be violent, to want to kill. I saw inside myself a terrible, ungovernable, raw need for violence, the diabolical child of blood-red jealousy. He had broken his promise, for June wasn't there nor Arthur who might have consoled me with kind, inconsequential words. The studio was a desert, the candlelight a blazing relentless sun, the wine like fire. Now Barney was humming strains from *The Chocolate Soldier*, *Come, come, I love you only*, and Poppy's white arms were fast round his neck. Her skirt was pushed up and I could see her lean buttocks, the pale skin through silk stockings and suspenders. She did not care. She didn't care how much leg she showed so long as she could have Barney. She was willing to sell her soul for him. The air was suddenly full of her sexual need. I turned. I tried to walk but my legs had lost their dignity. I tried to hold my head high, to thrust my nose out like an eagle's beak as I strode towards the door, but the waves from my jealousy were as strong as those from the seductive and seduced Poppy. They pervaded the room. A silence fell, heads turned. The gramophone had reached the end of the record and someone lifted its head. I opened the door. "Christabelle," called Barney thickly. "Don't go." The stairs carried me down like a river, bearing my legs away. The air outside was cool on my face, a little wind shivered between the houses; a few stars glistened in a velvet sky. I stood with my hands clasped, fighting back the hatred. From the distance came the sound of cars and now and then the clip-clop of a horse and then the rumble of trains.

"I shall go away," I whispered. "Go right away."

I started to walk. The adrenalin must have been pumping into my system, for my legs just went on and on as though they were automated, as though their energy came from a force outside myself, while in my brain a vision of Poppy was like a film still – the unbroken suspenders (had she known Barney's liking she would surely have torn one in half), the lean legs, the flesh above the silk, the glossy mouth; above all those, green eyes. How could I compete? All my self-confidence vanished. For a time I thought I wanted to die. If only I had a pistol I would shoot myself. What a sensation it would make! Barney would carry the blame. Or would he? Would he not shrug it off with a quick toss of his head? Put the whole sad incident down to my innate failings, my in-built neuroticism? Now I could imagine him developing a wonderfully involved Freudian story around my suicide, thereby taking any responsibility off his shoulders. "Poor little devil. Never ever knew who her parents were." And why should I hate him when I had turned him down so often? Why should he not take Poppy instead?

By midnight I was back in my little room staring out of the window at the rooftops, but still seeing only Barney and Poppy, still fighting hate and longing for revenge.

Chapter Nine

THE NEXT day feelings of hurt pride and self-disgust washed over me, roughly like the damp flannel used by the grey nuns to clean me when I was small. I drank endless cups of tea and eventually went out to Spitalfields to visit an artist whom I had known slightly at college and more closely when he came to Clare's house. Ludwig Rottheimer had changed his name to Larry Russell in the war, because of anti-German feelings. An orthodox Jew who lived with his parents, happy with the marriage which had been arranged for him. The girl's dowry and business flair would give him a good financial background, so that he could work without worrying too much about money. He was to be the third artist in three generations, while his wife ran a clothes shop and produced a son. When Larry looked at me, I think my situation confirmed for him the wisdom of the Jewish system; for girls like me, born out of wedlock, unblessed by a dowry, were sometimes objects of pity, even irritation, unless we made it obvious we were invulnerable because we had our own unique careers ahead of us.

Larry, who was at this time exploring dream imagery, showed me some of his latest work in the studio his parents had built out at the back of the house for him. We walked about as he earnestly expounded his theories, and explained his views on a symbolism which owed much to Jung. He was a cerebral painter, I told myself, while I was a soul painter; I let the inspiration flow from the deeper recesses of the heart and brain, while he painted self-consciously, assessing, considering, reshaping at the brain's dictates as he went along.

"And what are you doing now, Christo?" he asked at last,

sitting down, looking at me from cupped hands, his dark eyes very sincere, glasses slightly askew.

"I'm going to paint jealousy," I said quite suddenly, the words coming out unexpectedly. "Knives and daggers, searing red, a stockinged leg, a broken suspender, a face, no, two faces, and another in between, a man's face in between."

I jumped to my feet. The picture was so vivid in my mind that it almost hurt.

"All the old symbolism," said Larry.

"No, the new," I said. "Something different. A jumble of searing emotions. Thanks for the lemon tea. I like your new work. It's stunning."

The sun was shining on the streets. A rainbow dived behind the church tower and umbrellas were being closed, shop blinds rolled back; trees dripped and suddenly it seemed as though all the birds in London had started to sing. "Scarlet," I whispered to myself. "Scarlet for the bleeding heart, black, deep black, for jealousy and silver, cold and metallic, for hate. And the leg! The flesh behind the broken suspender above the silk stocking, with just a hint of satin petticoat, and then the faces!" Should one be a self-portrait? Would that be baring the soul too much? Whose face for me, then? "No," I whispered, "this shall be my own secret picture; the faces shall be true. It can be seen only after I'm dead. This will express hate and torment, love gone sour, a whole gamut of human emotion."

I worked for the rest of the day. First preparing a canvas, then making drawings while it dried, trying to decide how I would position the knives and the faces, the leg and the background of whirling colours which symbolised the feelings of the three, jealousy the strongest of them all. The next day I drew the design on the canvas and, like an Old Master, I covered the whole with a layer of monochrome, then, very carefully, I started to apply the colours using both glazes and scumbles. Usually when working with oils I put the paint straight on and if the picture didn't turn out right, I rubbed it all off and started again. But this was to be, I thought, my greatest work. It was to be also an act of therapy, although I did not realise this then, seeing it only as divinely inspired by the gods, the muses of art, something unique, almost spiritual.

Within three days it was finished and for an hour I loved it. Then dissatisfaction started to creep in like a wood fly laying its eggs to bring forth worms that make holes and spoil something beautiful, the first little thoughts that would eventually destroy the pleasure I had experienced when the picture was just finished. It now seemed to me that the work was too studied for its subject, that direct painting would have achieved a better result. I twisted my hands together, then, hearing a knock at the door, shoved the picture under the bed.

"Coming," I said.

"It's me," said Barney.

"Oh!"

I leaned against the wall for a moment trying to slow the beating of my heart; I took three deep breaths.

"What do you want?" I asked.

"You to come to the flicks, to see Buster Keaton, or, if you prefer, Charlie Chaplin."

"No," I said. "No, I'm busy. Barney, please go away."

I went to the window to try to gain comfort from the familiar rooftops, but today in the pale sunshine they looked dusty and untidy.

"Won't you forgive me?"

"There's nothing to forgive. You go your way, I go mine."

"You haven't locked the door."

He turned the handle. "Did you know you hadn't locked the door? Anyone could have walked in, a thief, a maniac."

"Or Barney," I said, realising that my total absorption in the picture had made me absent-minded. "No, I didn't know."

"Don't you want to lock it?"

"It's too late. You're inside."

It was fate, I decided in a flash. Oh fate, make him love me. For ever and ever!

"Shall you come?" asked Barney.

I could not look at him. Instead my glance fell on the picture under the bed.

"You've hidden something, Christabelle. You've got a guilty look." He started to peer under the bed.

"Come away, at once."

I seized him by the arm. "No," I shrieked. "No, you're not to look. No, no!"

I thought he would grab me then. I thought he would pull me to him, that in an instant we would be on the bed, but he did not. Instead he pushed me aside and walked to the window.

"Are you coming to the pictures?" he asked again.

And some rising emotion in me died. My body's sudden longing started reluctantly to subside.

"All right, thank you," I said.

"Well you'll have to powder your nose or something. And take off that smock. You look awful," he said. "I'll go downstairs and wait for you in the lobby. What about your red skirt, you look nice in your red skirt, I should wear that."

I was shaking. Why had I always refused to live with him? I tried to assemble my reasons. I was afraid of a later rejection. I had not the self-confidence to suppose that I could hold him for a year, let alone three. And I did not want to sink deeper into what was becoming a suffocating mire of emotion and lust. One day I might want marriage but a liaison with Barney would end all hope of wedlock. You could fall once perhaps and still hope, but twice was too much. I should be considered a loose woman. Would my pride and the long-term influence of the Anglican nuns allow that? Was he not Satan? I sat down on the bed, clasping my arms around my body in a self-protective fashion and crossing my legs. It wasn't right for a woman to want a man so much. It wasn't ladylike or normal. I was a freak. But what about Lady Hamilton? I asked myself a moment later. And Lillie Langtry? Perhaps I was one of their ilk, a great lover.

"Christabelle," called Barney from the stairs. "Are you coming? If you don't hurry we shall be late. We'll miss the beginning."

"Coming," I called back. "Coming, Barney."

In the cinema, in the interval, I said quite suddenly, "I'll live with you. I'll pack up and move in with you, Barney." He turned round in his seat, took my hands in his and squeezed them so tightly they hurt. "You mean it, really?"

"I always say what I mean, you know that," I said.

"This evening?"

"If you'll help me bring my luggage."

"How matter of fact you are." He started to smile. The smile spread right across his face and I hoped it expressed only love not triumph. I hoped that he did not think his trick had worked.

"Such a calm little voice," he whispered. "So collected."

"I have an awful feeling that I love you," I said.

"Yes, I know," he said.

Happiness is an activity of the soul, who was it who said that – Aristotle, Plato, Socrates? I have not a book to hand to tell me. For me the assertion is not quite right. For me happiness is to be in accord and living with someone you love (and also in the moment when you lay down your brush after a good day's work). And I moved into that happy state when I took up residence with Barney. Of course there were moments of disagreement, moments of hurt and dismay, but these were overridden by joy and contentment, which have stayed in the mind while the more distasteful experiences of those first months have faded like blue cotton in the sun.

Barney's three great releases were painting, talking and sex. Deprived of any he would turn to drink for consolation, but in those first weeks he enjoyed them all, and I was his ally and opposite number. We listened, argued, made love and painted, relishing life with a rare passion which was never quite to return. That time must have constituted the largest, the most magnificent pool of bright water in the grey sea of my life. I was lifted up by Barney's enthusiasms. I grew, took on new wings, developed into a woman who began to know her own mind. If that kind of life is sinful, surely we should have suffered; surely I should look back to it now as a time of misery and despair, not a golden time.

We both painted together. Barney criticised my work mercilessly. I praised his, genuinely believing that it was better, bolder, more original than my own. I envied him his spontaneous brushwork, his self-confidence, his quick, decisive mind. I thought that he was a great artist, perhaps even a genius, and I was proud to be working in his studio. This must have been pleasing to his ego, although my admiration was entirely unselfconscious, so I did not for one moment see it in that way. I wakened slowly, lazily, and then felt for Barney, ran my hands over him, whispered in his ears. "Oh, go away," he would rumble, his face twitching into a half-smile. "Lie down, you minx, or otherwise make me a cup of tea. It's too early to communicate."

He was a slow waker, a late riser, a man at his best after ten o'clock at night, a person who liked to drink tea and coffee on and off all morning to bring his sleepy being to life. And, dozing, he was to me like a ruffled lion, stretched out in the sun, his beard beginning to show blue on his remarkably fair skin; his mouth the brownish red you find on some apples; his eyes sleepy as those of someone who has wakened to find the afternoon half spent and a golden haze lying across the landscape, dazzling the eyes that are coming back to life. Sitting on the bed drinking mugs of tea, we would find our way into conversation and, always in those first months, he would remember to say that he loved me. "I'm so glad you've come, Christabelle, my darling friend from nowhere," or some such words of encouragement. "You mean you're glad to have a tea maker," I would joke. "A skivvy!" And sleepily he would touch my hair.

There was a warmth and magic about our love which I cannot now convey. Looking at each other, we would see our own happiness reflected in the other's eyes. We seemed to make each other whole, almost to be one. Occasionally, of course, there were clashes. The first was when Barney introduced me to a couple, who had come to see his pictures, as "My little concubine." He thought he was funny and followed this introduction with a bellowing laugh. But I was hurt. Thinking that he considered me to be his kept woman, that by giving me a bed he somehow owned me, paid for me, I ran from the studio and sat in a park weeping childish tears, my pride torn like a flag seized by enemy soldiers who had no respect for the defeated. He had made me feel as though he had won a battle. But I had come to him because I loved him, I had come of my own free will, and refused to see that he had in any way engineered my decision. Whereas at bottom he was congratulating himself on what he saw as my eventual capitulation to his charms. My presence proved to him once again that he had a way with women, that if he persisted long enough he could win the favours of any female he wanted. I was, in short, a great boost to his ego, which flagged from time to time, unless stimulated by conquest.

I did not realise for a long time that Barney was attracted by all but the ugliest women. Some people are dog lovers; others are horse or cat lovers. Barney loved females in the same way. He found it hard to pass a woman he knew without touching her affectionately. He loved to be surrounded by women, to hold court to them, expound his theories on art, his short hands pounding the air, his plump, cheerful face lit up and smiling. He simply loved the female race without necessarily wanting to exploit it and much of his pleasure was purely aesthetic and warming, without being sensual. He could be wheedled by females, although wheedling was never one of my arts. And his liking for women inevitably drew them to him.

The studio consisted of one large room, about twenty feet by twenty-five with a kitchen and washroom off. It had a spacious northern window reaching from floor to ceiling and the huge stove right in the middle, with a flue taking away the smoke, and a back boiler with a tap from which we drew hot water. Every morning at about eleven before breakfast Barney would wash himself sitting by the stove in a hip bath, and looking for all the world like a plump bear. While he washed he would invent vulgar limericks shouting them out at the top of his voice. They were not very clever.

He had been through the war as a balloonist and in a cupboard I found his drawings and poems of that time, lively sketches illustrating verses which seemed to show a side of him I did not know, a merrier more innocent Barney.

"Oh I was daft in those days," he said, reverting to a Yorkshire accent which he claimed to have been part of his youth. "I was a patriot and a bigot and I thought I would be a great big writer, not rich, but famous. My head was as big as a mangold and about as thick, too. I actually believed in the goodness of the ruling classes. I saw myself one day in a pretty little house with a pram in the porch and a little blonde wife with curls and a rosebud mouth, yet I was quite willing to give my life for my country, poor bloody fool that I was. To sacrifice all those hopes in an effort to wipe out poor old Jerry, who didn't want to fight anyway. Oh, my generation was conned! We went like sheep to the slaughter, singing songs of exultation, worrying about whether we would die nobly and be an honour to our country, while the brasshats enjoyed their wine and brandy, swaggering about with their Sam Brownes shining like polished mahogany and their bellies full of roast beef, hushing up the casualty figures!"

Under Barney's influence my style of painting changed. My street scenes became less detailed and at the same time less impressionist. This sounds perhaps contradictory. What I mean is that my lines became harder and the faces of the people were sketched in with fewer strokes of the brush. I do not think my work can be labelled, but I think I probably came nearest to being an expressionist, although here and there the influences of Steer and Wyndham Lewis mingled unhappily.

Rouault and Henri Rousseau were two other artists whose work affected me deeply. I was always to be a figurative and landscape painter rather than an abstract and my vision was, I believe, very idiosyncratic. Unlike Barney I did not and could not theorise. When he asked me what I meant by a picture or what precisely I was trying to do I was unable to give a coherent answer.

Meanwhile he was jubilant when Lady Ottoline Morrell swept into our studio and bought his abstract study of roof-tops which had a beautiful steely quality, combining a marvellous mixture of slate greys, varying blues and sea green into a whole, which both excited and pleased. She came without an appointment, having heard of Barney through Roger Fry, and sadly for me I was out shopping. Characteristically Barney forgot to show her my work. Looking back, this omission was, I think, largely due to his chauvinistic attitude towards women. Although he loved and admired me, I was always, in his mind, a lesser being who could not compete with men in the world of art and work. Although he would never have admitted it for one moment, I think he patronised me. It simply did not occur to him that Lady Ottoline might have been interested in my paintings. I was to him then a charming, gallant girl trying rather hopelessly and endearingly to make my way in a man's world. Such criticism was largely necessary if he was to remain in the superior position he felt was his natural place. Of course I did not see this then, although I reproached him for not thinking of me when that famous collector visited.

"You never know. She might have seen something she liked."

"Oh my little Christabelle. I do apologise. What an egotist I am! How shameful!" Outwardly he was contrite; inwardly I suspect he felt glad and safe. "She likes men best, anyway," he said, holding me close. "How divine your hair smells today. What have you washed it in? Honey, nectar and all the scents of heaven? You know I worship you. Darling, I'm sorry."

Other times he could speak roughly. "Come on, you silly old cow, aren't we ever going to eat?" But his roughness was always leavened with a smile, a ruffling of hair or an artful look which was waiting for the reaction which he knew would come, for I always rose to a jibe like a fish to a bait.

I refused to allow Barney to paint me naked. The influence of my bloody convent upbringing, he said, for he liked to imagine nuns around me crushing my natural instincts. Barney possessed strange emotions about the brides of Christ. He saw in them Freudian complexes while at the same time being in awe of their purity. Since we were lovers he could not understand my prudery, which also made me ensure that we only made love in the dark, insisting that sex should be both nocturnal and private.

"Why can't I see you naked?" he would ask. "What are you afraid of? The human body is beautiful. I want to paint it. In particular I want to paint *you*."

Sometimes, switching on the light suddenly, he would catch a glimpse, but always I would clothe myself as quickly as possible. "Oh Eve," he would moan. "Are you to be for ever overwhelmed, crushed, by the thought of original sin?"

So a year passed, and then two. I continued to sell a few pictures in the street each summer month and to sketch the passers-by, and Clare's friends patronised me from time to time, prompted no doubt by her letters. She wrote to me too, monthly, and eventually there arrived news of her second marriage, to an Austrian banker, and a request for me to send her some of my latest pictures. I feared she was simply being kind, supporting a friend rather than buying work that pleased and stimulated her. But Barney said I was being too modest; my pictures had a certain charm that appealed particularly to women. I might not be very adventurous, but my eye was original and clear. I spent a long time choosing, turning down those of Barney, most of which depicted him in the bath or lying in bed. In the end I sent her three street scenes in oil, two gouaches of rooftops and a portrait of June, as well as a few charcoal sketches of the local market and its characters. She wrote back by return saying that my work showed a new and wonderful vitality and enclosing a money order for one hundred pounds which in those days was double the yearly salary of a cook general. Instead of feeling elated I wondered whether this was an act of charity, for she was not keeping the pictures, apart from the portrait, but giving them to friends as Christmas presents. "Your pictures," she wrote, "will hang in some of the choicest houses in Vienna."

"There's fame for you," declared Barney.

"She just feels somehow responsible for me," I said.

"So now you are going to torture yourself. You can't accept good fortune when it comes your way, but you must turn it over and over like a woman at a market looking for a hole or stain in some garment she is about to buy. You don't believe that life owes you anything, do you?" complained Barney.

"I just wondered. They don't seem that good," I said.

"How can you judge? How can anyone judge? It's just a matter of opinion. If they say something, if they arouse in her some emotion, they've succeeded. You're damned lucky. You have a patron, which is more than I can say. My dear, be thankful."

One day an academic from Boston came to see Barney's work, a tall man thin as a fir tree with meagre grey hair and gold-rimmed glasses. His voice was very controlled and clipped for an American so that I decided he was probably of East Coast Scottish origin rather than Irish or English. His mouth hardly moved when he talked and his deep grey eyes were unnervingly expressionless so that it was impossible to guess what he was thinking. He used very long words and was apt to launch into a complicated monologue about the theory of painting which left us both speechless.

An excited Barney brought out more and more pictures for

this would-be patron to see, and the fewer the American's comments were the faster Barney talked, explaining, expounding, performing like a clown who is afraid his audience has not spotted the joke.

"Remarkable," or "Ah-ha, most interesting," seemed to be the man's highest form of praise, for he lacked both spontaneity and enthusiasm. It was like talking to an animated dishcloth as far as I was concerned. After a time I sensed that he was disappointed with Barney's work and was therefore somewhat embarrassed. Then, saying, "Do you mind, may I?" he started to pick out pictures for himself.

"Ah," he exclaimed suddenly, "now this is very interesting. I like this."

He leaned the oil against a wall. He stepped back to get a better view. "It's very English," he said. "Full of the atmosphere of London."

I turned cold, seeing that he looked at one of my Lambeth market scenes. "I'll buy this one, I think," he said. "It's a fine study, full of character. Have you any more of a similar nature?"

"Oh, they are Christabelle's," said Barney.

"Yours?" The man looked at me with just the tiniest glint of surprise in those inexpressive eyes.

"Yes, I'm afraid so," I said.

"And why the fear?" he asked.

I wanted to say, because I think you're prejudiced against women, because you've ignored me until now, but that seemed too rude.

"Well, women are still expected to be amateurs. I mean most people don't take us seriously."

"Well, perhaps I can help to put that right. Things are changing," the American said. "We are more forward-looking on the other side of the Atlantic."

"I'm glad," I replied. "I often think that Gwen John is as fine a painter as her brother; the only reason that her work does not win similar acclaim is because she's female."

"Sure," said the American, picking up one of my pale still lifes from those days with Clare. "This is remarkable, too."

After half an hour he had gathered together six of my pictures.

"Now we come to the little question of price," he said. "Say, what are you asking?"

"Oh five..." I began.

"Twenty each," cut in Barney as though he were my pimp.

"Fine," the man said, bringing out a cheque book. "I have an account in London. Now I must ask you to arrange for packing and despatch, so let us add six pounds for that."

After he had gone there was an awkward silence. "You've done well," said Barney at last, and the very modulation in his tone seemed to indicate the strength of his jealousy. "The man was a fool, mind you," he added a moment later. "I don't think he picked the best of yours."

"He just wanted the London atmosphere, like a tourist," I said, trying to soften the hurt for Barney. "They are his souvenirs."

"He had no idea..." began Barney, then realising that he was being unkind to me, he went on, "no taste for the modern. He was a traditionalist; that's the tragedy for people like me who are trying to blaze a path – so few understand what we are trying to say and do. I have little doubt that he was an admirer of Steer, that's why some of your less adventurous works appealed to him."

This visit by the American seems, looking back, to have marked a very subtle, almost imperceptible, change in our affair. There was a new touchiness in Barney when we looked at our pictures together and sometimes a fever of activity as though he was trying to compete with me, to produce more work. He had to be better than me or lose his self-esteem. He could not bear to be beaten by a woman. The ethos of the minor public school which he had attended as a boy had dictated that girls were considered as a different and certainly inferior species to be conquered and won, but not lived with on equal terms. Barney was, despite his bohemian ways, very much a man of his generation.

Now sometimes he went out drinking in the evenings without me. "If you come you'll be the only girl, and you wouldn't enjoy that. We're a coarse lot," he once said by way of excuse. Left alone, I frequently sank into despondency. If, as occasionally happened, Barney returned boisterous and rather drunk, he would prance round the room wearing my only hat or sing rather *risqué* songs in a loud voice, or simply talk too much with a slur in his voice. I didn't disapprove. I accepted that men got drunk while women stayed home. This was after all the custom of the times.

Then, out of the blue, after a drinking session, he blurted out, "I've been awarded a travelling scholarship to study in Italy for four months, to travel through the Dolomites, and stay in Florence and Rome."

"Couldn't I come, too?" I cried.

"Well, if you can get a scholarship, too," replied Barney uneasily, his eyes not meeting mine, so that suddenly I knew that by going to Italy he hoped to get ahead of me, that he was frightened of me as a competitor, and professional jealousy was as dangerous to us as frost is to spring buds. The warmth of our mutual feelings was threatened. The man from Boston had served to crystallise some fear and make it real, and now the ice was there setting our faces, freezing our spontaneity. We trod carefully, on our guard. I praised Barney's work too much; he spoke of mine with a touch of sarcasm in his voice. We were not partners any more; we were competitors. If Barney went alone to Italy he would come back with his self-esteem restored, with sunshine and ruins, palaces and mountains in his work to which I could not aspire. I saw that it would be better if I stayed behind.

"Of course, you can go on living in the studio. Aunt Daphne won't stop paying the rent just for four months. I'll leave you plenty of wine to help you pass the lonely hours."

"You'll be like Turner," I said.

"Oh, my pictures won't be so atmospheric. They'll have more body, more form to them. I long to reduce a baroque church to a few shapes, a three-dimensional picture presented from different angles with the utmost simplicity. Do you see what I mean? No one will ever have painted a baroque church like that before. No one will have seen it like that before. I want people to see those churches with new eyes, to take in the unique line and form rather than become immersed in the glass and decoration, the lavishness."

He was very excited. He bought himself a painter's big hat, a blue smock and leather sandals. He meant to play out his role to the full. "The Italians really appreciate artists," he told me. "They are not philistines like the blasted Londoners."

He did not ask what I was going to do. He did not actually seem to want to know, although he remarked once that he hoped I wasn't going to get "caught up with the intelligentsia," in his absence, meaning people like Clare and June and various vaguely literary people who he felt talked about art rather than created it, and were therefore suspect. I made no reply. I did not want him to go; his preparations felt like the hand of doom on my shoulder, but since I had left Sam as easily, I could not now reproach Barney. I thought of Georgina but decided not to give him her address for fear that she might seduce him.

"I'm afraid that you will fall for some deposed princess and not come back," I said.

"More likely a countess. The place is riddled with countesses," he retorted, unaware how closely his thoughts matched my own.

"Is this to be the end?" I asked suddenly on a wet afternoon when all the world seemed grey and the rain beat mercilessly on the wide northern window.

"No, of course not, you little minx. I'm coming back, rejuvenated." He grabbed me and held me close. "Keep faith, won't you," he said. "I love you, love you, love you. Come on now, why not now?"

"It's light."

"Do you call this light?"

"Tonight, tonight. Later," I said.

"You're a dark lady, a dark, dark lady," he said. "If I were rich I would have a room full of mirrors so that we could see ourselves and each other making love."

"Now you're being coarse," I said. "And we would look ridiculous. Surely you can imagine how ridiculous."

"Oh my darling Christo, how matter of fact you are! There's something very practical and down to earth about you. Did you know that?"

"I expect so," I said.

"Not like a young girl," mused Barney. "Not romantic at all. It must be the funny beginning you had, the coming from nowhere. It's given you a sort of toughness which I rather admire, vulnerable and yet so sturdy. Oh, I don't know. Just remember there's never been anyone I loved as much as you, and your hair smells wonderful. It smells of sunshine even when it's raining like today. And your skin. I'm so glad you don't spoil it with lashings of scent. It's *you*, Christabelle. And there'll never be another you." I buried my head in his shoulder. I did not want to speak, for suddenly I was almost overcome by a sense of impending loss. And I thought, this is how Sam must have felt, as I walked away down that unmade road in my new shoes. And I did not realise. I did not care enough. And now the positions are reversed. Someone upstairs has decided to punish me, to give me a dose of my own medicine.

"Write every day," I whispered. "Please do. I will. Don't forget. Let me have your news."

"I don't know how you could have been so foolish," said June sternly. "Didn't take any precautions? I mean nowadays, it's so easy."

"Ah, you haven't tried," I said. "Of course I did. Barney sent me to the doctor who keeps Poppy in the clear, a lady, who I believe once fitted out Dora Carrington – although that's only rumour. I mean, I didn't exactly like to ask."

"And didn't it work?" asked June, prim and unused as a piece of new crochet work.

"It was embarrassing. I hated every moment. You won't believe it, but I'm dreadfully tied up when it comes to bodily things."

"But what went wrong?"

"Well you know, well, precautions do rather take away the spontaneity, the romance, and when Barney was going away I got a bit abandoned. Don't look so shocked. I am his common-law wife after all."

"What a perfectly frightful term."

"It's his. He once introduced me to an American that way."

"That doesn't surprise me. So it wasn't just a slip. It was intentional."

"Please, this isn't the Inquisition. You've no right to pry. I've got to straighten out my thoughts. Suddenly my life has become very complicated."

"You can say that again. Frankly, Christo, I am amazed. I

thought you were so sensible about that sort of thing, responsible."

"I don't know my own mind. I don't really know right from wrong. Has that never occurred to you? I'm without guidelines."

I stared at her bony face; her wide unlined brow, her unswerving eyes. Her conscience, I thought, was clear, unstained; whereas mine, for as long as I could remember, had been marked, pitted with misdemeanours, thoughtless acts and later by what respectable people call sin, sin which I saw as love and good intentions.

"I suppose really underneath it all I actually wanted a baby," I admitted at last. "A bit of Barney before he went away, perhaps for ever, and it isn't such an awful thing in our world after all, is it? Think of the children fathered on intelligent women by Augustus John, to give but one example."

"Well, John is John," replied June firmly. "A world full of little Johns might not be such a bad place after all. But Barney, Barney is a different kettle of fish altogether. He hasn't made a contribution yet."

"Success," I said, "is often a very transient thing. You can't judge someone in his lifetime, think of Gaudier-Brzeska famous now, and of lesser people who appeared great in their time but are now almost forgotten. And I must ask you not to criticise the father of my child."

"Oh, now you're mounting a white charger," said June. "Well, it's your life not mine, and I wish you well. Come and stay a weekend in the country with my people before it gets too obvious. The air will do you good."

"Kind," I said. "You're very kind, like an elder sister, taking me to task and then suddenly throwing out a hand of friendship. At least, June, this baby will be a child of love, and love children are always beautiful. They have something the planned children don't, a gift from nature."

"I'll design it a christening pot – today. Can I be a godmother?" asked June, "even though I'm pretty exasperated by the muddle in your life. You know how I like things to be neat and tidy. I can't bear frayed edges. Little imperfections drive me mad."

"Shall I tell Barney now?"
"No, leave it."
"But it's half his."
"He might not be pleased. The studio isn't big enough to take a baby. He might not return to face his responsibilities."

The thought turned me cold. Sitting down on a stool, I said, "But I think he cares for me."

Chapter Ten

WHAT RIPPING news, he wrote, like an excited schoolboy, to hear that we have made a baby despite our precautions. If she has your eyes and my hair she will be a stunner. Are you looking after yourself? My darling, take care.

A warm glow of pride and joy seemed to suffuse my body. I was loved and cherished. Our child was a wanted baby. I took up knitting, which I had learned to do at the orphanage. I thought of the baby as a boy. Barney thought of her as a girl. I made little jerseys in white and yellow, snow and sunshine, purity and riches. I sang as my needles clicked.

Then one day there was a knock at the door and there stood a middle-aged woman in a hat, coat and gloves, a respectable person with greying hair and trout-blue, rather prominent eyes.

"Miss Lang?" she said. "Barney asked me to call to see whether you're all right and looking after yourself."

"Oh, please come in. I'm afraid the studio is rather untidy."

I stood back wondering whether this was his mother. We had never talked about his relations and, unaware of the significance of childhood experiences, I thought the present and future mattered, not the past. Besides, I had sensed in Barney a reluctance to refer to his family, which suggested that there had been a rejection either by him or them. In addition I had no wish to talk about the orphanage and would not have benefited, I thought, from an exchange of confidences.

Now I asked my caller to sit down and she accepted enthusiastically an offer of tea. She had, I noted, the trace of a Yorkshire accent and Barney's nose which sat uneasily on a face which called for a smaller less bulbous affair. Her even white teeth were clearly false and she smelt vaguely fragrant, like clothes stored with cachets of lavender. Two large pins with blue tops secured her hat against the antics of the wind. Her dark blue dress, which was lightened by a touch of white at the throat, matched her accessories.

"I'm Aunt Daphne," she said, taking a cup of tea.

"Oh, you're our Guardian Angel, then," I cried. "How kind you are! Barney could not afford to paint but for you."

"Yes, I know," she said. "He wrote to me. He's a bad lad. Some would call him a ne'er-do-well, but I know that artists are different. They cannot live like the rest of us; they have to be wild and unreliable, selfish and greedy, because art can be like a religion. I am sure that Our Lord forgives painters in their efforts to portray His world."

"You must be very fond of Barney," I said.

"He's all I have." Her secretive smile suggested she was looking inwards to herself rather than outwards to me. "He is one of six," she went on, "the third, quite unlike his brothers who have all gone into business – following father. My side of the family were mill owners, so I have the money to help you see, and my own needs are small. And when I think of the great painters, Gainsborough, Constable and our dear Landseer, who have given so much pleasure, I am glad to be of use, even though I cannot appreciate Barney's work."

"He is lucky," I said, "to have so understanding an aunt."

"And you have no one. He told me you had no one."

"But I manage very well on my own."

"But it's hard now with no mother to turn to and with Barney abroad. I know. I understand."

I looked deep into the respectable, ageing face, the eyes which were an anaemic version of Barney's, the mouth that trembled a little with emotion, and thought *how can you?*

"You are surprised," she said. "You do not think I know what it means to be alone and pregnant, without a gold ring on the finger and money in the bank."

"No, I'm sorry. No, I don't think that," I cried, unnerved to find my thoughts so easily read.

"You young people never believe the old might have been daring too. You think of us as fogeys, who have never experienced passion, wild hopes, or black despair. You are blazing new paths, forging ahead where we hesitated, grasping with both hands where we fumbled."

She was sitting very still; her small feet in their little lace-up shoes placed closely together, her back very straight. Her hands folded neatly in her lap. But through her came an echo of Barney's voice, Barney's vehemence and sincerity.

"Well, I don't suppose you ever quite found yourself in my predicament," I suggested gently after a pause.

She smiled, that strange inward smile again, like an author with a bestseller about to break into the market with a fanfare of publicity, meaning *Ah-ha, if only you knew, you wouldn't look at me like that.*

"Have a biscuit? Can I cook you lunch? I have some eggs."

"No, no, you mustn't feed me. You must feed yourself. I hope you are eating enough for two. Now I want to help you financially. I feel somehow responsible." She brought out a cheque book.

"No, no," I cried at once. "No, certainly not. I have plenty of money. I've sold some pictures to an American. No, please not. You are in no way responsible. I am, and glad of it."

"But I want to," she insisted. "I have always felt a special responsibility towards Barney because he was the least loved of the six. He never quite fitted in with his father's ideas. He had to fight to keep his end up. I was his ally. He knew that."

"He's thirty," I said. "Old enough to stand on his own feet. Anyway, I have the money, so why should you pay? You've done enough already by relieving us of the rent, by giving us security."

"Barney has wronged you, my dear, and as a relation I want to make amends."

"To buy me off?" I suggested with dignity. "There are no rights or wrongs in our affair, Aunt Daphne – may I call you that? – we are in it together as equals. I am glad to carry Barney's baby because I love him. But I have no intention of asking him to sign a legal document, to tie him to me for ever."

"I see you are one of those people who must give, who must sacrifice themselves, who can never take. You are a have-not by choice." Her eyes suddenly looked like Barney's when he was criticising one of my pictures, taking me to task for some obvious faulty technique or some banality of design.

"But why should you?" I demanded jumping to my feet, to stare right into her face. "Why on earth?"

"It won't be the first time," she replied quietly, fiddling with her handbag.

"What do you mean?"

"It has happened before."

"Other babies?"

"Two."

"Well, I'm not surprised," I said, after a pause, while I took in the information and set my face in what I hoped was a cheerful understanding expression.

"No, he's a bad lad," she said again, "a little like the father he dislikes so much."

"But it doesn't make any difference," I insisted. "It wasn't my first time either. I don't mean I have had another baby, but another man." I eyed her carefully. Would she be shocked? No, there wasn't even the flicker of an eyelid. "I don't want your money, thank you very much."

"Perhaps I must let you into a secret," Aunt Daphne said, two tears suddenly rising to her eyes. "Very few people know, and Barney must never know. But I like you, my dear, because you are so forthright. You have the courage of your convictions and that is rare."

"Yes," I said, sitting down, waiting for the next shock, feeling the baby in my stomach kick, bracing myself.

"Once I was like you."

"You mean forthright and all the rest?" I asked.

"No, expectant," she said. "It happened with my kind too you know. We were also capable of reckless love, even if we came from respectable homes. It wasn't just the little servant girls who went astray."

"Oh," I said. "Oh, I see."

"Thirty years ago," she continued, "I was twenty-five, almost past the marrying age. I had only fallen in love with one man, who had married my younger sister who was prettier and livelier than I. That was Barney's father, a big, bumptious, full-blooded man, full of jokes and good humour. The grandson of a blacksmith he had made good in trade and become a town councillor, a man of note in the area. When my sister was expectant I went to help supervise the house, for she had difficulties and was ordered to stay in bed, and in a moment of need he turned to me, and there I was with open arms, for I truly loved him to distraction. We decided that Barney should never know, that he should be brought up as a third child, following seven months after the other. My sister went away for a time, and I too in another direction, and we told everyone that he was premature. But, of course, I've always had a special interest in him for he is really mine."

"I see," I said. "It must have been very difficult for you to keep silent, to watch him being brought up by someone else. I could not bear that." And rendered phlegmatic by pregnancy I spoke as though nothing would ever surprise me again.

"You are less disciplined, less capable of self-sacrifice. And I had to think of my parents, well-respected mill owners, why the disgrace would have killed them. So now will you let me contribute a little to the child's welfare? Do you see that it would give me great pleasure?" She brought out her cheque book and wrote in a spidery looped hand. "There, for a secret grandchild."

The cheque was for one hundred pounds.

"Get the best care you can," she said.

The baby was born without difficulty two days late, after the usual pains, in the studio with the help of a midwife. He was a big boy with a great bald dome and Barney's eyes, and he looked like a judge in miniature, or rather like my idea of a judge, for they can't all look the same. We called him Daniel. Barney wished that he was a girl.

"Damn it, I've fathered two boys already!"

But, unaware how much his words hurt, he held the child tenderly and said, "A definite look of Aunt Daphne about him."

Barney was brown, Barney was rejuvenated, talking too much, bubbling over. A man who spoke his thoughts aloud, who edited nothing before it took the air. Just occasionally I wished I could cut his tongue out for there was so much that he should have left unsaid. But then a man brought up with five brothers and educated among boys cannot be expected to understand the female mind. And, I reminded myself, he had never been close to his mother.

Daniel was strong-willed, windy and demanding. As soon as he was big enough he used to bounce his pram so high that he turned it over and then he crawled out of his harness and rushed across the studio upsetting everything he could find.

"He's like *my* father," Barney said. "He rushes in where angels fear to tread. He's grab, grab, grab. He'll be a rugger player, you'll see, Yorkshire to the core. And a bloody pompous mayor, no doubt."

"I'm hoping he'll be an artist, born in a studio, conceived in a studio, brought up in a studio," I said.

"Poor devil. Far better be a businessman, make money and own a mock Tudor house in Beaconsfield," Barney said. "Defeat is so depressing."

"I don't actually feel a failure," I said.

"Women set their sights so low," complained Barney. "They're pleased with minor successes, men want big successes or nothing. We're bad at compromising. We turn bitter."

"You've brought so much more colour and light into your pictures since Italy," I said, wanting to encourage him.

"They don't compare with Wyndham's," grumbled Barney. "Think of his superb 'Crowd' and that marvellous war picture. What is it called? You know, the one I liked so much."

" 'A Battery Shelled', " I said. "Some of the figures look to me like matchstick men."

"Yes, for in war we are no more than matchstick men manoeuvred by the giants, the generals and the politicians. We are shelled; we fall down broken, helpless as toys. If I could do something half as fine I should feel a whisper of triumph. My blood would run faster."

"You're better than Wyndham Lewis. There's more human warmth in your pictures," I said, as Daniel started to cry.

"No one else thinks so. For heaven's sake fetch that baby, stop his mouth, strangle him, crying drives me bloody mad." Barney threw down his brush; his eyes blazed. "For God's sake," he said.

As Daniel began to crawl my suggestion that we might find a larger place increased Barney's fury.

"I'm not leaving my studio for any bloody baby."

I should have known that babies and art don't mix. It is impossible to create even a sausage with a child yelling in your ear. I gave up my own work to protect Barney from Daniel's noise, pushing a pram for hours in the parks, and then, when winter came, it was often Barney who went out, striding miles, coming back contrite but still frustrated. He couldn't bear toys on the floor or the stench of dirty nappies or fingermarks on the doors.

"Train him, discipline him, whack some sense into him! And if he gets amongst my canvases again, it's death."

"You're not being reasonable," I would plead. "Daniel must exist too. He didn't ask to be made. We did it, together, you and me, in that bed over there – remember? Wasn't it fun?"

"I never meant it to happen."

"When he's ten you'll feel differently."

"Ah, children," said Barney ruefully, running a hand through his hair. "I think I only love little girls, and the irony is that I father little boys so easily. I expect there's another little one in Italy by now. Hurray for Anglo-Italian relations! My children are becoming two-a-penny, two-a-penny I tell you! God, just think, lots of little Barneys!"

"In Italy, Italy? You mean you had a girl in Italy?" My voice was like the wail of a car that won't quite start.

"Yes, didn't I tell you? Listen, our love bond means nothing if we cannot allow each other the freedom of an occasional frolic on the side. We don't have to cage each other. I don't ask you to wear a chastity belt. I've never put limitations on your behaviour. That's why we aren't married, isn't it? That's why we didn't go all bourgeois and exchange fancy rings. You're not going to reproach me because of two nights with another person across the sea, in a different country, almost a different world! I'm a man, Christabelle, not some poor downtrodden, lovesick clerk. We're free, adult people. Love is only strong if it is free, you know that, you said that. We used to talk about it, in your little flat, high up in Earl's Court, don't you remember?"

"I've always been jealous, you know that. You got me by arousing my jealousy."

"Oh, my poor Christabelle, you must grow up. We are not characters out of some sentimental novel. We know sex for what it is, a demon to be fed." He held out his arms.

"You make it all sound so cheap," I said, turning away. "While I was carrying the baby, you were lying with another woman. Isn't that loathsome?"

"A pure Madonna," he murmured. "Straight out of a stained-glass window. And she offered herself. The old story: married off young; neglected by her husband, left alone while he amused himself in Rome. How could I refuse? She had the most perfect features I have ever seen on any woman and that wonderful golden skin some Italians have, like beaten honey, and tawny eyes. God, what eyes. And the profile! Hair looped either side. Christabelle, she was a poor, starved, deserted beauty who yearned for me. I painted her, but she tore the painting up. She said I distorted her. Under that Madonna-like serenity there was a strange serpent. Extraordinary. Totally fascinating!"

"You want to hurt me," I said, standing by the sink in a checked skirt and a white embroidered blouse, dirtied by Daniel's chocolaty hands.

"You came to me as an advocate of free love!"

"A baby changes everything. Another life."

"A natural product, no more," Barney said. "And never forget, you're the one who let it happen, not me! I trusted you!" And now there was menace in the room, like a bad smell, and my voice shouting.

"I love you, I love you. Don't let Daniel come between us, or anybody else!"

"No." Barney put up an arm to ward off my embrace. "No. Don't let's get emotional. Let's look at this in a rational way. Why don't we find you and the baby a room somewhere and I will visit you? Wouldn't that be best? I mean we can't go on like this, rowing all the time. Our work is suffering. To be blunt, it's bloody awful, and I haven't sold anything for ages. Aunt Daphne will help out with money, if I go and see her and talk nicely. She thinks of me as a son, the poor thing. She has no one else. We can't go on sleeping three in one room. It isn't decent. We shall be happier apart."

I felt in that instant as though someone had removed my

stomach. To me the studio was home; its walls enfolded me like arms, its warmth protected me. Its wide northern window greeted me like a loved familiar face each morning. I did not want to sleep again in an alien bed. I wanted to waken with Barney at my side.

"Don't look so crestfallen!" he shouted. "You knew this might happen. Things don't go on and on for ever and I'm a bloody awful companion these days. There was never any suggestion that our arrangement would be permanent, rock hard. In this world we all have to adapt to changed circumstances. It is part of living in the new time, the modern time. That's what makes everything so exciting. For heaven's sake stop wilting like some disappointed Victorian girl of seventeen. You knew the ticket when you decided to live with me. Everyone knows I'm an old rogue. I'll come and see you, and, if you can find someone to mind Daniel, you can paint here as often as you like just as it was before, when you had that little place in Earl's Court. I'll pay my share."

"Nothing is ever just as it was before," I told him. "Nothing at all."

"Look," said June. "I should get away. I shouldn't take a room nearby. I've known Barney for a long time you see. His love affairs usually run for three years and then he starts casting his eyes around. It's nothing to do with you as a person. It's his sort of biological rhythm. He's got his eye on someone else. I *did* warn you. Why don't you take the baby away into the country? Get some fresh air into his lungs. You both look pale."

I sat down. My legs were aching and the skin of my face seemed stretched as though set in one immovable expression.

Outside spring was in the air; snowdrops shone white in the parks, one could almost feel the sap rising in the trees, and everywhere was turning green. It seemed the wrong time to end a love affair; the wrong time to feel sad, to walk alone with no one's arm to take. In the Gloucestershire woods, the shoots of the bluebells would be pushing like spears through the brown earth. Soon the yellow forsythia would sparkle on bare twigs, exquisite as a Japanese painting, and then the brash daffodils would add their own louder tones, and all the gardens would be ablaze with colour, and the scent of mown grass and flowers would drift through windows open to the sun.

Sitting there my legs drawn up, I felt all at once a deep ache for the Randolphs' landscape, for the blue light in the woods, the smooth bareness of beech trunks, and the quietness of a country lane sweet with cow parsley and dandelions, and all the weeds of heaven. I would be able to show Daniel lambs, cows, gentle hills, honey-coloured walls, a winding village street and the dark yews of a country churchyard. I could almost smell the sweetness of it all wrapped in the soft tissue paper of a romantic haze.

"I should have to find a job," I said at last. "I should feel cut off." June advised me to insist that Barney signed a written statement assuming some responsibility for the child, but I baulked at that.

"I refuse to haggle over my baby," I shouted. "He is not a piece of property; he is my little darling whom I love more than anything else in the world. There is to be nothing sordid in his background. He is a love child and love children are special, a gift of nature. I look at other people's children and then I know that Daniel's unique. He has a special aura, a charisma." I was getting wound up, for only by believing such nonsense could I bear to face the future.

"I'm simply trying to be practical," said June gently. "Extra money can help tremendously."

"I would rather do it all."

"But you *shouldn't*," cried June. "Can't you understand? It's Barney's baby too."

"It's not in my nature. I want no alms. Besides I'm a romantic."

"You're proud," June said. "In the worst possible way."

"So you don't think I should look for a room?"

"No," said June. "You will be humiliated. He'll call for a while and then the visits will become fewer and fewer and shorter and shorter. You will be duty rather than pleasure and, in the end, Barney always hates duty. It spoils his fun and takes him away from painting, which is all that matters to him."

"How many times has it happened before?"

"Three to my knowledge. After that party at Clare's when he decided he wanted you, Celia moved out. She went to Baron's Court, so that he was free to woo you, tempt you to share his studio. Oh, what a privilege that is! The great master instructs his female pupil!"

"You sound very bitter."

"I was fond of Celia. Well, the awful thing is that I'm fond of Barney too, in a maternal, exasperated way. And, of course, you enchanted him; he told me so. It's just that the enchantment never lasts. It's so powerful that it can't last. And he's addicted to the sensation. He can't do without it, so he has to find someone else. Do you see what I mean? There's no permanency in Barney, not in his style of painting or anything else. Fidelity is not his line. He must have change or pack up and die."

"What happened to the other girl?"

"To Celia? Oh, she found another chum. She's settled. They're getting married."

"Was she an artist?"

"No, a colonel's daughter seeking adventure, very upper class, but trying to slum, with her head full of the most modern literature. She read Maupassant and Flaubert, but took Barney to tea dances. The contradictions in her nature fascinated him. He had never known a really upper-class girl before. She had actually come out, done the deb thing, been to college balls and in the Royal Enclosure at Ascot. She lived with him for just over a year and then he began to edge her out for you, but they had been going together for a long time before she moved in. Now she's settling down with a very respectable young man in publishing with a place in Surrey, and ten servants, and no one will ever guess that she was once an artist's mistress. I expect all the local ladies will call and she'll open fêtes and be lady of the manor."

"And who is it now?"

"Who?"

"The new girl."

My voice seemed to have shrivelled, to be a small rather pathetic sound that carried no weight. I wanted to hate, but, just then that luxury would not materialise.

"Oh he's back to the Mimi stage. This time it's a little thing who works herself to death in a laundry. He's going to rescue her, educate her, show her what happiness is. She's much more deprived than you were and she's willing to pose in the nude."

"Did you know I wouldn't?"

"Yes, Barney indulged a moan once about the absurdities of a convent upbringing and the wickedness of those who sought to make girls ashamed of their own bodies. I don't blame you. I wouldn't pose for Barney. He would turn all one's curves into angles."

"You've been brutally frank. You've left little unsaid."

"I don't think you're as tough as Celia. And I don't want you to harbour false hopes. Barney talks to me. He pours everything out, pacing up and down, banging his right fist into the palm of his left hand. He can talk to me because he doesn't desire me. I don't count as a female as far as he's concerned. I'm blotting paper. Sometimes I think I'm everybody's sister. I live through the affairs of my friends. Sometimes it makes me feel very dried up. But I think for you a clean break will be best in the end, don't you?"

"Supposing he changes his mind, wants to find me?"

The hope hung in the air for a moment like the last sparkle from a firework, glistening and beautiful.

"Then he'll come to me, and I shall give him your address." June stood up. "I'll write to country friends to see if there's a job for you. Can you type?"

"No," I said, but I was a good letter writer and I could do basic accounts. "I was well educated at that convent school," I said. "But something inside me has gone."

I wanted to be hard, strong, unforgiving.

I hate Barney. I hate Barney. I wrote it ten times on a piece of lined paper, wanting to believe it, for there seemed nothing between the two emotions of love and hate, and I did not want to love. I despised myself for loving, now that I was no longer wanted. I had moved into a rented room, after all, for a job in the country had not been immediately available. We had rowed, of course, and I had thrown china, and slashed one of Barney's pictures, and he had held me by the wrists until the tears poured down my cheeks and I had called him every horrible name which existed in my vocabulary. Afterwards he had asked me to forgive him. But love, he said, could not be manufactured like chocolates. What was the point of going on, once it was dead? What was there left? He had, he pointed out, never promised to love me for ever: he had suggested marriage after three years only as the faintest possibility. He had always been honest with me, and had imagined that we were two of a kind. Artists, he said, were not expected to be respectable. The work itself was not conducive to stable relations. Painting had to come first. Change and constant stimulation were an essential if inspiration was not to die. I would, he said, find other men. I was far too attractive to live a lonely existence. And he would visit me until I had adjusted.

"No," I said. "No visits, thank you. This is goodbye. You condescend, you patronise. You take, take, take and give nothing back."

"Yes," he said. "Yes, you're absolutely right. I am not a nice character. I am a grabber. My father was a grabber. I broke with my father when I found he had betrayed my mother with three of his secretaries in turn. I hated him for it, but now I see that I am the same. I understand him now that he is dead and it is too late to tell him so. I am not a nice person to know, Christabelle. But, all the same, you have not wasted your time with me. You've learned so much more about art. I have opened your eyes, and you have a lovely baby, a fine son, and you wanted that. I know you wanted that. Whatever you may say now, Daniel was your decision. And together we have enjoyed nearly three years of happiness. Some people go through a lifetime without touching the heights we have reached together. We have enriched each other, Christabelle. Let's be thankful for that small mercy. Happiness is so rare an achievement."

"Words, words, words," I shouted and then I said something that I shall always regret and I saw that lively face suddenly straightened and still with astonishment, and the sight turned me cold. I left, carrying Daniel while the wound still lay fresh on Barney's face, wanting to escape from the damage I had done.

Chapter Eleven

THE MOST exciting thing happened this morning. Sitting with a cup of coffee and slices of toast, butter and marmalade I turned to the middle pages of my newspaper and read in NEWS FROM THE SALEROOMS the following:

A revival of interest in the art of the twenties continues. Yesterday saw a record price paid for a picture of Barney Copeland, the Vorticist, in his bath by the little known painter Christabelle Lang. A small oil, exquisitely executed, fetched three thousand pounds. The buyer was an American collector. Two weeks ago a charcoal and wash drawing by the same artist was sold for six hundred pounds.

I put down the paper, sat very still, my hands lying quietly in my lap like dead hands. At last people are beginning to understand, to feel what I felt with such piercing intensity, to know what I knew. I remembered painting the picture, working on it each morning for just as long as I could keep my boisterous lover in his hip bath. I remembered how tiresome the sponge was, how difficult it was to get the shade just right so that it contrasted with the paler colour of Barney's robust body. I remembered how Barney had cried, "You witch, you crafty little witch, you are turning me into a teddy bear. My stomach is not as big as that, and my fingers, what have you done with my fingers? They're too short. Jesus, they look like bent cigars." And I had redone the fingers but left his stomach, because I knew I had the lines there just right. I knew that it was Barney's stomach to a tee, and that somehow its size balanced the composition. But afterwards he had said "Another dead picture," and so I had invented a red curtain that wasn't there, and somehow that splash of colour had highlighted the soft shades of flesh, of yellow bath and sponge, while the blueness of Barney's eyes had managed to convey the joyfulness of his nature which I had loved so much, the high spirits which had made him such fun to be with. I had liked the picture for a few days and then suddenly I had hated it. Finally I had just dumped it on Patrick Guggenheim along with the others, wanting to forget it because the painting seemed to speak of a happiness that I had lost, and one does not want to be reminded of such things.

Patrick Guggenheim? – I took a sip of coffee, stroked Marco, who had climbed on my lap, and went back over the years to the day when June had introduced me to the young dealer whose dynamism had impressed me so much. Sleek he was, quick on his feet as an alley cat with lovely slim hands and a smile that caught the heart. His nose was pointed and sharp, his brow towered, his hair grew in wild curls like Shelley's. He was a god of a man and it was no wonder that attentive girls seemed to hover round him like bees after nectar, and that somehow one knew that he knew how devastatingly attractive he was. Born of Irish–Jewish parents, he had the charm and wit of one race and the intellect, cleverness and business sense of the other.

"I'll make you, Miss Lang," he had said. "Just go to the country and send me everything you do. I'll build up your reputation brick by brick until you are as strong and firm as a house. I like your work. You have no cause to worry now. Leave it all to me. It is my job to sell."

There was in his voice the trace of a Yiddish accent mixed with the softness of an Irish voice. "And is this your little boy?" he asked. "What a delightful child." He crouched down until his eyes were level with Daniel's. "Here," he said. "Come to me. Tell me, are you going to be a great artist too?" But Daniel had clung to my skirts and then the dealer had screwed up his mouth and made a funny face and the little boy had laughed, and Patrick Guggenheim had said, "I understand. I was shy, too. I know what it feels like. Don't worry."

And afterwards I had done what the dealer asked. June had found me a situation in the country as general dogsbody to a widow who had been left to run a big estate; a job with a tied cottage right on the edge of a wood, a pretty red-brick place with two rooms up and two down and violets by the front door. There was no hot water, no refrigerator, just a little range and two fireplaces and a number of oil lamps. And here Daniel grew up. I bought him four beautiful bantam hens and a cock who sported all the colours of heaven, and a big grey rabbit with outsize ears, and later a bicycle.

The widow, Mrs. Henrietta Spilsbury, was impractical, selfish but kindly and as time went on she relied on me increasingly to manage her affairs. I found in myself previously unsuspected strengths. I became an organiser. I dealt with the semi-literate farm manager, with the tall, inscrutable housekeeper and the touchy head gardener. I booked the widow's holidays, reserved her seats on trains and ferry boats. I wrote her speeches when she agreed to open fêtes and made her excuses when she wanted to avoid callers. I became her buffer against the world. And the servants in the big house helped me bring up Daniel; he became their darling, while to me he was everything. My only day off was Sunday and so jokingly I wrote to Patrick Guggenheim that I had become a Sunday painter.

Later I sent Daniel to a private school, the second best in the neighbouring town because I could not afford the finest, and I drew him over and over again; and then, when I could afford a canvas, I painted him in oils. My wage was two pounds a week, but the cottage was rent free and my milk, fruit and vegetables came from the estate and cost me nothing. After two years I asked for a holiday, which caused some consternation.

"I can't do without you. I can't spare you," said Henrietta Spilsbury, her hazel eyes watching me like the bantams when I came to them without their corn. Her face was thin and aquiline; her voice a slight drawl touched by petulance.

Despite her helplessness she was a woman who carried herself as though she had worn a back board as a child, straight as a staff, unbending as steel. All her life she had relied on someone to do her dirty work. First her Nana, then her husband, now me. Yet she commanded respect and her social inferiors fell back when she came among them, the older women curtseying as though she were a queen, the men touching their forelocks. Gradually many of them started to use me as a go-between.

"I want to take Daniel to the sea," I said. "He has never been to the sea. Other people take their children to the sea. And I have the money, because my friend in Austria has just bought six of my pictures. I have a little following in Vienna."

"I did not know that anyone had any money left in Austria. I thought they were a bankrupt country," said Henrietta Spilsbury. "You know that the Conservative Association is using the park for their annual fête. I shall need you to liaise. I cannot bear their chairman, that dreadful man Barclay. He is so vulgar."

"Afterwards then," I suggested. "September, early September."

"But then we have the harvest and all those extra hands to employ. And you know I have a house party and the Duchess of Atholl is among the guests, and she's so particular. I count on you to supervise it, to see that everything runs smoothly."

I would have given way had it been just for myself, but, fiercely protective towards Daniel, I stood my ground and went. We stayed in a small boarding house at Bexhill and I longed to paint the sea, but Daniel needed all my attention every moment of every day. He gave me no peace, and I would not chastise him because I wanted to make up to him in every way I could for being born illegitimate. I spoilt him. Gradually I turned him into a tyrant, although I thought at the time that I was simply loving him.

Back home, I felt only partly rested and slowly as the weeks passed I painted less and less, my time divided between Henrietta Spilsbury and Daniel, each resenting the other. Looking in the mirror I saw a tired, white-faced girl with shadows under her eyes and lank hair and shoulders that drooped.

Then June, who knew Henrietta, came to see me and her godson.

"I'm getting married and you look dreadful," she said all in one sentence.

"I think I'm overworked," I replied, "and I have to suppress my longing to paint, and when Patrick Guggenheim has sold all the work I have done, what am I to do?"

"Go and get your hair done, buy yourself new clothes, eat more meat and spinach. You're neglecting yourself," replied June. "And get someone to mind Daniel for several hours a day."

"I do when he's not at school, but then Mrs. Spilsbury needs me."

"Paint her portrait. Go on. She'd love that. Now none of your humble 'I'm no good' stuff. We all know you are a very competent painter. I'll speak to her myself."

I realised now that June loved power, the power to help people and rearrange their lives. It was the breath of life to her. Her young man, a sandy person with pale hair, pale lashes and hesitant, short-sighted brown eyes like toffees which have been sucked for a few moments, needed her strength, her decisiveness and perhaps her contacts too, to bolster him against the winds of life and she needed someone to manage, to fuss over in her calm direct way which was without sentiment yet touched at times with a rather endearing affection.

I went to their wedding held in a village church near her parents' bungalow which was called Poona. Following her advice I had bought myself a yellow dress and a hat with a little veil, and new shorts and a darling grey jacket for Daniel. I kept thinking this could have been Sam and me, promising love until "death us do part". And I thought there was something rather grand, even noble, about the vows. The idea that two people loved each other so much that they swore to stay together for ever and ever come what may, in sickness and health, and all the rest, suddenly seemed to be the only kind of love worth having. Much later, after we had made the long journey home to be met at the station by Mrs. Spilsbury's chauffeur, Daniel asked me about my marriage and where his daddy was. And all my old resolutions to tell him the truth melted like ice under the eyes of the sun, and I said, "In heaven, darling."

"Was my daddy a nice man?" asked Daniel.

"Wonderful," I said. "An artist."

"I wish he was still alive," mused the small boy. "Other people's daddies buy them all sorts of lovely things. Did you promise for ever too?"

"Oh yes," I replied, despising myself for the deception, yet wanting desperately to protect Daniel from my unhappiness. "I loved your father very much."

Having told the lie I had to live with it and in many ways it was not the most comfortable of companions. I was known in the village as Mrs. Lang, but the servants of the house suspected a mystery behind me, for once again I had come as if from nowhere. Mrs. Spilsbury on the other hand knew the truth, but never discussed it.

But now I have travelled a long way from Patrick Guggenheim whom I had meant to discuss earlier. A sharp-minded man, as you needed to be to survive the slump of the thirties when few people were buying pictures, he had encouraged me to sign a contract in which I agreed that he would handle all my work. In exchange he was to take a commission of one third on sales. At the time of signing I had been in a miserable state, afraid of the future, unsure of myself, a sense of rejection hanging over me. Above all I had needed to store my work, which consisted of thirty oils, about fifty charcoal and wash drawings, a few watercolours, five tempera works and countless sketches, all of which were still residing untidily in Barney's studio. But now when I sold pictures to Clare I had to do so through Patrick, so that I lost a third of my usual Christmas income from that source. At the same time Patrick's sales were few and far between, and the promotion he had promised did not materialise, although some of his other artists seemed to be exhibiting fairly frequently. Most of the trade I enjoyed came through friends I had made before meeting Patrick, but I was usually too busy to write to ask the buyers' names.

As Daniel grew older he went out sometimes on Sundays to play with school friends and then I would paint with the desperate haste of a soldier who has been able to grab a few hours' leave in which to find a woman. There was not time to walk far, so I would paint the landscape around the cottage or individual trees, becoming obsessed with a nut walk which climbed towards the horizon like a peasants' path to heaven. I wanted to catch the transient beauty of light at the end of the passage between the trees, but I always had to break off too soon, to fetch Daniel or put on a meal to cook. In this way I seemed to become two people, the artist and the employed mother, while struggling to serve three masters: the creative instinct, the woman and the child. Mrs Spilsbury and Daniel usually won because they were vocal and outside myself, while inside the other fermented like wine which must in the end blow off the cork or break the bottle.

Still, following June's advice, I painted Henrietta Spilsbury, and that commission led to others which sometimes she would allow me to execute during a weekday, and the money for these I kept for myself without telling Patrick Guggenheim. Occasionally, when I was unable to paint or draw for several weeks, I would come out in a rash, which I would scratch until I bled. Eventually I recognised this to be a symptom of frustration.

Meanwhile I saw in Daniel all the waywardness of Barney: a face that turned pugnacious in opposition, a mouth that could pout or break into the most delightful smiles, a great crown of curls and short, gesticulating hands. He was a beautiful child, but his school reports spoke of what today would be known as bloody-mindedness. He was not going to be pushed around by anyone. Henrietta's cook said I spoilt him. I had made a rod for my own back. When he flew into one of his tantrums, the head gardener suggested that he needed a father to thrash him.

At nine Daniel was playing cricket for the Colts at his school and beginning to be spoken of as a possible rugby player. At ten he took the lead in a school play. At eleven he started to order me around as though I was a servant. There were rows. The first awful one occurred when he came home from school and found me still out in an orchard trying to paint the duck pond.

"Where's my tea?"

"Please," I said.

"You haven't answered."

"No."

"Where's my tea? I asked a question."

"When I've finished I'll get it. If you're hungry, help yourself – there are plenty of biscuits in the tin – and have a glass of milk."

"Other people's mothers have tea waiting."

"I'm not other people. I'm *me*. Now please go away and just let me work a little longer."

"Why should I be neglected for a silly old picture? Anyway those things don't look like ducks, and the water's too grey. Water never looks like that."

"Don't teach your grandmother to suck eggs." I was squeezing more pigment on to my palette.

"Mother, you never even said hullo."

"Hullo then. Now please, darling, leave me alone just for a few more minutes."

I held the brush very tightly, too tightly; there was a feeling very near hate rising in my stomach. Just now I loved my picture; it was all and everything to me. I was utterly committed.

"I hate your work. I could do better than that. The weeds in the pond are too big," his voice droned on, spoiling my concentration. "Nobody will want to buy it, because the ducks are wrong, real ducks are more rounded. And you've made the grass too silvery. How did you get round the old Spilsbury to let you off work? She treats you like a servant. Other people's mothers don't have to work. Smithers has a splendid tea waiting for him when he gets home, fish paste sandwiches, chocolate cake and iced biscuits. Why don't we have iced biscuits, instead of the boring plain ones? Why don't you make a chocolate cake like Smithers' mother does? Why don't you tell the Spilsbury to go away and shut up? I would!" My hand began to tremble. I felt a sort of tightness in my throat. I had been so delighted to steal this hour from Henrietta and now Daniel was spoiling it. How could he be so horrible when I loved him so much?

"Why don't we just chuck the Spilsbury and go and live somewhere decent, somewhere with a lavatory inside the house and electricity? I'm the only boy at school without electricity in my home. Other people's mothers don't paint. Can't you see, you haven't made the grass green enough? That won't do for London. The dealer will never sell that. When did he last sell one of your pictures?"

I turned round at last. Daniel stood four-square, sturdy as a young pony, a forelock of pale hair protruding from under his school cap, his rather small blue eyes periwinkle-bright, his chin thrust forward. His mouth was set in a familiar pout, hands thrust deep in the pockets of his grey school shorts.

"I don't think you'll ever make a first-rate artist," he said. "Women never do. All the great ones have been men."

"Go away," I said, in a strangled voice. "Just go away and let me finish."

"All right, all right. No need to get ratty."

I felt my scalp pricking. Every pulse in my body seemed to throb at twice its normal speed.

"Go away," I shouted. "Go away. Now, at once! Do you hear? Do as you're told! And shut up! Leave me alone, alone, alone." For a few moments it seemed as though he was going to obey. He turned away, began to walk, then stopped. Suddenly his eyes grew larger; two red cherries appeared on his cheeks then spread all over like squashed plums; he leaned down to pick up earth. "I hate you," he shouted. "You're an old sow!" His right hand went back and then he hurled the earth, so that it spattered my picture. "And I hate your paintings, too, so there!"

I stood quite still, feeling my head shrinking back to its normal size, the pounding pulses slipping back into their regular rhythm, a coldness creeping over my body and then remorse nibbling at my mind. It was all my fault. Everything in the end was my fault. How could I expect the boy to understand? I was ashamed of my temper, dismayed by the hatred I had heard in my voice and shattered by Daniel's action. I waited, not trusting myself to speak sensibly, while the boy watched me.

"That was a very silly thing to do," I said at last. "Now I shall have to take the mud off before we can have tea." I turned back to the picture, heard his feet in the grass as he walked away to the cottage and closed my eyes, trying to fight back my conflicting emotions. One half of me wanted to run after that retreating figure to take him in my arms and cry, "Oh Daniel, please don't let's fight. I love you, Daniel, every fibre in my body loves you. You are mine. You are me!" And the other half knew that he would push me away, that this was the beginning of an end; that nothing would ever be quite the same between us again; that the little boy phase was over, and now it was the long haul to adulthood. And in the end, I thought, he would want to know the truth about his father, because Daniel was not, like me, content not to know, afraid of what he might find. Like Barney, he was obstinate, self-willed, a seeker after truth. I did not think Daniel would take anything but death lying down. And suddenly I felt too tired, too weak, to be the sole recipient of the fruits of his disillusionment.

So the years galloped by as they do when you have too much to fit into every day, when nightfall always comes too soon and daylight nudges you back into a world that you are not quite ready to face again.

The world slump crept into the estate like a thief in hobnail boots, causing misery and blighted hopes. The farm ran down as cheap imports of grain flooded the country. The manager was retired on a pittance; fences rotted, hedges ran riot, blackberry bushes flourished and nettles proliferated where hens once scratched busily for worms or pigs had lain obscenely fat, suckling their young. Henrietta Spilsbury's chauffeur left for better pay in London.

"You must learn to drive. We'll have a little Austin. It will be such fun," she said.

A mechanic at the local garage gave me three lessons. Dark with a neat moustache, heavy brown eyes and hairy wrists, he let his hands lie too long on mine, as he taught me to double declutch, and pressed his knee against mine on every bend. Away from men for so long I was uneasily aware of his masculinity. He wasn't the sort of person to whom I was attracted, but he must have sensed my vulnerability, because he called round at the cottage one evening to see me. Smelling of Lifebuoy soap, he had put on a shiny blue suit and smeared down his hair with brilliantine and scrubbed his hands until they looked as smooth as pumice stone.

"Is this your boy?" he asked. "What a good-looking little fellow." I said yes, he was, but I did not ask the man in; instead I stood firmly in the doorway barring his way. Eventually he asked me whether I would go to the pictures with him to see a film in which Robert Donat starred. I said I could not leave Daniel, but the mechanic said he would drop the boy off at home and his mother would keep an eye on him.

So then I said I had given up going out since my husband died and preferred to lead a quiet life. The mechanic said it seemed an awful waste for a nice pretty girl like me to live like an old woman, and jingled the money in his trouser pockets. Then he said he hoped that he had not caused any offence, and I said, no, of course not, and good night, and shut the door.

Afterwards, cooking supper, I wondered why I was now so reluctant to start any association with a man; how, since Barney, I had almost managed to shut them out of my mind after once being so aware, so easily attracted. Part of me had died, I thought, and, looking in the mirror, I supposed this was because I was so tired, washed out, pallid as milk. My whiteness made my eyes look abnormally bright, blue stones in a silvery setting, and now my hair had darkened with age becoming brown as beechnuts. As I looked, my face suddenly interested me and the next evening when Daniel was struggling with his homework, I started my first self-portrait which was to occupy my spare time on and off for the next fortnight. Thinking again about my appearance, I began to use rouge and sometimes varnished my nails just for the pleasure of seeing them pink again. I felt as though I were waking up from a long sleep of the senses.

Then, one June day at half term Henrietta allowed me an extra day off so that I could be with Daniel. It was one of those silvery dew-wet mornings with a shy summer sun trying to break through thin mother-of-pearl clouds, and everywhere trees whispering in a soft breeze. The air was very light, the woods fragrant with bluebells and the garden with the first roses. Daniel demanded that I should bowl for him, being anxious to get into the cricket eleven at his new school. But I remember that first we ate a good breakfast, porridge, boiled eggs and toast, and afterwards took the broody bantam off her eggs which I sprinkled with water while she ate her wheat, grumbling and puffed out, her comb pale from lack of exercise and fresh air.

"Only two more days, and then you'll have your chicks, won't that be lovely?" I said, as I allowed her back.

"Mummy, I do wish you wouldn't talk to the hens," complained Daniel. "It sounds so peculiar. And you did it in front of Rookman when he came to tea and I was so ashamed. He must have thought you were a loony."

"But animals like it," I argued. "It calms their nerves." Yet even as I spoke, I knew that I talked only to fulfil a need inside myself, that there was no altruism involved, only perhaps some maternal urge on my part.

We started to practise cricket. I was a rotten bowler to the despair of Daniel, who found me grossly inadequate, and soon we broke off for elevenses, tea or squash and digestive biscuits. My right arm ached and it seemed to me as though a wad of cotton wool lay between my brain and the world outside; my immediate surroundings seemed far away and slightly blurred, as though I was looking at a bad photograph.

"Try to be more accurate," pleaded Daniel. "It's more fun when you are not so far out." He hit the turf with his short-handled bat, which I had bought him after I had been paid for my portrait of a local woman.

"You shouldn't do that. You'll spoil the bat," I said.

"No, I won't. I know what I'm doing. I know more about bats than you do." He made a face. "Come on, let's start. Hurry up!"

We began again.

"Try to do a fast one," shouted Daniel. "I need to practise those. Come on, put some power behind that elbow."

The sun was hot on my back, and a little cooling sweat ran down my sides; bees were buzzing in a border of flowers, and the birds were singing as though they would never stop. I remembered someone telling me how they had continued to sing after the Battle of Ypres; how incongruous their voices had seemed as thousands of dead and dying lay in the fields. But, why, I thought, should they care a jot for man's idiocies, for man's cruelty to man?

"Come on," shouted Daniel. "Why have you stopped?"

"To get my breath," I said, and then I saw a figure walking up the track to our cottage, a slightly bent figure with hunched shoulders and a stare which seemed to be taking in everything. Slowly the cricket ball fell from my hand, the cotton wool padding seemed to swell, then suddenly to drift away, so that my brain was clear again.

"Barney!" I said.

"Much older," he replied. "Christabelle, how are you? So this is Daniel, my son? Playing cricket like his uncles." He kissed me on the cheek; his breath smelt of brandy and tobacco; his eyeballs were threaded with pink.

"I'm so glad I've found you," he said. "But you look pale. You're not eating enough. You're working too hard. You women beat yourselves into the ground. Daniel, you must look after your mother, carry her suitcases, bring in the potatoes."

"She doesn't have any suitcases and you're dead," said Daniel.

"Is that what she told you, the little fox! Well, you see me here, as large or larger than life. Barnabas Copeland, artist. Aren't you going to offer me a drink, Christabelle? I've walked a mile or more, and I'm sweating like a pig."

"Are you any good at cricket? I need a decent bowler. I want to get up my batting average," said Daniel.

"No bloody fear," replied Barney. "But I'll tell you something. I have three sons and you're the best looker of the lot. Do you paint?"

"I used to, but just lately I've given up. We've got a rotten art master."

"Oh teachers!" exclaimed Barney. "They're a bloody waste of time. Your mother can teach you all you need to know about art. She's an accomplished painter. Much better at that than cricket. Don't let him wear you out, Christabelle, boys can be tyrants if you let them. Take a firm hand with him."

"There's only sherry, I'm afraid," I said.

"All right. Let's have a cup of tea to start with."

"I suppose I'm a bastard. I suppose you never married. That's what a kid says at school," said Daniel, later on, and I thought then that only a child of Barney's could come straight out with a question like that; in most children it would linger unspoken at the back of the mind, breeding poison, nibbling at the roots of self-confidence and respect.

"Quite right and we don't give a damn. Your mother and I believe in free love, not a life sentence."

"All the same it's bloody awkward for me sometimes, especially at school," said Daniel.

"Don't swear," I said.

"But *he* does," the boy replied, pointing at his father.

"I like you. You must come and see me in London. You've got spirit and that's the best thing anyone can have, and you speak your mind loud and clear, and no one is going to push you around." Barney clapped the boy on the shoulder. "Keep it up and you'll be a great man."

"Are you a great man?"

Barney did not hesitate. "No," he replied. "Artists are only great after they are dead. One day my pictures will hang in the great galleries of the world and you will stand before them and say Christ, he was my father!"

"Is that why Mummy said you were dead?"

"What?"

"Because she knows you will only be famous then?"

"Oh," replied Barney, after a pause. "I'll let you into a secret: women sometimes say odd things for odd reasons. There's no telling why. I shouldn't take the fact that she made me dead too seriously. Now you know I'm alive and kicking, so it doesn't matter. The whole thing is my fault for not having come to see my most delightful son before. My dear Daniel, I am most heartily ashamed of myself. It must be thirteen years since I last set eyes on you, and that's no way for a father to behave."

The boy was captivated. Talking, the mantle of tiredness had fallen from Barney's shoulders; his eyes had brightened so that I no longer noticed that they were slightly bloodshot; the old dynamism was back, the hands gesticulated again; the words flowed and the friendly teddy-bear geniality had returned. He seemed the kindest, most exciting person in the world. And he was clearly flattered but not surprised by the boy's admiration for him.

"You must come to see me at the studio," he suggested. "I would like you to see my work."

"I haven't been to London," Daniel said.

"What? Never been to London? What a dreadful omission! We must soon put that right. Get your mother to bring you up at the first opportunity."

"If the Spilsbury will let her," said Daniel.

"And who might that be?"

"My employer," I said. "She relies on me rather too much.

Sometimes there are things to be done every day of the week including Saturday. It doesn't leave much free time."

"Don't let the old bitch exploit you. Those bloody nuns have given you a martyr complex. Be firm. But what about your paintings? Let me see your work, where is it?"

"I send it all to Patrick Guggenheim."

"Jesus. I shouldn't trust that smooth bastard a bloody inch! Watch him, Christabelle."

"June recommended him."

"Ah June," mused Barney. "June wants to run all our lives. June always knows best. Did you know she was head girl at her school? Jesus, just think of an artist being head girl! But then she isn't an artist. She's a craftswoman, and there's the devil of a lot of difference between the two. Yes, I think June has gone off that young man a bit. He's on the sharp side. But you must have something to show me somewhere. What's this?"

He snatched a cloth off my self-portrait which was on the easel. "Ah you, the new you, the pale you, the tired and wilting Christabelle, a fragile flower, with all the bounce gone. Listen darling, you're anaemic. You need to go to the doctor and get liver capsules. A girl I know turned pale too. Women do sometimes. It's lack of iron or something. You were not built to be pale, to droop like some rain-beaten snowdrop. You're a full-blooded girl, with natural curves, so, for God's sake, seek advice."

"You don't like the picture?"

"Oh, it's very accomplished. You're rather slamming on the pigment, but I can't fault the technique. It's simply not my idea of you at all, that's all. The sad little orphan image carried a bit too far."

"I only painted what I saw."

"You mustn't let that Spilsbury woman turn you into a slave. You must stand up for your rights. How much does she pay you? And why hasn't she put electricity into this cottage?"

"Would you like lunch?" I asked. "I have plenty of sausages and a jam tart I made yesterday."

"Absolutely scrumptious," said Barney, glancing at Daniel. "And what about booze? Where's your local?"

"About a mile away, up the track and turn left on the road."

"Right, Daniel will show me the way, won't you?" He turned again to the boy. "We'll go together. It's not every day a father renews acquaintanceship with such a splendid son. All right, boy, tophole? Is that the phrase schoolboys use these days, tophole?"

"Sometimes," replied Daniel. "Will you buy me a cider?"

"Yes, of course, and crisps, a big bag of crisps. Come on, then."

I watched them walk away, both sturdy in build with short necks and thick hair, and suddenly I felt very much alone, a woman left in the kitchen to do the work.

Years ago I had decided how I would treat Barney should he dare to return, how I would keep Daniel from him and arouse his sleeping conscience with my biting words. But when I had seen him walking up that track I had felt nothing but compassion for an ageing man, and then fondness for an old and much loved friend who had come back. Now cooking the sausages I could not feel angry with him because of those last words I had thrown at him like bricks before I left the studio. My treachery, my broken promise lay before me like an object smashed in a moment of senseless anger. And suddenly his jolliness, his enthusiasm for life, had seemed so heartwarming that I could forgive him everything. He had come into my cottage like a wonderful being from the past, making my present life seem stunted, half dead. For years, I thought, I have worried about how I would explain to Daniel about his illegitimacy, about the lies I must tell to protect him, and dear Barney just walks in and speaks the truth with such disarming simplicity that the boy is captivated. June is wrong, I decided suddenly, when she describes Barney as a hypocrite. He is the most honest of us all, and he never takes second best. He is after all a self-confessed egotist full of good intentions. He has never pretended otherwise. He is, in short, rather a marvellous person despite his shortcomings, because there is nothing shifty about him, nothing mean; above all, nothing devious. Suddenly I longed for him to hurry back from the pub so that we could have a long talk about art, so that I could catch up with all the news about the people we had both known in London.

But when he came back, when we had sat down to lunch with tall glasses of beer and cider, Daniel dominated the conversation and Barney gave the boy all his attention, reducing me to the role of parlour maid and cook.

"You are so articulate!" Barney exclaimed. "It must be thanks to you, Christabelle, you have let him talk, haven't you? So many parents don't. There's this awful idea that children must treat their parents with deference and respect which stifles everything. I can see you've brought him up as an equal. You've listened to his views. You have a remarkable mother, Daniel. Never forget that."

"Then why didn't you marry her? Then the three of us could have been together and maybe we could have had a bathroom like other people," suggested the boy, turning his blue-eyed gaze on his father.

"Oh heavens, how young people do love to conform! My dear Daniel, I have told you already, we did not want to tie each other down, and bathrooms really do *not* matter; a hip bath in front of the fire is infinitely cosier than a zinc affair in an icy bathroom. It is the human spirit that matters, not where we wash. Souls, dear boy, souls, not bodies. Now what are you going to do? Be a painter, a writer, soldier, sailor, tinker, tailor? Made up your mind yet? Have you got a vocation?"

As he spoke Barney leaned across the table and looked straight into the boy's face. "Come on. Out with it."

Feeling that he had somehow said the wrong thing, the boy looked crestfallen. "Haven't decided yet," he muttered.

"I think he wants to be a great cricketer," I said.

"Well, so long as he wants to be a great something I'm not going to grumble," Barney said. "Now I want you to send him up to see me in London, Christabelle, put him on the train, and I'll meet him the other end and take him round the galleries." He turned back to the boy. "Have you ever been to the theatre?"

"No."

"Terrible, never been to the theatre! We'll soon put that right. Can't have you growing up a philistine."

"He's seen a few local productions in the village hall, that's all," I said. "But he knows lots of poetry."

"I like A. E. Housman *And here's a bloody hand to shake*

and Oh man here's goodbye, we'll sweat no more with scythe and rake my bloody hands and I," cut in Daniel.

"And so do I. Isn't that extraordinary? My own son with a vengeance. Here, you've been away from me all this time and yet growing up with exactly the same likes and dislikes. Incredible! What my father would have called a chip from the old block. A great man, my father. Terrible old rogue, but great all the same. A town councillor, mayor, the lot! Could twist anyone round his little finger. A great talker too and a wow with women, women really loved him. A rugger player, too, a great rugger player. Centre forward, really tough, my father – your grandfather – and Yorkshire to the bone."

"And your mother, my grandmother?" asked Daniel.

"Oh, a different kettle of fish altogether," replied Barney without batting an eyelid. "Gentle, a little withdrawn, demure almost. In our house the male ruled absolutely. The women never wore the trousers."

"You sound nostalgic in your old age," I remarked, putting on the percolator for coffee.

"Ma will never tell me about her parents," complained Daniel.

"Your mother's different. She's unique. She came from nowhere," said Barney.

"No one comes from nowhere. And it's awkward at school; other people have grandparents. I say mine are dead."

"Very wise," said Barney. "And almost certainly true."

"Most people get ten shillings from their grandparents on birthdays and at Christmas. I don't get anything."

"I've told you. I am an orphan," I said.

"But you told me that my father was dead and he isn't. You're a liar, and you always tell me not to lie, and you've been lying all the time."

"Steady on, and don't speak to your mother like that. Life, my dear Daniel, is not as simple as you think. If your mother lied she did so painfully because she thought it was for your own good. It's my fault. I should have come sooner. You are not to blame your mother for anything, or I shan't show you round London. Now look you here, I've brought you a little present which might make up in a small way for all those missed ten-shilling notes." Barney dug into his pocket and brought out a wallet from which he extracted a five-pound note. "Don't put it in any savings account, spend it on anything you like as soon as you like." The boy took it. He read it carefully as though it were a letter. It trembled a little in his hands.

"I've never seen a five-pound note before," he said in tones of awe. "Thank you, thank you very much."

"Not at all, don't mention it," replied Barney with a little bow. "Did someone say coffee was coming up? I could do with a drop I must say, Christabelle!"

Chapter Twelve

FINISHING the last chapter I decided suddenly that I would go to see Patrick Guggenheim, for surely, I thought, if my pictures are selling for so much he must owe me some money. I had not been to London for fifteen years, but intoxicated by the thought that my worth might be recognised at last, that I had after all contributed something of note to society, I felt as though I could face even an avalanche with a certain equanimity. For me there are few stimulants more powerful than the smell of personal success. I threw off all memories of Barney as though the very act of writing had exorcised his influence for the time being, and telephoned the nearest taxi owner from the village call box. Yes, he said, he would be pleased to take me the next morning to catch the nine five train. Then I rang Patrick's office and made an appointment to see him at eleven and noticed with relish how startled the girl was to hear from me. "I bet she thought I was dead," I told Marco. "I bet half the world thinks me dead." (Of course I was being somewhat megalomaniacal because probably only a few hundred art-minded people actually knew of my existence.)

What should I wear? And what about my hair? Looking in the mirror I saw an old gipsy, weatherbeaten, lined, with two very blue eyes, peering out from under thick eyebrows. How could I make a grand entrance into Patrick Guggenheim's gallery like this? "No, Christabelle, it simply won't do," I said aloud. "No, no, no." I checked my money which I kept in a jam jar in the store cupboard. There was forty-seven pounds saved from my pension to pay for coal and emergencies, so I thought I could easily afford to have my hair restyled. But now I had no change left for telephoning, so I went to see Ellen, who was in bed with a touch of bronchitis, and her servant, the straight-faced Miss Elmwood, gave me silver for a pound.

"Getting quite adventurous, then, in your old age," she said. "Won't you be needing some new clothes as well?"

"No time for that," I said.

I returned to the call box and managed to change my appointment with Patrick Guggenheim to three o'clock. Cold, hungry but elated, I made my way home through a gentle fall of snow, hoping fervently that the taxi driver was right about the train times. But surely, I thought, he must know. He must be up to date if anyone is.

I cannot now describe with what excitement I made that journey to London, how avidly I looked out of the window as my hopes soared like swallows homeward bound to Africa.

I thought: if I make enough money I might go to Madeira or why not Arles or Provence? Would I paint again? After all I was not too old, not when one thought of Grandma Moses and of Henry Moore and Picasso going on and on. I began to see pictures in the landscape, in the canal and a white house and a lock keeper's cottage. I began to look at the sky again, the wonderful whirling clouds, the dense whiteness and the blankets of grey; to see them with an artist's eye, to transfer them on to paper and canvas. I began to long for the feel of a palette in my hand, for that intense and unforgettable moment when you make the first stroke in a new picture which you hope will be the ultimate masterpiece, when you feel that perhaps at last you are going to get it right, that your vision will transfer on to paper or canvas like a miracle clear and beautiful for all to see, that you can stand back at the end and say, "This is *it*."

I found it hard to stay still, and I thought that my companions, a middle-aged man in a grey suit and a dowdy young woman in spectacles, looked at me oddly. Living alone I had become unaware of my little eccentricities. How sometimes my lips moved as I talked silently to myself or how unselfconsciously I would jump to my feet driven by a sudden impulse, which in company I would have subdued until the acceptable moment.

In London everything seemed changed. I did not understand how to manage the entrance barriers at the underground station until a young girl came forward charmingly to help.

"You put your ticket in like this and it pops out here, and the barrier drops. See."

She might have been speaking to a child of five or six, so kind and encouraging was her tone. But I did not care. Refusing to feel diminished, I thanked her with all the grace I could muster. I found an Italian salon down a side street, and was welcomed like royalty. My shabby clothes did not matter. I was sat down. I was offered coffee at once, since, the young man said, I must be tired after a long journey up from the country. My new style was discussed with great seriousness. I was informed that my hair was wonderfully thick and in excellent condition for my age. I was offered a manicure which in a mood of extravagance I accepted. An hour later feeling cherished I emerged with smooth glistening white hair cut so that its "natural movement was exploited". Gently wavy it now reached just below my ears. Too smart for my face it was nevertheless a tremendous improvement: the gipsy look had gone; from between two wings of white a serene woman seemed now to look out on the world, battered, of course, but undefeated. Walking up Piccadilly I felt ten years younger. But my coat was the wrong length and all the other women seemed to be wearing boots, some with false spurs which I thought a ridiculous touch. And where were the smart hats one used to see? And why were there so many foreigners?

With the hair style and the train fare and a hastily eaten porkchop in a restaurant, I had now spent nineteen pounds. Never mind, I told myself, if my pictures are selling for three thousand pounds, what does it matter? I shall be a rich woman. I wished that Oliver was with me, walking at my side with that straight, slightly old-fashioned gait, that he was talking to me about poetry or the latest novel he had read, his voice reassuring as the murmur of a gentle, well-loved river. His presence would have routed at once the panic which was mounting inside me at the thought of seeing again that young curly-headed god. Oliver, I knew, would have backed me up with the assurance of a man well established in a respectable profession, a man to whom others listened. "I feel so alone," I said aloud.

I was early. All my life I have been early, except when I have been painting. A secretary sat me down in a small waiting room, but I could not stay still. I went out into the main part of the gallery where the pictures were, and there hanging on the wall, I saw "The Nutwalk, The peasants' path to heaven", and the light in it shone like the light in a cathedral at the end of the centre aisle, like a gift from God. It was right after all, exactly as I had wanted it, but perhaps a little too theatrical. No, but it *was* like that, I told myself, it *was* theatrical. That was the whole point. You've captured it, Christabelle, you've achieved your aim. Yet unable to accept success, I started to look for flaws. Were nut leaves really quite so green and was the path truly as steep as that?

"Christabelle Lang. Hullo, how nice to see you after all these years." I turned; a figure approached, grey-suited, shorter than I remembered with just a hint of a waddle in his walk; the nose was still strong, the mouth mobile, but above the dark eyes the head was smooth as cheese.

"Patrick Guggenheim."

I must have hesitated, for he said, "Yes, much changed, I'm afraid."

"Me too," I said.

"Ah, age catches up with all of us in the end," he remarked. "It is the one experience we share whatever our circumstances."

"In a way I feel very much alone," I said.

"But you wanted to be alone. You ran away, hid yourself in your cottage. God knows why. Do you know that June Haycraft is still alive, still has the old flat in Queen's Gate as well as the house in Hertfordshire? These publishers don't do badly for themselves do they? Do you remember the day she brought you in here? How green we all were then, but how eager. I don't think the young are so eager nowadays, do you? There's a certain languidness about them. They have done too much too soon. Life has been too easy for them."

Thinking of James I said I wasn't sure – some were motivated.

"And do you remember that young fly-by-night, Poppy?" continued Patrick. "She settled down in the end, made a most respectable marriage to someone in the wine trade and produced six children. Isn't life extraordinary? What tricks fate plays!"

We were walking round the gallery as we talked, stopping here and there in front of pictures.

"I believe absolutely in fate, don't you? It's all pre-ordained."

"I don't know, I'm not sure," I said. "I used to, but now I think that I could perhaps have altered the course of my life, by a different decision here and there. Perhaps I should not have run away."

"A fallacy," he said at once.

"I don't agree. There must be freedom of choice; otherwise there is no such thing as good or evil."

"Ah, the orthodox Christian view," he remarked with a quick smile, which reminded me suddenly of the young Patrick. "What do you think of this?"

"It seems too easy," I replied. "Just black on white and red. I suppose it says something to some people."

I was astonished to find how easily I had slipped into conversation with the dealer. It was as though we had been close friends for years, whereas we had only met two or three times in our lives. And here we were touching on fundamentals.

"What do you think of assemblages?" I asked tentatively.

"Not much, not much at all," he said. "But then perhaps I have hardening of the arteries. My son, Jacob, is loud in his enthusiasm for these modern concepts. He even likes the bricks at the Tate. He makes me feel old and out of date. Maybe they are the Van Goghs of the future and you and I are now too prejudiced, too blinded by influences on our youth to see. We have a few. Look, here, in this ante-room. This is Jacob's little corner."

"I don't understand it," I said.

Suddenly I was tired of looking. I wanted to sit down and talk about money, *my* future, my escape to Madeira or Provence; my beginning again. "It's beyond me."

"It's beyond a lot of people," said Patrick, his eyes looking black as sloes in the sleek whiteness of his face which was almost unhealthily flabby, as though he spent too much time under artificial light. "But it sells. This one has been bought by a museum in Belgium."

"Well, there's this great worship of youth now. Think of the pop stars."

"Youth by youth," said Patrick. "It's rather narcissistic, isn't it? I don't know whether we were wiser."

"We simply didn't have the money to spend," I said.

Now we were back at "The Nutwalk", and suddenly I was assailed by a longing for the lamplit cottage, for a small boy struggling with me to master Meccano, for the moment when he had crouched beside me as we watched the first bantam chicks pecking their way out of their eggs. Nostalgia smoothed away the frustrations of that time, leaving only a sense of sunshine and warmth, a woman's love for a loving son.

"Well, there's certainly been quite a revival of interest in your work. Did you see the Barney Copeland?"

"The photograph in the paper? Yes."

"And we're hoping to sell this wood of yours. There's a Canadian interested."

"It is one of my favourites."

"I will tell him that. Come into my office. Sit down. Do you smoke? Drink? A glass of brandy? Or is it too late in the afternoon?"

"No, I would love a brandy, thank you. It's so damned cold."

"I'll keep you company. Good of you to come up."

"Not at all," I said.

"Still painting?"

"No, but I think I may start again."

"I admire your spirit. I'm thinking of retiring, shall hand over to my son, retreat to my villa in France. But of course we shall always be interested in anything you have to offer."

"I shall have to see whether I've lost what little technique I had. Fingers stiffen and so on," I said.

"Oh, surely not. Do you mind if I smoke?"

I nodded. "Please do," and he lit a cigar. "You like the country then, don't feel too cut off?"

"I'm not sure. One can slip away into a sort of Cotswold coma," I said.

He laughed. "Still the same old wit," he said.

"I was thinking about money," I said, plunging in too bluntly as the warmth of the brandy raised my spirits.

"Aren't we all in these dreadful days of inflation. Why, do you know? This suit I'm wearing now actually cost me three hundred and fifty pounds, and the cloth isn't even superior, just an ordinary suit and it's not even Savile Row. Where will it all end?"

"Well, you and I haven't much longer," I remarked between sips of brandy. "But to get back to my point: my pictures are fetching a good deal now, so that sales must have covered all the eight thousand pounds you let me have to buy the cottage and pay my debts. I mean you must have made quite a lot on top of that." Now I took a gulp of brandy, then choked. Patting me on the back, Patrick Guggenheim said, "It wasn't a loan, my dear; it was a payment. I bought all your work for eight thousand pounds. I took the risk. I've kept them here, with rents and rates going up and up, and any profit belongs to me. That was the arrangement. A gamble. I gambled and won. I might equally well have lost. I might still be paying storage for fifty or more paintings that nobody wanted. As it is I'm letting them go gradually. I'm not flooding the market. The Barney Copeland picture that sold for forty-five pounds twenty years ago came back on sale because the owner died. And Sotheby's are about to auction some of your paintings from a private Viennese collection. You're on the up and up, Christabelle, my dear." He patted my shoulder.

"And I get nothing now?"

"Well, fame is not to be sniffed at. Not many people achieve it in their lifetime and if you've got anything else, anything new ... "

"I'm not famous," I said. "And I painted the bloody things."

"Yes, but we dealers take the risks. We put up the money, gamble with our capital. Five thousand pounds was a lot of money to advance in 1962."

"But 'The Nutwalk' will fetch at least three thousand," I protested.

"Not necessarily," replied Patrick in measured tones. "The hip bath picture is doubly attractive because Barney Copeland is gaining quite a following. There is something so intrinsically lively about his work."

"But the paper was wrong. He wasn't a Vorticist. He was greatly influenced by them, but he wasn't *one* of them."

"No, he was a little late for that," agreed Patrick Guggenheim. "Well, you must forgive me, dear Christabelle – I have another appointment, but it's been a great pleasure meeting you again. I'm only sorry it's been so short. When I heard you were coming I wondered whether it might be rather worthwhile having a few photographs taken now that the experts are beginning to re-assess your work. A bit of publicity might help. There's a chap coming at four o'clock. It may be that an article or two might not be such a bad idea. I was thinking of *Vogue* or *Harpers* or even the *Burlington*. They get to the right people."

"To help you, not me," I said, getting slowly to my feet. "No, please let the earlier photographs speak for me. They show Christabelle the painter. Anything else now would be out of place. I'm too old."

"Do call again – it's been such a pleasure – any time – always delighted." Patrick removed the cigar from his mouth to shake me by the hand. "My secretary will see you out. Very courageous of you to come so far in such terrible weather. We do appreciate it. And if you do change your mind, we shall be happy to send a photographer down to your home. It will be no trouble. I'm sorry about the little misunderstanding, but you did sign a receipt, it's in the files. I know one is apt to forget things like that as one gets older. I do myself. 'Time to retire' I say. But I don't seem able to take the plunge, been at it too long I suppose. It becomes a way of life. But if you do produce any new work I shall be very happy to handle it – I'm thinking of an exhibition. My commission is fifty per cent."

He was ushering me towards his secretary as he spoke. Outside the flakes of snow were thickening. "Hope you get back all right," he said. "Take care."

On the long journey home I wished again that Oliver was with me, for he always made everything slide into perspective. As a doctor, he recognised the difference between real suffering and hurt pride or disappointed hopes.

But now I have gone on too far, because we have not yet reached Oliver in the story. We are still with Barney and the methods he used to steal Daniel from me. At least that was the way I saw it at the time, although I now know the word steal is too strong. All boys must grow away from their mothers and Barney only helped Daniel grow a little faster than he might otherwise have done. Perhaps the real hurt, the deepest, was that Barney no longer wanted me, that he could look at me without the tiniest bit of sexual interest, that as a woman I was no longer of interest to him. I was part of his past and his motto was *Never go back*. At forty-four Barney inherited a small fortune from his real mother, so that he could do what I had never been able to achieve: buy Daniel's love. But even without money he would have won anyway at that stage in the boy's development, because he was so amusing, so alive. Because he seemed, above all, to be a man of the world, and every boy of fourteen surely wants a man of the world to show him the way to manhood and the sophistication and self-confidence for which he longs. Daniel's visits to London became longer and longer. (Sometimes he missed school so that I was afraid he would not get his school certificate.) And when he came back he was always rude and off-hand with me, showing none of the tenderness which I, with no experience of family life, felt a son should feel towards his mother. Now I know that often the stronger the maternal bond has been, the greater must be the rebellion of the child against the mother, if he is to grow up normally and marry happily and produce a family. But then, forgetting that the revolt had started much earlier, I blamed Barney for the boy's constant criticism of me.

Our rows were terrible. I threw china at Daniel, slapped his face, confiscated his cricket bat, refused to cook him supper, but he never fought back physically. He did not, he said, hit women. His weapons were words and keeping company with Barney had sharpened his tongue until it cut like a sword, deep and clean. And underneath my growing hatred was the idiotic assumption that boys naturally love their mothers, that sons are automatically protective towards those who have brought them into the world.

Meanwhile as Henrietta Spilsbury grew more arthritic her mind began to weaken. She found it increasingly hard to make decisions. Gradually I found myself running her life as well as the estate. At the time of Munich, she was slipping into senility.

"Chamberlain, who's Chamberlain?" she asked. "And I've never heard of a man called Hitler. The Kaiser is Germany's emperor. I don't know how you can be so ignorant, Christabelle. Were you never at school? Don't they teach children history these days?"

Now mindful perhaps of her will, her two nieces called more frequently to see her, and, hardened by my struggles with Daniel, I asked that my wage should be raised.

"You do have the cottage," they said, plump as pampered cats, stoles of fox fur adorning their necks. "And free milk and eggs."

"But I'm companion and chauffeur as well as everything else, and I'm afraid I must go if you can't pay me three pounds ten shillings a week. I'm not a servant. I am an educated woman."

"All right," they agreed. They would speak to their aunt and to her lawyer.

Then I suggested, while the going seemed good, that they should modernise my cottage. "Otherwise it might be condemned."

"We would much rather you lived in the house with poor Aunt Henrietta," they said.

But I said that was impossible. I was an artist, not simply a companion. Under the terms of my employment I had free use of the cottage. As I spoke, only the convent-bred conviction that I should not desert a demented old woman prevented me from giving in my notice. For since Daniel had grown out of the cottage and me, there was no other reason for staying.

Now with the wisdom of hindsight I know I should have left much sooner, for an artist is not the right person to care for an increasingly tyrannical woman. To make matters worse, the silent housekeeper retired to live with a daughter, the long-trusted house parlour maid, Elsie, left to care for a chronically ill sister and the cook walked out in a rage after Henrietta had accused her of stealing money. I was told to engage replacements but my employer's notorious behaviour ensured that only moronic, dishonest or ill people applied.

Matters came to a head on a spring Sunday when I wanted

to paint. Daniel was in London; the nieces were coming to lunch. I had decked out the house with vases of flowers, supervised the menu (a local woman was coming to cook), written a letter to a local government office to explain why Henrietta had been late in paying the rates. Now my easel was up. I stood on the edge of a wood determined to catch the curve of copse and hillside, the light coming through the trees on the crest of the horizon and a sky of wonderful, shifting clouds.

"Christabelle, Christabelle."

A little bile seemed to rise in my throat at the sound of that dictatorial voice. "Where are you? I need you. The telephone keeps ringing. Perhaps it's Bertie, Bertie back from the war."

"Bertie's dead, you know he's dead. Now go back and wait for Martha and Betty," I called. "I'm busy."

"Bertie's not dead. Don't tell me fibs. How dare you tell me fibs? I always thought you were such a nice girl, Christabelle."

"Go away," I shouted. "Please go back. Go away!"

Bertie, her husband, had been dead fifteen years. Her assumption that he was still alive proved to me how drastically her memory had deteriorated. Childhood was now the only part of her life which she could recall with clarity.

"But I don't want to go back, not alone. You must come with me. We have things to do. Letters to write. Bills to pay. Fred will be coming round soon for his orders." She sounded petulant, half child, half woman.

"Fred left years ago, and it's Sunday anyway."

"Then why aren't we in church?"

I turned back to my painting. My behaviour was following the same old pattern; the clash was again between two calls on my time. I always resisted my natural impulses of rebellion against tyranny for too long and then the explosion when it came leaped beyond my control and took its own course. Now I felt my scalp pricking. All the frustrations of a thousand years seemed to rise up of one accord in my body and mind.

"No, I won't come. I won't! Go back! Go home," I shouted at her as though she was a stray dog who wanted to take up residence with me. "You're a dictator. Hitler! Leave me alone."

"How dare you speak to me like that! I am your employer. You are my servant. I have treated you like my own daughter, given shelter to you and your illegitimate baby. And where is the baby? Do you now neglect him as well as your duties?"

"The baby has grown up, you silly old woman. Now go, before I hit you. Go on, back to the house! This is my day off. Go and get ready for Betty and Martha, do your hair, clean your shoes."

"Clean my shoes? I have never cleaned shoes in my life. Elsie can do that. Where's Elsie?"

"Left," I said. "Now please go away. I want to paint."

"How dare you speak to me like that, you a fallen girl who I gave a home out of charity! For who else would employ an unmarried woman with her bastard son?"

I dropped my brush. For a moment a red flame burned before my eyes. My voice rocketed like a stone from a catapult. "Go!" it shouted. "Go!"

I must have moved, although I have no recollection of doing so, for the next instant Henrietta's white, strained face was close to mine; its thin lines criss-crossed over the faded flesh like network; her lips pale as pearls. My right fist was clenched very tightly, then it opened, thank God it opened – and struck the frail cheek just below the accusing left eye. Then I watched in transfixed horror, as the look of utter astonishment and pain flooded the old woman's face, before her knees gave way and she sank slowly to the ground like a puppet whose strings have broken.

Immediately an overwhelming sense of exhaustion and despair swept over me. She was ill, poor woman. Supposing I had killed her? I knelt at her side.

"Mrs Spilsbury? Are you all right, Mrs Spilsbury?" I was shaking. "For heaven's sake speak, speak!"

I imagined in seconds that seemed more like minutes her coffin and the hangman's noose for me.

Lady artist kills widow. But I wasn't a lady.

"How dare you? How dare you?"

"I'm sorry," I said.

"You have assaulted me. The police must be called."

She had lost her bottom denture. A little spittle formed at the corners of her lips.

"Give me your arm."

I helped her up, saw the white teeth snarling, their gums piercingly pink in the pale greenness of the spring grass.

"Here," I said, "your teeth."

"Who are you?"

"Christabelle. Now let me help you back to the house." I felt wrung out. My legs would scarcely move. The blow, I thought, had made her worse. She could no longer recognise me. How could I hit a helpless old lady? What demon lived inside my brain to drive me to commit such atrocities? I hated myself.

"The police must be called. I have been knocked down," said Mrs. Spilsbury.

"Come to the house and rest. Your nieces will be here soon. You're all right."

But even as I spoke I saw a bruise spreading, purple as squashed damsons, on her left cheek. "You had a fall," I said, disgusted at myself. "A fall. Tell your nieces you have had a fall."

I was suddenly frightened, but middle-aged and staid, the nieces accepted my words rather than their aunt's.

"Old people fall so often," they said. "She'll be breaking a leg next time."

"She needs a nurse, not me," I said. "Regretfully I must hand in my notice."

They exchanged glances; they were very alike, their hands lying on their laps, homely hats solid as brass bedknobs on their grey heads, blue eyes watching me from behind glasses.

"Could you not give us a little longer?"

"No, I don't want to be responsible. I haven't the right temperament. Perhaps one of you should come, a member of the family."

"I doubt that we could manage her," Betty said. "She's always had a strong will of her own. Uncle Bertie spoilt her. Could you find someone else? She's always relied on you."

No, I said, I must go. I was sorry, but my son was in London. I rose to my feet, feeling the burden of my guilt as a horse must feel the dead weight of lead when he begins a race under handicap. Before me the future did indeed seem to stretch as formidably as the Grand National course, full of almost insurmountable obstacles.

"She was fond of you," Martha said, getting slowly to her feet. "Perhaps you would like to choose a little object as a memento, a sort of thank you. I am sure she would have wished that, had her mind been sounder. We are sorry to lose you."

"No, nothing, no thank you. I would rather not. I'll see you again before I go." I slunk out, ashamed that I had taken advantage of someone so helpless, that my word had been believed against hers; yet unable to retract. For years that memory was to leave a bad taste in my mouth: haunting me sometimes when I could not sleep, but now as an old lady I see it differently. I know that should I be in Henrietta Spilsbury's shoes I would rather the younger woman's violence and treachery be known only to herself. I see that I could become as tiresome as my old employer had been; and disbelieved so often myself, I have learned that this is but a facet of old age that we all must face. In short I have at last forgiven myself.

Soon, middle-aged too, I left the country for London, but I felt that I looked and was younger than many of my contemporaries. My return to the capital seemed an inevitable step now that Daniel no longer appeared to need me. He had taken school certificate and was not anxious to stay on to matriculate. Photography had now become his main interest and Barney found him (through June I later discovered) a job with a well-known photographer, where he could work and learn at the same time, a sort of apprenticeship. Barney was now tiring of this third son so the boy found lodgings, which were not hard to come by in those days just before the war, where he was provided with bed and breakfast and his evening meal. He was only sixteen, but in an age when most children left school and started work two years earlier, he was ready for independence.

By a stroke of luck the day after I had given in my notice I received a cheque for two hundred pounds for twelve watercolours I had sent Patrick Guggenheim, which enabled me to put money down on a two-bedroomed flat in Chelsea close to St. Luke's Church. Soon, as always in London, I plunged into work as though running away from life. I painted St. Luke's

Church, the cottages in Cale Street and the studios in Jubilee Place and then I persuaded a restaurant owner to hang these pictures in his King's Road restaurant and at ten pounds each they soon found buyers, and, through these sales, I built up a small business painting views of people's houses for them.

I wrote to June, who responded by inviting me to all her parties and when I met Barney there, rumpled, rather drunk, rebarbative, but warm-hearted, I half wished I could pick up with him where we had left off, but he treated me on meeting like a favourite if exasperating sister, and never asked me back to his studio. He continued however to make my health his concern and when I collapsed with 'flu and sent for a doctor, Barney was proved right. I was anaemic. And, within weeks after treatment started, I realised that it had been a weakness in my blood not temperament which had caused me to be so down-hearted, so feeble as Henrietta's companion and Daniel's mother. And so in times of isolation my failure to consult a doctor earlier become another *if only* in my repertoire. And I decided that body chemistry was as important as fate in life. Or could it be fate, I asked myself the next moment, which decided that the red corpuscles in my blood should become too few?

The day war was declared I was out painting by the river, but when that first air-raid siren sounded I was not afraid of death. There seemed so little to lose. My only joy was my art, and that could be a tyranny and a disappointment too. I wasn't unhappy. I was making friends among the people who lived nearby, and I loved the long hot days which followed one another that summer. But I had no commitments, no dependants and forty seemed to me an unenviable age.

Chapter Thirteen

SUMMER brought James back to my doorway with Belinda at his side.

"So nice of you to come," I said. "And how, James, is the thesis?"

"Half-way through, thank you so much for asking. And this is Belinda."

We shook hands. She was tall and rangy like a half-grown horse, and not the sort of girl I would have expected James to choose. There was a touch of arrogance in her walk and a touch of mockery in her smile both, in a strange way, rather magnificent. The hair I had once glimpsed in the Mini still flowed like a golden river and her skin reminded me of apricots which have just caught the sun. Watching my two visitors together I decided on reflection, however, that their liaison was not after all to be wondered at, for exquisite and delicate men are often attracted to women like Belinda who have about them the scent and strength of an animal.

I suggested we sat outside and, when we had settled down with mugs of coffee, James said he expected his thesis to take at least two years.

"And how's the biography?" he asked.

"Stuck," I said, and then I surprised myself by asking impulsively whether he would care to read it.

And immediately, because the offer of favours always encouraged his natural and sometimes irritating diffidence, he dithered.

"Are you sure? Really? You don't mind? It's tremendously kind of you."

"Oh, for Pete's sake!" cried Belinda. "Of course he's

longing to read it, Miss Lang. Don't take any notice of his hesitation."

"I've reached the war and lost heart. And I don't know why. Listen," I said, "I'll bring it down from upstairs and go for a walk while you read it, James. Is that all right, I mean, do say if it would bore you? There's a lot about Barney in it."

"Marvellous," said James. "Belinda is absolutely right. Of course I'm dying to read it."

"He is incredibly lucky to have your co-operation," added the girl. "I went through hell with my dissertation and he's got his thesis made, thanks to you."

So I left the two of them sitting side by side on the seat half shaded by the lilac bush. I walked across the fields that lead to the bluebell woods and sat on a bank and worried about what I had written. Would they despise me for my weakness with Daniel and my subservience to Henrietta Spilsbury? Had I made plain my difficulties with Barney and my subsequently shattered self-confidence? Would James understand how an institution's upbringing may deny its children a proper understanding of family life and love? Would he despise me for my jealousy, for my hatred of Poppy? In today's climate would my story seem unbearably trivial, my observations banal, my behaviour a disgrace to the memory of the feminists who had struggled so long to give women a rightful place in society? Would my disclosures embarrass my young friends so that they would find it hard to meet my eye when I returned? And why had I forgotten to stress in my story how often I had lain awake at night wondering whether I could lay the blame for my actions on the genes of my parents who had turned their backs on me for ever? What were their names, their talents, their professions? Did either paint? Was it their fault that I wasn't able to settle with Sam and that I could not give my whole self to Oliver? And that sometimes there were times when only painting seemed to matter and others when I sank into a trough of inertia? Days when nothing seemed worth doing? James, I reminded myself, had promised to find out my parents' names, to go to the place which had replaced Somerset House as the centre for births and marriages. When I returned I would reproach him for not doing so.

I scrambled stiffly to my feet cursing old age, stretched and walked on across the June fields. And as I walked I was overcome by the beauty of the landscape and the trees, the foamy white of the may and the elders' first rosettes, and the leaves – Oh my God, the leaves! So many greens, so many shapes, nature in all her opulence. In the face of such glory, how could my own small life matter? Could I really take myself seriously when such miracles of loveliness returned year after year? I had heard it said that an intense love of landscape is a form of sublimation of the sexual urge, but I swear that as I stood there that June morning the sap which seemed to rise in my body was quite quite unconnected with the desire to make love; that it flowed from my soul and from my eyes and made me feel close to God.

Belinda spoke first when I returned.

"Wonderful!" she exclaimed with a sideways smile. "We couldn't stop reading!"

"So sensitive," murmured James.

"Now the truth," I demanded. "No pussy-footing."

"There are one or two questions," James said, looking down at me in a rather fatherly way, for he had leapt to his feet on my approach.

"Oh dear, not too near the bone, I hope. Let's have a drink. Gin?" I suggested. "I stocked up the other day."

"Superb," said Belinda. "How kind you are."

"I think I may need it," I said.

"I don't want to be too personal," began James, when we had tumblers of gin and tonic in our hands, "but I was wondering about Oliver."

"What's Oliver got to do with Barney?" I asked.

"You had better come clean, James," said Belinda, nudging him with her elbow.

"I thought I hinted last time. Perhaps I didn't make myself clear, I feel a bit awkward. In a way, I've changed horses mid-stream."

"He wants to switch to you," cut in Belinda. "He thinks you're more interesting than Barney."

"I've discussed it with my supervisor, and he's quite agreeable."

"Because my *life* is more interesting or my painting?"

"Both, and because you're here, the authentic voice."

"No one is entirely authentic about themselves or those they have loved," I said severely. "You're quite intelligent enough to know that. But I feel very flattered. I really don't know what to say. I'm quite overwhelmed!"

"But now you see why Oliver is important," said Belinda.

"His influence brought your paintings into a more purely descriptive phase," added James.

"That was the war," I said at once. "I wanted to record. Suddenly I saw that I was living through history."

"But did Oliver encourage you to do that?"

I refilled my glass, offered Belinda and James more, sat down again. Was I right to talk? Was I not being vain and self-centred? I took another sip.

"Not exactly. Listen," I said. "I met Oliver in an air-raid shelter; the bombs were falling. We had been at one of June's parties. We were just a little plastered, but I kept drawing; drawing quietened my nerves, hid fears. Oliver knew June because June's husband was publishing some of his verse – he was a poet, as well as a doctor – not a great one, but pleasing and sometimes profound."

"How romantic!" sighed Belinda.

"And he liked your drawings?" asked James, leaning forward, his glass held between his knees.

"We got talking, he saw me home."

"And what did he look like?" asked Belinda.

"I'm not sure his appearance ever affected my art, I mean the way I painted," I said, feeling warm inside. "Oddly enough I never drew or painted him. He was tallish, a well-preserved fifty; he wore black library spectacles and his hair was streaked untidily with grey which somehow fitted in with his rather crumpled suit. He looked as though he had come up from the country for the day, although in fact he had a practice in Battersea. I was a bit the worse for drink as I have told you, so I became very dogmatic about myself and my future. I told him I was going to make a full pictorial record of London at war, so I was glad to be in a shelter. The idea had been lingering in the back of my mind for some time, but Oliver made it leap into words. He had a wonderful way of encouraging people, so that talking to him made one resolute. In his company half-thought-out plans crystallised. I suppose that's one of the reasons why he was such a good doctor. Sitting in that shelter which smelt of urine and damp dust he suggested he might help me in my work, because, though he was a general practitioner, he was on duty twice a week in one of the big London hospitals and was frequently on call for emergencies. He could phone me if there was a dramatic event to record. But would a hospital scene be too grisly for me? I said no, I was tough. Then, when the All Clear went, June, a little gaunt in a black dress with pearls, saw us off as though we were leaving her house, rather than a shelter. Oliver fell in step with me and asked to see me home. And that's how it all began."

"You hit it off first time? You clicked?" asked Belinda. James winced at her question.

"It just seemed right that we should be walking side by side, and when he left me outside my flat, there was a gap. I wished he was still beside me."

"But you never married?" said Belinda.

"Oh for God's sake, give her time," cried James, losing a little of his poise for the first time in my presence.

"We did not even live together," I said. "After my failures with Sam and Barney, I was afraid of giving too much. Sleeping together, yes, but the thought of being with each other all day every day, sharing the same mundane things, frightened me. Too much would kill our joy, and bring back the old conflicts. Besides Oliver was married to a Roman Catholic, who had found him too wrapped up in his work for her taste and moved out. We were friends more than lovers, we were two of a kind. I told him everything. He was my priest, my confessor, my psychiatrist. And yet most of the time when I was with him, I felt on holiday. Is that a contradiction?"

"I don't think so," said James. "Wait please, while I change the tape."

"Oh Lord," my voice exclaimed with a giggle. "I really am telling all, aren't I?"

"But James is very discreet," Belinda assured me. "He'll only include things that are relevant to your art."

"It was rather terrible in a way," I continued, for the gin had wound me up; indeed I might often have been wound up without alcohol, had the nuns not tried so hard to make me demure and subservient. "It was rather terrible because in a strange way the war became for me a time of great happiness which passed with regrettable speed. Of course I wanted to help the national effort, as it was called, so I answered an advertisement and became a post office engineer. I had nimble fingers, you see, good for cleaning all those uni–selectors. I trained at Dollis Hill which was then the dullest place on earth, and eventually became a supervisor sitting all day by a telephone. My job was to send the engineers out to work where they were most needed. Often there wasn't very much for me to do, so I spent hours sketching from memory.

"I was happier as my failure with Daniel became less painful to me, more matter of fact, for Oliver explained to me how normal it was for sons and mothers to quarrel, and since as a doctor he was sometimes in the thick of family disputes, I believed him. He told me I had probably given the boy too much, rather than too little. And so, after a time, I was able to say quite casually, 'My son and I don't get on', without any bitterness towards Barney or myself. I had, as Oliver said, 'done my best'."

"So your relationship with the doctor was really happy. I'm so glad!" exclaimed Belinda, while James winced again.

"I think so, but not ecstatic," I said, weighing my words, as I caught sight again of the recorder. "Our physical love was the coming together of friends, mutual sharing, not wild passion. I suppose we were old birds. Oliver said our partings made our reunions sweeter – he had a sentimental side to his nature – I think after my refusal he decided that my decision was right and that if we lived together the sex side might fade out. We needed the stimulus of uncertainty which the war of course helped to engender. But now I'm about to return to Barney, so let's have a bite of lunch to give us strength. I'll open some tins, or will omelettes do again? I'm rather proud of my omelettes," I said.

"I love your writing. But I did wonder a teeny bit whether the Spilsbury incident wasn't just a little melodramatic," suggested James.

"It was like that, exactly like that. She was a Victorian, you see. *How dare you* seemed a normal thing for her to say to a child or a servant, who was answering her back." I was surprised to find myself sounding nettled.

"And the coffin?" queried Belinda, separating off a piece of omelette. "And the hangman's noose?"

"Not poetic licence," I replied staunchly. "Not at all. I remember the whole incident most clearly."

"And who are we to argue with that?" asked James. "Please may I have a little salt? Do you feel like talking a little more about Oliver?"

"He was a very *good* man," I said. "Once or twice a year we rented a cottage, usually in Scotland or Devon where we lived as man and wife. We hardly ever quarrelled. Well, he wasn't a person you could quarrel with. He soothed when another man would have shouted, and that must have infuriated his wife who liked scenes followed by forgiveness and sex. He always arranged our times together with the greatest care; he took me to good restaurants and hotels. It gave him such pleasure to see me happy. Oliver was a giver, you see."

"He must have lost his temper sometimes," Belinda said.

"Not with me, never with me; maybe with other men, at work – I don't know," I said. "Love was just one part of his life. I think I always knew the patients came first. And he wasn't like Barney, forever trying out new positions. But that's off the record, wipe that off the tape," I said. "I am not going to put that in my book; that is private."

"Of course," said James.

"Would you like me to make coffee while you two talk about Barney?" asked Belinda.

"And Stevie came back," I went on, unperturbed. "I didn't tell you the whole truth about Stevie," I said, still feeling a little drunk, for I had been off all alcohol, except for an occasional glass of sherry, for a long time. "Stevie was quite dreadful. She kept inviting herself to supper in my little flat, and then one day she got me down on the ground, and said she had wanted me for years and years; she loved me, she claimed, utterly and totally. I never thought she was lesbian, although of course I should have realised, and I fought back, and she gave up, but when she left I saw she had a dildo in her bag, wasn't that quite dreadful? I mean that I could be wanted so much and not know, not sense it."

"Poor thing," said Belinda.

"I still feel quite awful about it," I said.

"Please let's get back to Barney," suggested James who was clearly bored now by Stevie, "because whatever you may say about Oliver, I shall always feel Barney was the man who meant most to you."

"That's because you want me to fit in with your preconceived ideas and you would rather I was influenced by a fellow artist than anyone else."

"Maybe, maybe, but please go on," pleaded James, while Belinda put a mug of coffee in front of me.

"I don't want to talk into that bloody tape any more," I said. "But there's a bit more writing you can see if you like. Only it's not joined up with the rest. I've skipped, because for some odd reason it's much easier for me to write about Barney than Oliver. I can't make Oliver come alive, you see, Barney takes over. The next Barney bit ties in with Daniel," I went on, "because Daniel was, of course, Barney's son. As Barney once said he was our 'product'. Anyway, hang on and I'll go upstairs and fetch the extra pages. They're only a first draft, a bit over the top. I got quite emotional and had a good cry. A good cry is supposed to do you good, isn't it? I read the other day that tears of grief have a tranquilliser in them. But I think I'm a bit old for tears, don't you? A young girl weeping is a rather beautiful and moving sight, but an old woman, that's a different story."

I fetched the extra pages. "In for a penny, in for a pound," I said, as I put them in James's hands. "Read on, Macduff," I cried, with a tipsy giggle. Leaning over his shoulder I watched him read.

In 1943 Daniel joined the ranks of the 60th Rifles and in 1945 he was sent out to Malaya where some months later he was reported missing, believed killed by guerrillas. I had so often expected Oliver to die in an air raid that I had thought my capacity for fear was exhausted when Daniel left for Asia and somehow that made the telegram all the more shattering and left me absolutely drained. My studio had no telephone so I couldn't follow my first impulse and ring Oliver; and then on reflection I knew it was Barney who should be contacted. I went to the nearest kiosk, looked up his number, and as soon as he came on the line, read out the telegram.

"Come round," he said. "Come round at once. We must talk. Such terrible news is far too awful to bear alone."

He was in bed unshaven. "I am ill," he said. "I drink too much. The doctors say it will kill me, but I can't stop. I'm destroying my liver. See." He put out his tongue. "Yellow as horse dung!"

It was the same studio, to which I had not returned since I threw the china and broke my word and told him he was a bastard, too. It seemed very strange to be back.

"You look better," he said. "I'm told you have a new bloke, a poet doctor."

"Daniel," I said. "Daniel is dead." My tears wouldn't come. Instead my throat seemed dry as sandpaper and my hands shook as though they did not belong to me.

"Only presumed dead," said Barney. "Be careful, don't break my teapot. It cost seven and sixpence."

"What did you want me to come for?" I asked.

"To talk. I'm all alone, and we've had bad news, both of us. Daniel belongs to a time we shared. Nothing can alter that. But I don't believe he's dead. Daniel is not the sort of person to be killed by guerrillas. Daniel is the sort of person who stays alive. I refuse to grieve until we have definite confirmation."

"Here's the telegram," I said. "I've brought it with me."

"I don't want to see it." Barney waved an imperious arm. "Once a thing is written it seems like fact. Christabelle, you've changed. Your eyes are bright again with that special misleading innocence in them. You looked half dead in that cottage like a diseased hen, but now you are alive again. Come and sit on the bed. Do you remember how you used to in the mornings? When I heard your voice on the telephone it suddenly all came back. I just had a longing to see you."

"But aren't you upset about Daniel?"

"Yes, of course, terribly upset. But his death doesn't seem real. Besides, as I keep saying, it's not absolutely definite. He was a sweet boy, but dreadfully callow later on. I didn't actually love him. It's awful how often charming children turn into ordinary dull adults with whom one has nothing in common."

"But he was so like you. You must have felt that."

"Was he? No, he was much more like my brother, Henry, keen on cricket, always talking about scores. You know how cricket bores me. But don't let's use the past tense. I suspect he's simply debunked. I'm not sure he was cut out for life in a smart regiment. I know he must have done well, otherwise he wouldn't have become an officer, but there is that streak of bloody-mindedness. He doesn't like taking orders, and in that way he resembles me. He has the artistic temperament, but not the artistic gift – a great handicap that, a bloody shame – makes for trouble in life."

"I'll buy you grapes and lemon barley water," I said, full of pity for this wreck of a man with bloodshot eyes sunk deep in unhealthy pouches of sagging flesh, a lover with skin pale and pitted as parsnips, and trembling hands.

"I suppose you think I look awful," he suggested with a ghost of the old boisterous smile. "I don't care. I've painted all I want to paint. If the bloody critics can't see genius that's their misfortune. I've always been my own man, and I've sired half a dozen children and by and large I've had a bloody good time despite two world wars. June wants me to go on a cure. She visits me once a week, you know. Still the old organiser, telling us all what to do."

"I think you should."

"But what for?" he asked, putting a hand over mine. "Tell me, darling, why?"

"So that you won't die, so that you'll feel better and your tongue will turn pink like strawberries and your eyes will shine and you'll be the old Barney we all knew."

"Oh Christabelle, you are adorable, you know. You are rather a sweetie. Stay a little longer. Don't go yet. Let's talk about all the people we used to know. Clare, what happened to Clare?"

"She died in Austria, don't you remember – she married a banker and became a good patron of mine."

"And Courtney . . . ?"

After half an hour I rose to go.

"Stay a little longer," begged Barney.

"No, I can't. I have an appointment."

"With your bloke?"

"That's right."

"What sort of poetry does he write?"

"I don't know, a bit like Auden or perhaps Robert Graves. I'm going to illustrate a collection, in pen and ink. They are poems about the war in London."

"A bit sombre," suggested Barney.

"Not really, because he has a feeling for eternity."

"Jesus," said Barney.

On the way back to my studio I reflected that we had hardly discussed Daniel, that in the end our main subject of conversation had been Barney and Barney's friends.

And I wondered whether Barney's break from his mother was to blame for his inability to stay with any woman for more than two or three years. Perhaps, I thought, he has within him some deep-rooted need to protect himself from giving too much in love, because of the first trauma. Perhaps babies feel more acutely than we imagine.

"It must have been terrible," Belinda said, as James handed back the pages. "When did he die?"

I told her "in a matter of weeks" and went on to describe how I had visited him again and watched his quick deterioration.

"The sight of him on that bed, shrunken, yellow, with those dreadful bloodshot eyes, haunts me still. For God's sake, I could have done so much for him if only he had let me. Although he had loved dozens of women in his life, in the end when he needed them most, there was only me left. His mother's money ran out, and June paid for him to die in a private room, in hospital. I still cry when I think of it. But sometimes I wonder whether it was divine retribution for a sinful life."

"I think you were noble to keep visiting," James said. "And Christabelle, I can't thank you enough for letting me read that account. It's so moving, so well done, and this tape will be invaluable not just to me but to posterity. You've inspired me so much that I want to follow my thesis with a book about the little group who were with you at St. Stephen's."

"I must see it, before it's finished, in case I have been indiscreet," I said, suddenly apprehensive. "I've let my tongue run away with me. For God's sake don't include everything

I've said, without checking with me first. Some of it will be in my book anyway, edited after much thought by me. You're going to help me with my book, aren't you, James?"

"Of course, that's a promise," he said.

"James never lets people down," Belinda added.

"I have a naive streak," I said. "People take advantage of it."

"I think we ought to go, but can we wash up first?" asked Belinda, glancing at her watch.

"Yes, come on. I'll dry," offered James, jumping to his feet.

I wondered cynically whether they had chosen that moment to leave because they had got the booty so to speak. But the next moment James disarmed me.

"There's a bit of good news, which I've kept to last," he said, young and distinguished-looking, standing in the doorway.

"About my father?"

"No. It's nicer in a way; it's about an exhibition of drawings and watercolours to be held in New York in November; some of yours and Barney's are going. I know the selector; he's a good friend of mine, very knowledgeable."

"America?" I cried. "America! When I was young it was my dream to make it in America, how funny that it's come now."

James smiled, rather as though he was about to give a small child a box of chocolates and would soon delight in the pleasure his present aroused.

"They'll want you to go, of course, all expenses paid. Only one or two of the artists are still alive," he said.

"Have you ever flown?" asked Belinda, smiling down at me.

Feeling like the child they seemed at that moment to think I was, I said, "No, but I always meant to," as though I was somehow at fault. "Is that an awful admission?"

"Of course not. Dashing around the world on planes doesn't make for wisdom, and all the other attributes we need, does it? Rather the opposite, I think," said James.

Then he told me the exhibition had been in the offing for a long time, scheduled eighteen months ago, but one or two pictures had not been available. So mine had been chosen rather at the last minute to replace them. "The catalogue is at the printer's now."

"Which ones?" I asked.

"Your drawing of Sam," he said. "And two splendid little watercolours; one called 'The Ossingtons', which shows a Gloucestershire hillside full of may bushes bursting with blossoms, and another of boats on the river at Wapping."

"What a turnabout," I said. "And Barney's?"

"A pen and ink drawing of you, and a more abstract work called 'Church without Walls'."

"I don't know what to say!" I cried. "I'm overwhelmed. Me in New York! It doesn't seem possible."

"We're so pleased you're pleased," said Belinda, carrying dirty plates through to the scullery.

"But what about Marco?" I cried in sudden consternation. "I can't leave Marco."

"Who's Marco?" asked Belinda, as she put the plates in the deep white sink.

"The cat," said James. "Part Siamese, and very beautiful."

"He's my only dependant," I said. "And all these years he's been my special friend. He's kept me sane. I can't desert him at the first scent of success."

"Kennels, a cattery?" suggested James.

"He wouldn't understand," I said.

"But to miss such a terrific chance, such an experience, for a cat . . . ?" began Belinda.

"It doesn't seem reasonable, but it is reasonable. It's a question of loyalty. No, I can't go," I said. "You can have the pictures, well I suppose you don't have to ask me for those, anyway, but not me. I'm very sorry; it is a question of integrity."

"Is there no one in the village . . . ?" Belinda sounded incredulous.

"Just Ellen; she's simple, but sweet and kind. My massive inferiority complex allowed me to make friends with Ellen. She has an old servant who lives on an annuity bought by Ellen's parents, but gossip has it that the servant, Annie, took over Ellen's money, too."

"Would they look after Marco?" asked Belinda.

"I'm not sure about the complex," said James.

"I don't know," I replied slowly. "I'll have to let you know, but I must say, James, I appreciate very much all your efforts on my behalf."

"Oh no, not at all; the boot is on the other foot. I am grateful to you," he insisted airily.

"Any washing-up liquid?" asked Belinda, "to get down to essentials."

"I don't use the stuff, but there's some soda in the cupboard on your left, drop a few crystals in," I said.

Chapter Fourteen

A MODERATELY perceptive American interviewer with a somewhat pseudo-psychological approach to life asked me about my "emotionally deprived childhood". She said a recently published book on nuns revealed rampant lesbianism in convents. Did I consider that my upbringing had made my subsequent relationships with men difficult?

"Well, I have certainly never wanted carnal relationships with women," I replied, a trifle sharply, unaccustomed to being asked personal questions by strangers. "Perhaps no school would have suited me; perhaps all artists have rebellious natures, but I have to tell you that I grew to hate those nuns, and hate, like love, blurs judgement, doesn't it? I'm sure some were very good women; others took out their frustrations on their charges. Several of the grey nuns – I refer to the habit – who did the manual work had been put there by unforgiving parents because they had lost their virginity before marriage or produced illegitimate babies – this was just after the turn of the century, you understand, when girls, rather than men, took all the blame when they fell."

"Did any of the nuns abuse you personally?" asked the interviewer, who wore a sleek beige suit, a blouse with a bow tie and blue-rimmed spectacles, and yet despite her slightly mannish clothes, breathed a rather bossy femininity over me.

I turned my mind back: Helen dying, the nun kneeling at her bedside praying but not touching, not comforting the patient. The Lord giveth and the Lord taketh away – what was the point of touching when you had a direct line to the Almighty, when you were the bride of Christ and the daughter of God the Father, whose will it was that Helen should die struggling for the oxygen her diseased lungs could no longer supply?

"No. Inhuman, but not consciously cruel," I said, and immediately another vision sprang before my eyes and contradicted my statement. Little Jane wetting herself in the chapel, after she had been refused permission to leave, at the very moment of transubstantiation (for mine was a High Anglican order) when we should all have been devoutly upon our knees. Now I remembered how when the service was over she was made to wipe up her pool of urine in front of us and then wear damp knickers all day.

"Sadistic sometimes," I added. "A few were wolves in sheep's clothing, but I think the tone was set by the Mother Superior. When I was fourteen we had a new one, and everything improved. I expect there were a few saints but I never noticed them. I don't think it was typical of that type of establishment. I *do* not want to make any generalisations."

"I think you are trying very hard to be fair," the interviewer said with a warm smile which showed perfectly capped teeth. "I think it was much worse than you are going to admit. I think it is now universally agreed that great art comes from suffering. Do you think, Miss Lang, you would have been an artist, if you had *not* been deprived in childhood?"

"Heavens, what a question," I said. "Nothing would have stopped me painting. It is impossible for me to imagine my existence without work. I do believe that even in an institution I felt an artist first and a female second. There was a girl who starved, who developed, what is the word . . . ?"

"Anorexia nervosa."

"That's it, but no one knew what it was then. I think I might have done the same, but for my art. I had an identity, you see; a great painter had put the seal of approval upon me, nothing in the world mattered to me as much as that. It was work rather than the nuns' influence that limited the devotion and time I was willing to give to the three men in my life."

"Even Barney?" she asked, as the tape whirred on.

"Yes, but he encouraged my painting, you see; that was a classic teacher-pupil relationship which began to flounder as soon as I became a rival."

"Sure, but I don't think we can deny that the nuns gave you

the motivation; you broke away from an atmosphere that stifled you, from loneliness, through your painting. But now, Miss Lang," my interviewer continued, glancing at her notes, "can you explain why, despite your claim of an inability to live without painting, you threw everything up in 1962 to hide away as a recluse in the Cotswolds? There seems a definite contradiction here."

"Sudden madness," I said, and then after proper thought, "Listen, my dear friend Oliver had died and my 1962 exhibition – my only one – had been the biggest flop in Christendom. So I ran back to Gloucestershire where I had grown up, to the womb – don't we all sometimes, in one form or another?"

"But twenty years? Wasn't twenty years rather excessive for someone unable to live without painting?"

"Very excessive. But then I am a woman of extremes. I was broken-hearted. And other people, for heaven's sake, have done the same: Greta Garbo, Dali, Salinger. I sold nearly all my paintings to a dealer, wiped the slate clean."

"But they ran from *success*," the interviewer said in the voice of a young person who is surprised at how much they know. And wishing she had reached the stage of realising how much there was still to learn, I said, "And I from failure. But I wasn't totally alone. Oh no, not at all, not at all. I rescued an abandoned bitch who I called Murdoch because she looked like the novelist – she had a lovely fringe of hair over slightly furtive eyes – and the mobile library came twice a week, and there was my radio and my gramophone and, later, my cat Marco. I didn't stop work altogether. I drew Marco."

"No television, no telephone?"

I told her about the television set which was always going wrong, so I gave up. "And no telephone because I'm not one for phone friendships. When I have friends I like to visit them, to see them – eyes mean more to me than voices. And as for silence, I grew used to it. Thanks to the nuns, I can to this day be very still, very silent. I either talk a lot, like now, or say nothing – there's little in between."

"Wasted years?" she asked, carefully blackened eyebrows raised quizzically.

"Oh no, not at all, not at all," I cried, appalled. "I read, I thought about life. And, anyway, as I've already said, I didn't stop work entirely. If you could have spared a moment to read your copy of the catalogue, you would see that I painted 'The Ossingtons' there" – I pointed – "during what I like to call my retirement. I had switched off the main, you might say, but the tap still dripped now and then. And, oh yes" – I was now fully wound up in my attempt to refute the accusation – "in addition to drawing Marco I used to make pictures for a little old woman with a young mind called Ellen, a wonderful person, full of innocent joy."

The tape stopped whirring, the recorder clicked, and James, who had been standing behind me, said, "Well done. That was marvellous." But my interviewer's biro pen was poised above her notebook. She had not finished.

"And now, what next?" she asked with a pleasant smile of encouragement.

"No stopping me. This is all I need, a little praise, a little attention," my voice rose; "if only critics knew how many people they paralyse with their cleverness, they might pause sometimes to think before sitting down at their typewriters."

"Are you bitter?"

"Sometimes," I replied carefully, thinking of my image. "Not always. There is so much beauty to see if only we can forget ourselves enough to look. There is actually too much beauty for bitterness."

I was rather pleased when I saw two days later that an editor had chosen that last remark to head the rather awful piece of me in the local Greenwich Village paper. "But I should have mentioned Lady Randolph," I told James.

"I wish the interviewer had talked more about the paintings. She never even touched on Sam," he complained. "And you will be remembered for your work."

I loved the exhibition. I loved Barney's pen and ink drawing which showed me as the young shy girl I had forgotten. I liked the way my own pictures were hung and was honoured to find my work in the company of drawings and watercolours by John Piper and the two Nashes. The buoyant air of New York seemed to lift me up towards the stars, loosening my tongue and exciting my hair which had been cut and styled in

Moreton-in-Marsh before I left. It now stuck out in all directions like a thick thorn hedge covered in snow. But James said I looked marvellous. "Every American adores an English eccentric."

After two gin and tonics I forgot my worries about Marco, and began to love the private view too, where everyone seemed to be making a fuss of me. All the other exhibitors were either dead, or too frail or too booked up with more important engagements, to come. The organiser, Bob Fletcher, a burly Courtauld Institute trained man, from Manchester, looked after me. His distinctive north-country accent brought back memories of a visit I once made to the Peak District and indeed he looked as though he would be more at home walking over the hills than gracing a New York picture gallery.

As guest of honour at the dinner which followed the private view I sat between Max Beaton, the public relations man from the firm which had sponsored the show and Ashley Cunnington, chairman of the gallery's trustees. And oh, how I talked! If only the newspaper interviewer had been present she would have seen that the nuns' influence had not been as great as she had suspected. With *nouvelle cuisine* now the fashion, the food did little to counter the wine's potency. As the meal progressed, Max, who assured me twice, in a voice increasing every moment in volume that he was no relation to the great Cecil, grew steadily drunker, to the annoyance of Ashley Cunnington, who as a perfect, Harvard-educated, gentleman wanted to engage me in civilised conversation.

Max felt he had a tremendous advantage over all the other guests because he had known Barney both in London and Italy. Max had studied art himself and knew St. Stephen's College. He had drunk beer, he told me, with Augustus John, had visited Piper at Fawley and D. H. Lawrence in Mexico. As time passed he reeled off the names of so many distinguished people he knew that my head began to spin. He had given up painting, he said, because he couldn't make enough money from it, but now whenever the opportunity arose he persuaded his firm to sponsor work by living artists.

At the coffee stage, Ashley Cunnington, elegant in a pale, double-breasted suit, made an accomplished speech, in which he welcomed me warmly and singled out my work for special mention. As he sat down, Max said to me, "Now it's your show."

"Really?"

"Sure thing," he said. "It's your privilege to reply."

So there I was on my feet, feeling about twenty-five years old, a sturdy old woman from England, a little tipsy, a little overwhelmed.

"Ladies and gentlemen," I began. "Thank you for asking me, thank you for coming here tonight to look at all these wonderful British pictures. It is my first visit to New York and I shall never forget it. Thank you, Mr. Cunnington, for the nice things you have said about my work and myself. On behalf of all the artists who could not be here I want to express gratitude and admiration for this wonderful exhibition. I want to thank from the bottom of my heart the Chairman of the Trustees, the Director of the Gallery, the organiser, Mr. Bob Fletcher, and everyone else connected with the show. This is for me a great and unforgettable moment, which I shall always treasure. I think that is all."

As I sat down I thought, what a lame ending to a speech! Kicking myself I remembered Barney saying once in connection with something else, "Always finish with a bang, Christo! Never a whisper."

"I should have thanked the staff," I said.

"They are *everyone else*. You were magnificent," said Ashley Cunnington.

"You have all been so incredibly kind," I countered, meaning it. "I have enjoyed every minute of my stay. Such enthusiasm, such friendship!" My voice rose a little for the drink had made me emotional and I desperately wanted to show my appreciation.

The meal over, the people at my table rose first and led the way to the restaurant's main door where a photographer was waiting to take our picture for the records. Feeling light-headed, I swayed a little, so Max took my arm which he squeezed, breathing wine fumes, mingled with whisky, into my face. His own rather fleshy countenance had turned mulberry red – "Very boozy," Barney would have said. Max stooped a little to speak to me, as we approached the front door, his full lips near my ear. "There's one thing about Barney Copeland which I've always wanted to know," he began in a conspiratorial whisper. "Folks gossiped about his conquests, but I guess only his women knew the whole story. He used to talk big sometimes, but do tell me, was he the great lover he pretended to be?"

"A lovely man," I murmured. "A male chauvinist, but they all were in those days. But so vital."

"What I am trying to ask, if you will allow me," said Max in a drunkard's irritable tone, "is this: did he bugger you?"

"What!" I cried. "What do you mean, Barney?..." "and then as the meaning of Max's words sank in, my right arm went up; my right palm flattened, rushed forward and met Max's cheek, and, as if that were not enough, in a flash my left hand quite subconsciously followed suit. Two slaps, two gasps and one look of horror on Ashley Cunnington's face, as he grabbed Max to prevent him retaliating. (But would he hit a woman? I doubt it.) And the next moment Bob Fletcher's arm slipped gently round my shoulders. "Come away, love," he said in that warm Mancunian voice. "It's been a long day, and now I'm going to take you home in a cab."

"Such an insult!" I cried, still wound up. "To a great artist. He's spoilt my evening!"

The whole incident cannot have taken more than a few moments but the reverberations were to affect the rest of my life. Next morning I was shocked by news of it in the papers:

Dismayed sponsor struck by British artist. Little old lady from England physically assaults leading New York businessman ... "Such an insult!" Leading British artist strikes back! ... "He's spoilt my evening!" cries elderly artist after New York Gallery Opening....

...and so on. Worse still was the picture of me, actually slapping Max's face, which illustrated these headlines, for I looked quite wild with my great thatch of white hair all on end, my eyes blazing, and my nose an eagle's beak.

"But Max looks awful too, sodden with drink," I told James as we breakfasted in the Rose Room at the Algonquin on West 44th Street, where we were both staying.

"Don't speak to any reporters, don't try to explain. The incident should die a natural death", said James.

"But I must tell them *something*," I objected. "I can't let them think I was simply sozzled."

"You haven't explained to me yet," James said.

"I have. He insulted Barney."

"But in what way?"

"He suggested sexual malpractices," I replied loftily.

"But they're so common these days. I mean nobody thinks anything of them any more. Anyway, was he right?"

"No, of course he wasn't. And if he was, it would still be a private affair. Barney was very prejudiced against that sort of thing."

"It would have remained private if you had simply said 'mind your own business', but to attack him...."

"I am an impulsive creature," I replied with dignity, "and they had stuffed me with too much drink with hardly a nibble of real food. All that grated carrot and lettuce – what use is that as blotting paper. I'm not a socialite, and I don't lick anyone's boots," I said. "And how could I have known that some money-grabbing photographer would snap me and sell the snap to the media?"

"That's what fame means."

"I'm not famous."

"You are now – you're infamous, which is just as good for publicity. You could have hit me or almost anyone else and got away with it. But to slap the face of the man who represented the sponsors who have given thousands of dollars, including the cost of your stay here – that to put it midly, is going over the top."

"I do apologise," I said, feeling both hurt and contrite. "But could you please pour me another cup of coffee? I never thought of anyone at all except Barney, his reputation. I suppose I'm not fit to be here. But all the same ... "

"More's the pity," murmured James.

"I must stand up for my friends when they are not around to protect themselves," I said, suddenly angry because James was being so Anglo-Saxon, "and I daresay those thousands of dollars are peanuts to Max's firm, and anyway they wouldn't do it unless they were getting something out of it. I don't believe big business is ever genuinely charitable. Barney and I and all those other artists have given them kudos."

"Well, certainly your behaviour has put the exhibition on the map," admitted James. "But not in the way anyone expected."

"Exactly, I made it front page news," I said. "Listen James, I'm too old for remorse. I struck a blow for decency and honour, all those old-fashioned things."

"Oh God, don't say *that*," pleaded James. "Artists are not supposed to be *decent*. If you get caught by a reporter just say *no comment*. The truth, whatever it may be, will only harm the sponsors, who are putting it all down to your age and drink."

"And, of course, the man will go scot-free," I said. "No one will judge *him*."

I was indeed very upset, for although I felt Max's words were deeply insulting both to myself and to Barney, I wished I could have behaved with more dignity and sophistication. "My dear, of course not," would have done, or "Certainly not, Barney abhorred all perversions", or "What a curious suggestion. No woman could have wished for a better or more considerate lover."

And then my self-dissatisfaction spread to New York itself, to James and the whole exhibition set-up. What was I doing here, when I should be painting? Why wasn't I at home with my dear Marco warm and purring on my knee? How was he managing without me?

"I'm leaving," I said. "Please book me a flight today."

"But Christabelle, you can't!" cried James, jaw dropping, eyes aghast.

"Why not?" I stood up. "Be an angel and phone for me. I'm sure my ticket is transferable. I want the next flight to London. I'm homesick, James."

"But I was going to take you to the Frick. You said you would like to see the Whistlers."

"Not any more," I said. "Listen I'll write lovely thank you letters to everyone."

"But you *can't* go alone."

"Why not?"

He hesitated, afraid I would be miffed if he said I was too old.

"Well?"

"You're not strong."

"Oh yes, I am. I've never felt stronger. And there's nothing tiring about sitting in an aircraft, especially in the Super Club class. The stewardesses love fussing over old ladies. It makes them feel important."

"I shall cut short my visit and travel with you."

"I don't want you to, James. I forbid it."

"You'll be tired out. You'll collapse."

"I've never collapsed in my life. I'm only tired when I'm bored, and flying excites me. Now go on, time's passing. The first flight you can get please, and I don't mind going tourist, if necessary. I mean I don't actually feel I am Club or first-class material, if you know what I mean." I laughed, for in a strange and rather awful way I was enjoying his discomfiture.

"I wish you wouldn't..."

"Please, I want to leave before the reporters home in on me."

He was away nearly twenty minutes, while I drank another cup of coffee and thought about my future. It hadn't been easy, he said on his return, but he had booked me a flight via Zurich. Did I mind that very much? It added a few hours and meant a bit of waiting around. He had promised to confirm within fifteen minutes.

"Wonderful," I said. "I've never been to Switzerland. Oh, I should love that. Thank you, James, you *are* splendid. But how awful of Max to tell reporters that the dinner was just a little too good for the dear old lady, that I went a bit over the top when he mentioned one of my friends, as though I was tipsy."

"He doesn't want to be fired," James said. "He needs a good reputation. You don't."

Travelling with me in a yellow cab to the airport James said he had so much wanted to show me New York; indeed his sponsors had agreed to pay him to do so. The sponsors loved artists and wanted to help them in every way possible, thanks partly to Max. It was so sad that everything had gone wrong, James said.

"Oh, it's been wonderful, but it isn't my scene any more. I don't fit in, James," I said, touching his hand. "Besides I want to paint. I've wasted nearly twenty years and I haven't much time left. But, believe me, I am *deeply* grateful to you, and please don't be hurt. I am an unpredictable and tiresome old woman, and I look on you as a very dear friend. You have done so much for me, James. You'll be able to move faster here without me. I've spent a lot of my life looking at pictures, because Oliver had this culture thing; he collected a little, you see, so he got lots of invitations to private views, and he hardly ever missed a major London exhibition. He used to take me along too, ask my opinion all the time, which he said was always highly prejudiced. He was a great National Trust man, too, liked driving out on Sundays, standing me tea in some great house, and dinner in a four-star hotel on the way home. He loved giving *treats*. And I made him laugh. So please never think I've been deprived, James."

"But New York is New York," he insisted, "and I looked forward to escorting you, and it seems so awful – this premature exit. I'm afraid everyone will be upset."

"Americans are tough," I said. "Tell them I was taken ill, had to dash back to see my specialist. They'll like that. They'll think it's a shrink. Oh James, I *have* enjoyed myself, and I *do* thank you. But try not to take life so seriously, see the funny side. It's the only way to get through to the end."

I felt very wise as I waited for my call to board the plane, and then rather ashamed. But I was used to see-sawing emotions and I recognised that this temporary "high" would soon be followed by a "low". But at least I was living again and when I began to feel the sense of failure and inner loneliness that living seemed to bring, I should want to work. Work is for me addictive, a drug, but never a tranquilliser, because the satisfaction my pictures give me is always so brief. In the end they drive me mad as life drives me mad. They are never good enough; like myself they always disappoint. So the whole thing, the whole effort is really quite hopeless.

When I bought the cottage I ran away from life and work. There were no failures because there was no effort; no friends to lose, no kicks, only a kind dog and later a charming cat and little Ellen, who was still a child although her face was middle-aged and eventually old. Little Ellen needed love as a domestic pet needs love, so I could cope with it, and I liked to see her pleasure when I gave her a present or took her out somewhere. But I have painted my best pictures only when strife has torn at my flesh like a cat tearing at a tree's bark; when fears and remorse have wakened me in the morning or frustrated love has filled me with a terrible energy that allows me no calm, an unanswered need which I cannot even put before God, because in His eyes it is supposedly sinful.

My time with Oliver was the best time, but not the most fruitful. He was anodyne to my nerves; he was the long, calm sea after the storm. He knew how to handle me. And I gave him the tenderness and warmth he needed. We listened to records together; went to concerts. Handel's "Where'er you walk" became our song. We were unashamedly sentimental. When he died I felt that henceforth I should be a handicapped person. When my exhibition was a flop I longed for him as a bullied child longs for its mother. And the mother wasn't there, the mother was dead, so I ran away. I existed rather than lived. But I suffered no hurts and had no chance to disgrace myself. Isn't that, after all, how many people survive this world?

And now as I flew to Zurich the need to paint was like a great thirst. The flight excited me: first the whirling clouds below, then the sunset of blue-grey islands in a sea of red and gold and, after that, the moon, so close, so large, so wonderful and, incredibly soon, the delicate shades of the sunrise, and then daylight, grey as a seagull's wing, and the snow-capped peaks and the blue lake shimmering. How could my fellow passengers bear to sit watching the in-flight movie with their window shutters down when there was such beauty to be observed, such colours as we rarely see on land to be enjoyed? I felt very alone in the intense pleasure that the sight before my eyes engendered, but, in a way, hadn't I always been alone, different? Even at St. Stephen's, where we all shared so much? The trouble, I told myself sitting at Zurich airport waiting for a plane to London, the trouble was that I grew up alone, because deep attachments were not allowed at my convent home nor at school which was merely an extension of the orphanage. Perhaps, like a dormouse, I had only looked for a mate when my body craved union. No, that wasn't right, I told myself. I desperately needed, although I might deny it, the warmth I found so hard to give myself. I craved the reassurance that I was worthy of love. Sam gave it at first and then made it conditional on my becoming a housewife; Barney gave it as long as I accepted the role of girl-pupil and lesser being. Oliver gave it wisely, I suspect, on the mutual understanding that we would not live permanently together, for he appreciated his bachelor-like independence. He alone understood that I needed my freedom, too, that my art must come first, that I had become a *driven* woman, who yet needed someone especially in moments of crisis, or when failure seemed to look me in the face.

I was, I admit, hurt when I found Oliver had left no will, so that everything went to the wife who had walked out on him, which was wrong of me because I despise filthy lucre and 'blessed is he who expects nothing'. Only to Daniel did I give my life, my time, my all, until Daniel became assertive, until he too qualified his love with all sorts of impossible demands, and then I fled back to solitude and painting.

The delay in Zurich allowed me time to buy crayons, pencils and paper, for now I knew that only work would blot out from my mind anxiety about my behaviour in New York. The flight to London was uneventful until we approached Heathrow and I saw for the first time those golden necklaces which were to inspire a series of pictures. It was raining and there they were far below glistening like jewels on the wet tarmac, sodium lights arranged in circles and oblongs at every roundabout where major roads met on their way into the heart of the metropolis. Why had no one mentioned to me the beauty of these man-made junctions shining through the blackness of the night? Why had no artists painted them? As we circled around Heathrow, I started to draw, to sketch, to use my crayons in a frenzy of activity, leaning forward to peer again and again through my porthole and, once or twice, I heard my voice mutter *wonderful, unbelievable*. Sometimes I heard also a little gasp, as I took in breath. A few people looked as me as though I were crazy, but I thought not *me, you*!

No one met me at Heathrow, because no one knew I was coming back, but I didn't care, not a jot. On the contrary I was euphoric because my eyes and my head were full of those necklaces which I would paint in acrylic so that they would glisten on the shiny black of the canvas as no lights had ever glistened before, except those seen from a plane on a dark November night by an aggressive old woman who had punched a drunken New Yorker in the face.

Still elated, laden with luggage, I took the tube to Gloucester Road where I changed for Paddington, from whence I caught the ten o'clock train for Moreton-in-Marsh. I was now very tired, and the tiredness must have showed for lots of people helped me, even ladies of sixty or more offered to carry my suitcase. But in a strange way I felt in love with life, as though buoyed up by invisible hands, and it suddenly flashed across my mind that this might be an indication that I was soon to die. Experience had taught me that the ill often enjoy a sudden lucidity, a lifting of the spirit before the curtain comes down. And if I were soon to die I must work quickly to complete my acrylic pictures, which would be for me a departure from my past efforts because I had never before worked in that medium. Then with that thought in mind I couldn't wait to be home with Marco and, tired though I was, I found myself fidgeting in the train like an impatient child who is tired of grown-up companions.

I rang for a taxi at the station and by the grace of God someone answered and when he came recognised me.

"Saw your picture in the paper this morning, Miss Lang," he said, with a jovial, teasing smile. "Seems you've taught those Yanks a lesson. I never knew you were an artist, and famous too. Quite a shock really! You could say you've been hiding your light under a bushel."

"Oh well," I said. "Oh well, I've been brought up not to boast you know. I've just come out of retirement, that's all. And the man was rude, lewd you know. I can't stand lewdness."

Chapter Fifteen

I HAD LEFT the village as a mad recluse nobody believed or trusted, and now returned famous. My incident in the gallery had been exploited as an ironic story on local radio and my picture had appeared in the national press. At last, through a misdemeanour, I was somebody because I had behaved in the way that was expected of artists, and made news.

I woke very late next morning to find Marco, who had refused to leave my cottage, purring round me. There were letters on my door mat and in no time at all a knock at my door.

I crawled out of bed and a voice called, "It's only me, Eva Sims. Don't get up if you're in bed and suffering from jet lag."

Eva was a neighbour who had not spoken to me since, years earlier, she had accused Murdoch of leaving turds on her lawn. Now I was inclined to turn her away, but then I remembered my resolution to *live*, my decision that tension was essential to my work.

"Just a minute, I'll open the door."

She came in, cold and breezy, wearing her green wellies with a wool dress.

"Are you all right for provisions?" she asked.

"I've got a few tins," I said. "Thank you."

"Look, I've taken it out of the freezer for you." She handed me a home-made steak and kidney pie in a Pyrex dish. "Made by my own fair hands."

I said I felt overwhelmed. "You are a village heroine," she told me. "None of us realised. Why didn't you say? An artist, exhibiting in New York ... and no one knew!"

"I've come out of retirement. I've been discovered in the

nick of time. It happens, think of Barbara Pym." I tried to be social although I longed to go back to bed. "Would you like coffee?"

"Oh no, you must come to *me*. *Do*, pop round when you've dressed, and have a spot of breakfast and tell me all about New York. Was it fabulous?"

Eva Sims wasn't my type, but I went all the same, and as I sat in her chintzy little parlour drinking coffee from a porcelain cup, I suddenly remembered that picture of Poppy. What did I do with it? I couldn't wait then to get back, for all at once there was nothing in the whole world I wanted to do more than see that picture. And I was in a panic in case I had lost it for good.

"Madeira," I said.

"Pardon?" said my neighbour.

"I was just thinking that if I sold a particular work of mine I could afford to go to Madeira."

"Oh, how exciting!"

"You see I am a person of extremes, all or nothing for me."

"You could have your kitchen modernised. *Country Life* units installed, the place painted."

"Oh, I'm used to the old dump as it is, and I don't hanker after suburbia, or, for that matter, a bijou residence! Such things don't *mean* much to me."

I was astonished how the words flew from my lips, how, despite the long journey, I felt wonderfully young, but my laugh belonged to an old lady – no mistaking that – and springing to my feet, I felt as stiff as an elderly dog who has spent too much time in the rain.

Consciously remembering my manners, for when you have lived alone a long time such things cease to be automatic, I said the coffee had been delicious and that the toast and honey had set me up for the day. "Now, if you will excuse me, I must dash back."

"Well, if the picture is preying on your mind ..."

"And there's a pile of letters too, and Marco to feed and things to buy."

"Well, if you want a lift into Moreton, don't hesitate to ask," offered my neighbour for the first time in twenty years.

Back in the cottage, I gave Marco a saucer of milk from the

bottle Annie had left in the refrigerator, and half a tin of meat from my store. Then I started to look for the picture, moving furniture, opening drawers, turning out cupboards, as though my life depended on finding it. Was it a work of genius? Painted, as it had been, at a time of great tension. Or was it overdone, overstated, too literary? I had kept it hidden because it seemed too personal to be exposed to the public gaze. To see it was surely to look deep into my soul, to recognise violent emotions which I did not want to admit to within myself. It was against convent life, against my upbringing, full of sexual suggestion. For years I had kept it wrapped in a blanket, hidden from Barney and then Daniel. But now with the passage of time, now that all passion was spent I thought I might feel differently. Knives and daggers, searing red, a stockinged leg, a broken suspender, a man's face, Barney's face between Poppy's and mine. What emotion, what jealousy! Although the two pictures exhibited in New York had been pleasing enough they were not *great*, not my best, my most spectacular work. They were all right for hanging in a boudoir or passage, but not moving. But the Poppy picture would show the world, if they cared, that the old lady had never lacked passion, had always been driven by emotions, that in this frail frame were the remnants of a wilder woman.

At last I found the picture behind an Edwardian wardrobe which I had bought over two decades earlier with some of Patrick Guggenheim's money, and I thanked God the picture had not fallen into his hands. It was undamaged, unframed and shocking to me in its outspokenness and lack of subtlety, but so is some Bacon and some Hockney, I thought. It's very modern, well painted, ahead of its time and maybe historically interesting for that reason. And it's alive. It sizzles.

"But not really me," I told myself, feeling suddenly tired. "Not typical. And yet it has power. And I've captured that terrible malevolence in Barney's expression which sometimes overrode the warm teddy-bear look which I so loved. It's an honest picture, isn't it? And as for Poppy and me – Oh there's love and lust in our faces; we eye him with longing and each other with hatred. You feel the tension and the sex and the need for possession."

And then the convent me and the artist me were at war again, so that I could not decide whether the picture was shameful or a small masterpiece.

I decided to ask James's opinion when he next came; if he came. For now I suddenly wondered whether he *would* come. He was so well-mannered himself that my outburst must have deeply offended him. Sitting down on the floor, I felt like a small girl who knows she is to be punished for disgraceful and ungrateful behaviour. It struck me that men probably never feel like this, and that it was very odd that I could still be so vulnerable at the age of eighty-three, as though all those years of struggling in an adult world to hold one's own had added up to nothing. Here I was in my shabby cottage, a motherless and fatherless child still in a muddle about life, love, our Blessed Lord, whom the nuns worshipped but failed in so many ways to emulate. I thought, sitting there before my picture: I shall never understand, never be whole. I remembered Barney saying that when you knew everything you were ready to die, and someone else, perhaps it was Oliver, saying that all artists possessed a childlike streak, for how else could they see so much anew?

Then I told myself that I had been absolutely right to slap Max; it was only the convent's influence which made me think otherwise, the turn-the-other-cheek moralising, the false demure-girl image, which made me feel guilty. My best painting I knew now had come out of the tension in my life, the confusion, the conflict between my nature and my upbringing, the blood in my veins and the spiritual aspirations fed into my mind. And the contradictory element, which had disturbed me so much as a child, between the prayers of some nuns and their cruelty. And, added to all this, the ideal of chastity imbued in me in early life, which was so much at odds with the notions of free love which had fired my imagination as a student. And genetics? Oh God, genetics! What did the sperm and the egg bring me in their shameful regrettable union, what programme for life, what pattern? Hadn't I always suffered, deep down, an identity crisis? Something I pushed aside, refused to recognise, joking, when I wanted to draw attention to myself, that I had come from nowhere. Had my first embrace with Sam been a search for identity, a wanting to belong? Or a desperate need for the warmth I had been denied as a child, which then, because I was by nature passionate, led on to more than I had intended? At that moment another knock on the door brought me to my feet.

"It's going to be like bloody Piccadilly Circus," I muttered to Marco who was reclining on my pillow, as I hid the picture in the dust under my bed. I ran a comb through my hair, went down and welcomed Annie and Ellen – the one so old, so shrivelled, the other lined but spritely with red ribbons in her white hair and a coal-scuttle mouth which split the curiously young face in half.

"You came back earlier than we expected. We've brought some provisions for you," Annie said, a large cardboard box precariously balanced on her arms.

"Marco wouldn't stay with us. Marco liked it here best. We visited him three times a day," Ellen cried, skipping on bandy legs.

"He ate a treat though. We hear you're famous," Annie said. "Picture in the papers and all. And you hiding yourself away like a nobody all these years, not speaking! You're a celebrity now."

"A temporary state of affairs," I replied ushering them in. "A flash in the pan, a moment's notoriety. And I was only asked to exhibit because someone else dropped out. I was second choice, Annie, so my head's not going to get too big."

"Oh, don't say that! Don't spoil it! Look, here are two little cutlets for your lunch and half a dozen free-range eggs, and a bit of plaice and veg and cheese ... and ... and ..."

She started to unpack the box and all at once I felt tears coming into my eyes because I had not expected such kindness, not since Oliver died and I had withdrawn and become spiteful, because life no longer appealed to me and all social intercourse seemed a meaningless game. I embraced both women and called them my special friends. And Annie, whom I had never really liked, because she exploited Ellen and spent her money, patted me on the back and said, "Don't cry, dear, don't cry."

The next day I went to Cheltenham on the weekly bus to buy acrylic paint and several canvases which I left to be delivered. I was now very short of money, because I only had my old age pension to live on and there had been incidental expenses in New York, as well as the train fare home from Heathrow. So, back in my cottage, I decided to offer some of my pictures to a recently opened gallery in Stow-on-the-Wold, where I thought I could now command the prices I wanted. Quickly I started to turn out drawers and boxes, which I had left closed and tied for years, looking for works which I had kept from Patrick out of sentiment or carelessness. There were many sketches of Daniel and one oil which sent the tears running down my cheeks, as I lacerated myself for being a rotten mother. At such times my capacity for self-torture seems boundless and the memories I conjure up almost more than I can bear. I put the pictures back in the box, retied the string, sorted out my drawings of Marco and set aside one small oil of Barney which I actually liked, and would, I decided, yield more than enough money for Madeira.

The gallery was tucked away down a side street, its owner a young man hiding behind dark glasses.

"Christabelle Lang," I said feeling nervous.

"I beg your pardon?"

"Christabelle Lang."

He took off his glasses and I saw that his eyes were green like pondwater. He looked down into my face as though I were a child.

"Yes, as a matter of fact I do have one picture by her, you're just in time, because her prices are set to go over the top."

"The American trip?" I hazarded.

"No, there was a piece in *The Times* on saleroom prices. Hers are doing rather well, so a person who lives nearby brought in a picture for me to sell. Are you a collector?"

"Not exactly." I realised this ridiculously young dealer must be the only local person not to have seen my photograph in the papers.

"It's a portrait," he went on, "of a Gloucestershire personality. Hang on a minute, I'll fetch it. She's no beauty, but it's an interesting work, and if you're thinking of an investment, something that will appreciate for your grandchildren ..." The next moment I was looking at Henrietta Spilsbury.

"It's not a terribly pleasant face," said the young man.

"There's something petulant about the mouth, but it's wonderfully alive, don't you think? There's a real person looking out of the canvas, isn't there?"

"Yes indeed," I said, for suddenly I realised the portrait was much better than I had previously thought, that, looking at it, I felt Henrietta's presence and heard her thin voice which somehow had managed to combine in old age a commanding tone with a sense of smallness and petulance.

"It's a good likeness. I knew her well. I'm surprised her relations want to part with it," I said.

"Second cousins once removed apparently, and she was quite a cantankerous old lady, I'm told. Apparently Mrs. Lang looked after her, had a little cottage on the estate where she lived with her son."

"That's me," I said.

"Pardon?"

He was leaning forward to bring his face closer to mine, for age has shrunken me; his lashes, pale as matchsticks, accentuated the remarkable muddy greenness of his eyes. He looked as though he needed a good meal, roast beef, followed by suet pudding, with vegetables and all the trimmings. His immense height and his thinness made me feel dizzy, as though I was a starved myrtle bush overshadowed by a pine tree, which might fall in a gale.

"I'm Christabelle Lang, the artist."

Too impulsive and taken aback to be tactful, he said he had thought me dead. "You must be very old."

"Eighty-three," I snapped. "And you're no historian. I'm in all the reference books."

He was still young enough to blush. "Sadly mine are out of date, and nowhere could I find details of your birth or parents. Information on you is very sparse, almost non-existent." He put back his dark glasses.

"Well, here I am, alive and kicking. And I've brought you some things to see."

I spread out the sketches of Marco. Off came the glasses.

"Oh super! Oh, I like these! Great, terrific, such sensibility! Cotswold people like cats."

Remembering Patrick's greed, I thought I must make my position clear in case this man's praise was laced with avarice.

"I'm afraid I can only let you have fifteen per cent now that I am so well established." I spoke too loudly out of embarrassment and he stepped back as though I might strike him.

"Isn't that a bit hard? In London some dealers take fifty."

"Oh I know, I know. But let's face it," I cried, "you don't have such high rates and rents to pay. All right, twenty per cent, and since I'm on the up and up, that'll be money for jam."

"Well not quite, but I understand how you feel. I'll accept twenty per cent if that is the most you can spare." His tone was conciliatory but his expression said, *You poor old thing, you haven't much time left, have you*?

"Good. Now please look at this."

I brought out from my canvas bag a portrait of Barney, an oil on panel, rather old-fashioned in style, almost Euston Road, but full of atmosphere. "It's better than the one which went to America."

"I know the face," the dealer said, suddenly brighter eyed.

"Of course you do. It's one of my best works, and I won't take less than three thousand pounds, and for God's sake insure it."

Unaccustomed to haggling, I sounded more belligerent than I intended.

"It will be covered, never worry."

There was now awe in the young man's voice. I had made his day, and in doing so broken my original contract with Patrick, but I didn't care about that, not a hoot; the bloody parasite should be taught a lesson. Hadn't he diddled me long enough? The very thought of him was like bile in my mouth, the bald-headed coot.

"It *is* Barney Copeland, isn't it?"

"Of course, we were lovers!"

His hand trembled a little as he wrote out a receipt for all the pictures. Then he apologised for not having recognised me.

"Don't give it another thought."

I was grand, all-understanding, full of largesse, pleased that I was giving the man a chance of success, perhaps even a *start*, for when you are doing well you must spread your good luck around, share it. Don't be selfish, Christabelle, and all that.

When I said I must hurry for my bus, the dealer told his mouse-haired assistant to run me home in her car. An honour, he said it would be, going over the top a little. So this is the beginning of fame, I said to myself. This is what it feels like, along with the American experience.

But my confidence dipped when I saw two policemen waiting on my doorstep.

"Miss Lang, may we come in a moment?"

My first thought was, *My God, Daniel!* which of course was ridiculous.

Drinking my coffee they looked around as biographers do. Casually almost, they mentioned the incident which had once loomed so large in my mind, until James came into my life. And I now remembered how these same two men had humiliated me with their suggestions of wish-fulfilment and fantasy – the frustrated old maid fancied by someone at last; their assumption that no woman could feel complete unless possessed by a male disgusted me. Today, however, they politely awaited my reaction.

"Refresh my memory, please," I said, playing the whole incident down.

"Last year you alleged, madam, that a man broke in and threatened you with a knife. Do you now recall the occasion?"

"Of course. Are you suggesting senility?"

"No, but time plays tricks sometimes," the taller, more intelligent policeman said.

"I shall never forget that night as long as I live." Hostility crept into my voice. Today I was a different woman. No trembling, no pathos, no tears, a woman to be reckoned with. "It was attempted rape. He had no trousers on. He wanted a female body, a hole. I was the best he could find. He wasn't sane, his eyes didn't focus properly. He was not seeing the old and tatty woman you have before you now, he was seeing someone else – his mother perhaps. I'm not a fool, no innocent. I know about men. I've been around."

"You didn't report all this to us at the time," complained the heavier-built constable, his helmet resting on his knees. "You didn't give us a good description."

"I had been through an ordeal, and you didn't believe me, you were, to put it mildly, cruelly sceptical; you made me feel old and incoherent. Why have you come back? What do you want now?"

"There's fresh evidence, Miss Lang. This is just a preliminary visit. One of our plain-clothes branch will come to take a full statement from you."

"You mean you believe me?"

I stared at them both with pounding heart and total disbelief as my mind went back. Now I was sitting up in bed again, listening to the scraping on the wall as he climbed up, hanging on to the wisteria and the honeysuckle. Then his face was at the window, blocking out the moonlight; his body was pushing its way through. He was breathing heavily. I switched on my torch, tried to dazzle his eyes. The scream in my belly would not rise fast enough and then it was jammed somewhere in my throat. Dropping the torch, I put out my hands to protect myself. He had a fair moustache and lots of greasy hair and eyes that were like pebbles yet bright with wanting. I knew what he desired because he was bare from the waist down, but he revolted and terrified me. I did not want him near. I would rather have died than submit to him. Without conscious thought, feeling very light, very small and quite soundless, I scrambled out of bed. In the orphanage we had not been allowed to scream, even when we were slapped with Sister Maria's slipper. Just punishment had to be borne without a whimper. We had to learn absolute self-control. Now as my heartbeats slowed, I fought back fear and threw my hair brush at his head and missed and he smiled as though I was a little girl he would soon master, as though he liked childish resistance because in the end it would make his triumph and rapture all the finer. He moved away from the window and a shaft of moonlight caught the flash of his knife as he raised it in the air.

"I'm too old. Go away. Now, at once." My voice sounded rusty. "I'm no good. I'm eighty."

But he was living in a dream. I could see from the glint in his eyes that he was seeing not me but someone else. The lust was from inside himself, not aroused by me, but by some image in his head. And there was an awful secrecy about his smile, and the scent of unwashed maleness and madness hung in the air like a bad smell from the bathroom. I thought that if I gave way, ignoring the nausea and hate which he aroused in me, there was always the chance that he would kill me afterwards. So why die violated?

"Are you all right? Is this the man?"

The older policeman passed me a photograph. "I need my glasses."

I wanted time to pull myself together, to speak and act in a calm convincing way. "Perhaps they are in the kitchen." I went through the door. If only I could drive the man from my mind and stop shaking, perhaps the dizziness would pass.

"It cost a lot of money having those bars put in," I said, coming back. "Now then." The photograph, a snapshot, trembled in my hands. The face was the face which had come so close to mine, tearing forth at last the thin scream from my belly, but the eyes were calmer, normal eyes, and the smile's furtiveness bore little resemblance to the mouth that had seemed to welcome with a callous teasing expression the ill-thrown brush.

"The same," I whispered, "the same man, with a different expression."

"What made him leave before he actually assaulted you?"

"I don't know. Perhaps it was God. Perhaps it was my guardian angel, or maybe my feeble scream, or perhaps sanity, coming back."

"He went down the stairs and let himself out?"

"Yes, without another word."

"And then you ran to Miss Elmwood's cottage?"

"After I had waited and made sure he had left." As I spoke I could feel again how my old legs had gathered a strength which I had thought long past them, bearing me down the street at a run, bearing me to the brown door.

"Annie! Ellen! Quick! Help!"

The avaricious servant had come.

"Whatever on earth! Miss Lang? Whatever is the matter?"

She had stood there like a Shamely maid, disapproving, reducing me to the size of a naughty little girl from the institution.

"I've been attacked. A man! He had a knife. Rape!" I was scarcely coherent.

"Oh you have, have you? You had better come in." Her

voice had been cold with disbelief. "Out in your nightdress at this time of night!"

"The police," I had said. "We must telephone them," and then everything had become distant with Annie's face growing smaller, fainter, as, with a warm sensation stealing across the back of my neck, I slid to the ground.

Pushing this memory back, I said, "Why are you reopening the case?"

"He's struck again, another elderly lady."

"And you've caught him?"

"Yes, picked him up on the street. She had a telephone. She dialled 999. We shall need you to give evidence in court."

"Has he confessed to breaking into my house?"

"Yes."

"So he isn't quite mad. He knows what he's doing?"

"Yes."

I should have felt triumphant, vindicated, for was this not a moment for which I had been waiting? But the day's events had been too much for me. After the policemen had gone I fell asleep in a chair and wakened to find the fire out and Marco mewing at the door. Snow was falling like torn paper and I was sad because I had forgotten to put an evening meal out for the birds. In consequence I was afraid that some might die of hypothermia. I opened a tin and fed the cat; then put sausages under the grill for myself. Poor little birds, I thought, with empty crops, so beautiful and so frail. I wondered whether birds' feet felt very cold perching on snow-covered branches. I could imagine their toes losing their grip, the bundles of feathers falling noiselessly to the ground and lying like broken toys. The whistling wind and rattling windows reminded me of a film I had seen of *Wuthering Heights* with Oliver years earlier. Then remembering that I should soon receive money from the young art gallery owner, I decided to seek solace from the bottle of sherry I now kept for James. Sipping gently I fell to thinking of James's work. I now saw that I had told him too little about myself, forgetting to mention the three Chelsea shows in which I had exhibited, and the one or two pictures which had been seen abroad. I had been too modest, and he was too gentle a young man to nag me for more information. I thought how much Oliver would have enjoyed talking to a clean-looking, well-dressed art historian. They would have discussed poetry and James's career and art in general and the Courtauld Institute. Oliver always drew people out, humans being his speciality. He only talked about himself occasionally and then in a mildly derogatory way. His poems, too, were always about other people, never about his own problems or adventures. He believed that there was an intelligence behind the universe and that there was some kind of life after death, but it was not a question that he discussed readily. On the whole he did not speak on topics that went down to the painful heart of matters. He skirted the surface charmingly, being careful always not to cause people pain or embarrassment. He hated it when friends started to talk about income tax or their overdrafts, believing that such behaviour was bad-mannered, even vulgar. His success as a doctor had lain almost as much in his bedside manner as his diagnostic skill. Because he always took off his glasses before we kissed, he had become for me two people: the kind, bespectacled understanding friend and the vulnerable, short-sighted, brown-eyed lover, who could not see more than a few feet in front of him, a man made suddenly helpless and dependent.

I took another sip of sherry and thought how differently Barney would have reacted to the pink-cheeked James. With the artist's habitual suspicion of a critic he would have eyed the young man with mocking scepticism. He would have thrown provocative questions at him with the studied carelessness of an expert bowler who knows he can get out a batsman whenever he chooses. Finally when the wretched victim had left politely but with his tail between his legs, Barney would have turned to me and said with the dismissive grin which I knew so well, "Just a sharp shit with cufflinks. Was I disgracefully rude? Well, he deserved it, didn't he? What does he know about painting? Never touched a brush in his life. What about a spot of booze? Let's wash the memory away."

At this point in my musings I was suddenly brought back to the present by the stench of burning – the sausages I had put on for lunch, and smoke drifting into the room. Throwing Marco off my lap I dashed into the kitchen. The grill seemed on fire. There was nothing to hand with which to smother the flames, so I filled a jug with water and threw that on them. With a great sizzle they flew up to the ceiling, blackened it and then died down. Feeling quite weak I leaned against the door. Tomorrow, I told myself, I must paint that ceiling because if the meals-on-wheels lady or anyone in the village sees the blackness, they will say I am unfit to live alone, that my mind is going. And then I will have a call from a social worker, and I cannot bear that. I cannot bear to explain everything, to see her mind clicking like a pair of needles, one plain, one purl, and the pattern means time to get Miss Lang into a home.

The cottage was so dark that I had to paint out of doors, between showers of rain or snow, standing by an old Valor stove, over which I warmed my hands between brush strokes. But the vivid and compelling memory of those necklaces kept me warm, and the local children who had once mocked me as a witch peered at me now with genuine interest. Of course I was to them still an eccentric old woman as I struggled with paint and canvas, bizarrely dressed with two scarves and an old felt hat over my head for warmth, and several sweaters under a sleeveless jerkin – a coat would have constrained my arms too much – and ancient corduroy trousers with unfashionably flared legs. And, when they crept in for a closer look, they were bewildered by the golden beads I was so painstakingly painting as through a haze of rain.

"What's it going to be, Miss Lang?"

"Dog's shit," a boy said, waiting for the laughs, that did not, I am glad to say, follow.

"Wait and see. I'm not sure myself yet. Be patient."

And then I stopped answering them, for I was determined that nothing on earth should distract me from this new development in my work.

I had only half completed two pictures when fresh falls of snow kept me indoors studying brochures of Madeira. "No beaches," I kept telling myself, "but white houses and steep streets and wonderful rock formations which will give solidity to my pictures, and donkeys." I saw myself setting up my easel, as I had all those years ago in the Kent hop fields. I felt again the excitement of starting out with a head full of ideas and eyes ready to see extraordinary aspects in objects and landscape which were to others commonplace. In between these fantasies came the questions, the hypotheses, the endless going back, useless exercises to occupy a lonely woman's mind. Supposing I had married Sam? Could I have survived the role of wife and mother? Supposing I had actually killed Mrs. Spilsbury? Would I have lied or bleated out my sad story to the nieces? Supposing I had never met Oliver? Could I have continued in London alone? Was my life made easier or more difficult by the lack of parents? Freud, after all, laid much blame at the feet of mothers and fathers, so perhaps it was best not to have them at all.

Such were my thoughts when the thaw came and soon afterwards without warning James and Belinda. And how happy I was to see them, for whatever I might have pretended to myself, deep down I was afraid that they might have grown tired of me after my outburst in New York.

Picture me running to open the door to them, a disreputable old hag (for don't let's mince words) in a shapeless sweater with holes in the elbows, white hair on end, anthracite dust under the nails; feet stuffed into the clogs which Oliver brought me back from Holland years ago. Clump, clump, clump – who cares? Now only my work matters. And James saw in New York that I can dress well. Standing in my hallway my young friends gaze at me fondly as though I am a domestic pet they have not seen for months. I am their tame artist.

"And how is Christabelle?"

"Getting old and dirty," I say, "but look ... "

I bring out the two acrylic paintings I have at last completed.

"Seen from Heathrow," I say, "when hovering to land."

"Good God!"

"Why Good God, James?" I ask.

"So different."

"You don't like them? Come through, where you can see them in a proper light."

"Almost Jackson Pollock," he comments a moment later, glancing at Belinda.

"Oh come on, absolutely original," I cry, deeply hurt. "My very own, influenced by no one else, unique."

"He's astonished, not critical," Belinda says. "May we sit down? We have news."

"Not bad I hope. Have the Americans forgiven me?"

"Of course. Secretly they loved you for it. The Americans always love a sensation. And you filled the gallery. You are the talk of New York."

I turn again to my canvases as a person returns to an obsession.

"They inspired these," I say. "They set my adrenalin going again. And soon I shall be off to Madeira."

"Why? Why Madeira?" My friends both ask at once.

"I don't know. It's just a name that has always entranced me."

"We've been skiing," Belinda tells me. "Have you ever skied?"

"I've never had money for holidays abroad, except when Oliver paid; artists don't make money, unless they're Henry Moore, or dead. Think of Giacometti and Bomberg – such financial problems! But now things are changing, so I must hurry before it's too late."

"And your biography?"

"No time, back to painting you see. You can have all my scribbling when I die, James."

"You must write that down," Belinda says, "if you really mean it!"

I look at the young man and I know I love him. "But are you rich?" I ask half seriously. "I don't help the wealthy!"

"No, he isn't," Belinda says. "He's the youngest of four."

"Listen," I say, longing to see happiness on my visitors' faces, to feel their pleasure. "I've something you can take away with you on condition no one sees it until after my death. A Christmas present!"

I go to my bedroom, crawl under the bed, come back carrying the Poppy picture.

"Here, for you!"

So suddenly the positions are reversed again. I look at James as though he is a child, I wait to see his face light up.

"My God," he exclaims, "the picture you mentioned, the

jealousy one. Christabelle, it's terrific, but are you sure? You could sell it for thousands."

"Because of Barney?"

"Because it's a great picture."

"Anyway, it's yours."

"It's better than the necklaces."

"Don't say that; they're my hope for the future."

I turn away. James's uncalled for comment is the kick in the teeth, like Sam's remark about the girl he took when the moon was full. The little dig that always stops anything being perfect. But I'm old now. I don't care, because I know that all judgment is subjective, that today's failure is tomorrow's success. I must do what I want to do and to hell with them all.

"Christabelle," James says, "you're going to need a drink."

"Oh why? What's happened? Something awful?"

"Something rather nice."

"Belinda, in that cupboard, the sherry."

We toast each other and the future.

"Now then, out with it!"

I feel blood pounding in my temples, a throb at the back of my head. I hold on to my chair.

"Your father," he begins. "I went back to the village where you were born. I spent a whole day there, put up in the pub, and someone remembered, as I knew they would, something her mother said, and then everyone got talking. Your father was a curate, Christabelle, Algernon Appleby."

"And my mother?"

"A farm labourer's daughter, pretty, flighty, always drawing."

"Poor girl."

"Oh, she married later. A groom, who was killed in the war. She had other babies; you have half-sisters and brothers."

"Algernon Appleby." I roll the name over my tongue.

"He became a bishop."

Now my heart begins to pound and bells ring in my ears. "Oh dear Lord, not *the* Bishop Appleby, the man who was always questioning the Immaculate Conception? I remember reading about *him*. James, I don't believe it, it can't be true! You're having me on. I'm dizzy with astonishment."

"Cross my heart. I've got a photograph here. I got a print from *The Times*. See, he has your nose, Christabelle."

"And a shock of white hair," I cry. "Oh, this is too much. This will kill me! No wonder that convent took me in. The old devil! A man of the cloth and all!"

"He had six sons, one still lives."

"He married?"

"A duke's fourth daughter."

"Bishop Appleby. What a sod! Well, all the same he wouldn't have approved of my loose life, would he?" I hear an old lady's laugh. "I say, what a turnabout."

"He was a bit of a rebel," James tells me. "Unpredictable, like you."

I ask if James is quite, quite sure he's right. I lean forward in my eagerness and, because the sherry has gone to my head, the room seems to tilt a little as I speak.

"I saw one of Lady Randolph's children, too. She knew."

"James is a brilliant researcher," Belinda says.

"Fascinating material for a future biography, after I'm dead." There's a touch of acid in my voice.

"Only if you want it." James takes my hand in his. "Not otherwise; we biographers are leeches, as your tone suggests, we live on other people's blood."

I make an effort to be nice, for truly I hate my caustic tongue.

"No, I want you to write it. I'm glad. Spill all the beans. A bishop's daughter! What a laugh! Quite a story, isn't it?" I look at the photo again. "He has my eyebrows, too, but not my eyes. They must come from my mother, like the drawing. Do you know, James, I'm rather glad I'm a love child! I imagine them lying together in the woods. Such passion! Now what time of year was I conceived?" Forcing a smile, I count on my fingers. "Bluebell time, bluebells under the tall beeches and primroses in the hedgerows, and cowslips in the grass. How romantic! But in the end Algernon put his career first, the sod, and married a member of the aristocracy. What a creep!"

"The Lady Anne, she was very beautiful, I've looked her up, too," James said, "and he was quite a stunner too. They were well matched. A handsome pair."

I must forgive my father, for, after all, but for him I would not have existed. I remember how quickly passion overrode my ignorance and fear the first time with Sam. How when you are young you can so easily mix up sexual need with love.

"Now take care of that picture," I say. "Here, take this blanket, wrap it up. And, remember, no one is to see it until I'm dead."

I want them to go now so that I can be alone with this new information, to reproach myself for not tracing my forebears and the circumstances of my birth. How different my life might have been had I known earlier the origins of the blood that ran through my veins and the genes that made me the woman I was.

"Choosing is so important," I say aloud.

"Choosing?" echoes James.

"To do or not to do – priorities."

"Yes, of course." He looks at me doubtfully.

"Free will, choices. In the end we have only ourselves to blame for most of our failures – those omissions ..." My voice tails off. I am tired, wrung dry.

"Fascinating," exclaims James, who clearly does not understand my meaning. "Christabelle, will you do me a favour?"

"Depends what it is."

"When you're tired of writing, when you feel lonely but talkative, please speak into this."

He hands me his tape recorder.

"Oh heavens! That's a tall order."

"Tell me all the details, what you do, what you eat, what you think. I should love that."

"Even the silly thoughts?"

"Everything. Look it has a ninety-minute tape inside already, and here's another. This is how it works. It will pick up a conversation across the room or as you walk about."

"The miracles of modern science," I laugh.

They kiss me on the cheek.

"Don't get up," Belinda says. "We'll see ourselves out."

"Happy Christmas! Take care driving. Look out for black ice."

My warnings follow them to the door. They pause on the step, look back.

"Happy Christmas and thank you," they say in chorus.

The cottage seems very empty as the Mini jumps into life and purrs away towards London.

Chapter Sixteen

THERE came a night when I went to bed feeling as weak as an ancient tree, torn by tempests, dizzy with the sensation of an impending fall and above all with a sense of utter fatigue which made even thought itself an unwelcome intrusion into that overwhelming desire to sink into oblivion.

In bed there was, however, no peace, for within half an hour a background headache had become one of the worst migraines I had ever experienced. The dizziness became a need to vomit, the pain both a saw at the neck, and a tearing behind the eyes, became a fire and then sharp tongs opening and shutting, squeezing. This pain became so intense that I was forced to hold my head in my hands in a vain attempt to comfort it and keep it still, for to move was agony, an experience so excruciating that I thought I must die. Indeed I felt then that to die would be a merciful physical release. Yet at the back of my mind there was a conviction that I had more to do, that I must not leave the stage when recognition was at last at hand. Through all the tangle of pain, the torture of raw nerves and pounding blood a small voice whispered, "Don't give in. Not yet, not now when everything has started to happen. This is a test." I tried to sit up, but the whole room moved, tilting like a big ship in very high seas. And now although my head was on fire my body seemed empty and cold. My headache pills were not within reach; my legs were pinned down by the blankets which had become heavy as sacks of flour. And inside myself a voice cried suddenly in biblical tongue to a God in whom I did not wholly believe, "Save me. Forget not thy daughter Christabelle!"

From my single pillow a fine duck's feather floated, caught by a little breeze from a crack in the door, and rose to the ceiling. And through all my body there ran a great coldness, while a sudden rigidity set my mouth so firmly that even my inner voice was silent. My eyes became fixed hard as marbles and when I tried to raise my eyebrows they seemed to meet a wall of solid flesh. With the setting of my features the pain went and neither my arms nor my legs would move. And then for a moment it returned, pulling at my chest, beating against the walls of my rib cage, yet bearable because all at once I was outside it. Lighter than gossamer, I was above the bed, flooded with a sense of happiness so golden, so profound that words cannot describe it. Below me, on the crumpled bed, my body lay grotesque and rigid as some broken horror toy made of yellowing plastic, a used, rejected thing, a shell from which life had been plucked, not to be devoured as a snail by the thrush but to fly as the angels fly. How shabby the room looked, how faded the objects which had meant so much to me. How could I have wanted to hang on to such a life? My nose was an eagle's nose, ridiculously large in that shrunken face, my lips were the dull purply brown of a turnip's skin, my eyes ... But now the door was opening a crack, another crack, as Marco entered, soft-padded, warm-blooded and alive; his eyes blue as sapphires, his voice a baby's wail. He raised himself a little on his hind legs and looked at my body and then recoiled. In those wide blue Siamese eyes there was a bewilderment I could not bear. Was it death he saw?

"Marco!" My cry was soundless and yet he heard. He turned back towards the body and the body became me again. The body sat up and I was inside the body, and, looking up towards the ceiling, I saw only the feather floating there.

"It's all right," I said. "It must have been a dream." But the more I thought about the experience the more certain I was that it was a spiritual phenomenon, that I had come back from the dead. "I have risen," I said, and in the next moment asked, "But why me? I have done nothing to deserve such an ecstatic sense of happiness and revelation. In all my life I have striven mostly for myself and my art. I have done no good works; worshipped, but rarely at the altar rail, and lived for years in what the Church terms sin."

Yet having once experienced that sense of indelible happiness I almost longed to return to the same state for all at once nothing else mattered. Then Marco came to me, lying on my chest and pummelling me with his paws, asking for food, for companionship and warmth. My headache had gone, but as I got up, my limbs moved clumsily as though my brain's messages were being held up on the way. Slowly I went downstairs to the kitchen. "It can't have been a dream," I told myself again. "This was a message from God not to fear death. Perhaps other people experience it too, but like me will never speak of it in case they are suspected of insanity or religious mania."

Perhaps, I decided, Helen met her end with such equanimity because she too had risen. "I rose from the dead. I rose!" It was very strange having no one to tell but a cat whose mind was on his dinner, but perhaps it was right that at this moment there was no other human between God and myself.

I could not drive the thought of Madeira out of my mind, sunshine and warm, brown wine, gentle waves lapping on pebbly shores, and a sky devoid of all those shades of grey that bedevil our winter horizons.

Christmas came with the usual loneliness, of which I cannot complain since I chose to retreat from my friends. I took Ellen a red scarf and chocolates and sent Oliver's one-time housekeeper a paperback by Victoria Holt. I posted a dozen cards and received a handful including one from Patrick Guggenheim advertising one of his abstract painters, and another from James and Belinda, who had chosen a detail from 'The Trinity', a kneeling angel with green wings against a golden background, which was the right sort of card to send a bishop's daughter. James wrote that he hoped to see me again early in the new year.

After Christmas the snow returned in all its cruel grandeur. And as my cottage became a prison, the vision of Madeira grew in my mind until it became a goal that must be attained at all costs. I justified this irrational longing for shores I had never seen by telling myself Madeira was virgin territory: no friend of mine had ever travelled there. But it would, I assured myself in less obsessional moments, be only the first of many painting trips abroad, for nowadays when there were so many centenarians, eighty-four was nothing. But I needed more money.

Eventually I managed to reach the telephone kiosk with the help of a stout walking stick and the thick soled shoes I bought to wear in Scotland when Oliver rented a cottage near Arisaig. Cars had pushed down the snow and turned the road into an ice rink. I reached the kiosk and telephoned the young art dealer.

"Oh, Miss Lang," he said. "I'm so glad you've called, because I have good news. I've sold a picture."

"Which one?" My excited breath clouded the kiosk's glass.

"The Barney Copeland."

"How much?"

"Three thousand."

"Should have been more," I said.

"Oh, I don't know. It seems a fair price. It's what you asked."

"Never mind, who did you sell it to?"

"To the trade."

"Oh yes, which part of the trade, another dealer or what?"

"A London firm."

"Which one?"

But before he replied I knew the answer.

"Guggenheims of Bond Street," he said. "I'll post your cheque today."

And I thought, struggling back, Patrick will sell it four four thousand five hundred in next to no time. Patrick, I thought, will always win where money is concerned, because he has made filthy lucre his business as I have made painting mine. He has succeeded, reached his objective through his own single-mindedness, just as I appear at last to be attaining mine. I must try, I told myself, to accept this with equanimity, not get steamed up. Since my spiritual experience I have become much calmer. I have a new perspective. There is faith in my blood.

Back home I find a letter from James on the door mat addressed in the familiar ink.

Dear Christabelle, he has written in his small academic hand. *We so much enjoyed our last visit to you and very much hope that you managed to splash out a bit at*

Christmas and join in village celebrations if any.

You will be glad to know that my research has been continuing with all speed and I now have further news of your relations. I am sure that you will be fascinated to hear that you had an uncle in the Foreign Service, Hubert Appleby, who somehow disgraced himself and left under a cloud. I suspect he slept with a native woman who was in touch with revolutionaries, but it was more or less hushed up. On your mother's side you had a half-sister, now alas dead, who taught Art at Putney High School. The other discovery, which is very relevant to your current aspirations and will intrigue you, as it does me, is that your parents ran off to Madeira, where they remained undetected for two weeks. Counting backwards on my fingers, I have come to the conclusion that you were conceived within sight and sound of the Atlantic, and not in some pastoral English heaven, a fact which must turn your holiday into a pilgrimage. Somehow your motivation for that trip has come from your earliest roots. Isn't that quite extraordinary? Belinda wonders whether you are sensible to go alone, and says she's found a tremendously nice art student who longs to be your disciple and would adore to accompany you – Belinda's words not mine. Do let me have your reaction to this suggestion.

We hope to be down in February, weather permitting. Meanwhile my supervisor is pleased with the way my thesis is developing, thanks to you. And the Poppy picture is well hidden.

I fear this filthy weather has put a stop to your painting. Now that a little money is coming in, don't you think it would be a good thing to have a telephone installed so that we can keep in touch?

Until then we send in writing our best wishes and fond love. Yours, James.

PS. Please keep talking into that tape recorder.

I pour myself a glass of sherry, fetch pen and paper and write a last will and testament, leaving everything to James except for the cottage and furniture which I instruct to be sold, with proceeds split as follows: one quarter to Ellen, three quarters to the PDSA.

James, I think, will deal expertly with my papers, James, who knows publishers and critics, is that enviable being, *a coming man*. Never mind Barney's view on smooth young men. Barney failed in life on all counts but two: propagating the species and art. He might have won acclaim earlier if he had not consistently rubbed people up the wrong way. But how tickled he would have been by this Madeira coincidence, this astonishing evidence of early prenatal influence; but now, eating lunch, I am annoyed with myself for thinking about Barney again, because Barney was really a blackguard. Deliberately I try to think about Oliver. I fetch out Oliver's gramophone (or should I say record player) which I have not played for years, and put on *Semele* by Handel, and when I reach "Where e'er you walk" on the fourth record I cry, because it was at the end of that record that we really came together, and we held each other close, and started the one satisfactory relationship of my life. We had both been incredibly tired because of the bombing. Oliver's face was quite white with shadows like ochre under his eyes, and there were hollows in his cheeks and, as we clung together, the siren went, but we stayed close and suddenly for a time the whole horrible war did not seem to matter any more, simply because we had found one another.

But it is no use going back and back, I tell myself sternly on this relentless January day. Now is the time to pick oneself up and begin again, not wallow in nostalgia and regret. I switch off the gramophone and take up the brochures once more and notice that when I put my head back the whole room tilts. Perhaps it is the sherry I think. But when I stand up the room straightens. I lie right back to test myself again, and find myself vomiting. I begin to feel very small, as I always do if I believe myself to be ill, and clearing up the sick, I decide to leave Marco to Ellen. I totter to the window. Snow is still falling and the sky is darkish like a seal's wet face. Now I dare not go again to the kiosk to phone a doctor, and I feel bereft, because Eva has gone to stay with her daughter in London and Ellen and Annie are too far to reach. I find paper and charcoal and try to draw but my head swims. What was the poem by Walter Savage Landor which Oliver used to recite?

> *I strove with none, for none was worth my strife.*
> *Nature I loved, and next to Nature, Art:*
> *I warmed both hands before the fire of Life;*
> *It sinks, and I am ready to depart.*

But I have often striven with people. Oliver did not, of course. Oliver only strove *for* people. He was a much better person than I am. His patients always came first, which is perhaps why he died intestate, leaving even some of my pictures to his wife. But I must not remember or I shall cry and I don't want to cry. I want to think about Madeira, the land of my conception, and the new rejuvenated me who will come back from the warm seas and stretching pebble-strewn beaches.

Deliberately driving out morbidity, I fetch my pen and start to write to one of the travel firms. Although I feel quite dreadfully ill, my words are well formed and I am pleased to see that no one could guess my age from the writing. My brain must be all right, I tell myself, because I have such good control of my fingers. If there was a cerebral tumour I should feel tingling or numbness. Perhaps it is just what the women in the orphanage used to call "a little turn". *Dear Sir*, I begin, a small hope hammering in my head that inspiration will come back in Madeira like the sap to trees at springtime, and I shall return picture-laden to fill these pages with fresh memories like a schoolgirl with her diary at the beginning of her first love affair. And if inspiration doesn't come, please God let me die, let me float again and find that golden happiness and those friends who have also risen. Oh please, God, turn your face to me and hear my cry. Oh God, thy daughter...

From *The Times*, January 16th, 1983

MISS CHRISTABELLE LANG

Christabelle Lang, the artist, who was found dead in a telephone kiosk near her home in Gloucestershire on January 16th, was a contemporary of Terence Courtney and David Werner at St. Stephen's College, Lambeth, where she studied under Professor Edmund Santbury.

Born on November 27th, 1898, Christabelle Lang was brought up in a Church of England orphanage, which she once described as "harsh, unfeeling and claustrophobically Christian", and later educated at the adjoining St. Catherine's Convent. From there she won a scholarship to St. Stephen's. She always alleged ignorance of her parentage, but recent research has revealed that she was the illegitimate child of an Anglican curate, who was later to become a bishop, and a farm labourer's daughter. In 1921 she won a Sheldon Travelling Scholarship and spent several months in Paris.

She first exhibited at the Circle Gallery, Charing Cross, in 1926 and her work was a regular feature of the St. Stephen's College exhibitions. Critics were however always cautious, expressing only faint praise of her feeling for light and form, and missing the wide range of her ability: from the fine delicacy of her tempera work to the bold brilliance of some of her landscapes.

Although in middle age she was to express a lack of sympathy for abstract art, as a younger woman Christabelle Lang had been much influenced by Barnabas Copeland, her close friend for several years, by whom she bore a son. Her early pictures of London Dockland and riverside are now in demand as much for their period and topographical interest as their intrinsic beauty. A long spell in the country inspired from her a number of landscapes in oil notable for the almost theatrical treatment of the play of light and shade on the woods and fields around her home. Her 'Nutwalk', which has recently been acquired by the Tate Gallery, is now regarded as one of the masterpieces of the inter-war years and has at last established her as an important and previously underrated figure in British art of that period. Much of her later work lacks her earlier intensity of vision, but her sketches of London in wartime, some of which are now in the Imperial War Museum, must rank among the best of the genre.

Personal relationships never came easily to her. A slightly formidable manner masked an emotional and impulsive nature. Strengthened rather than hardened by the vagaries of life, she described herself as a soul rather than a cerebral painter. Although she continued to exhibit with various groups, notably the Tempera Club, Hampstead, and the Twenty One Group in Lambeth, she later eschewed movements and abhorred labels. She wanted to stand and to be judged alone. After the death of a dear friend in 1964 she retreated to her last home, in Wrighton-under-Blockwood, Gloucestershire, stopped painting for many years and was so rarely seen that many people thought she had died. Recently, however, stirred by new interest in her pictures, her thoughts had turned again to work.

She died alone, attempting to summon her doctor in freezing weather. She leaves no survivors; her only child, Daniel, was reported missing believed killed while on active service in Malaysia in 1946. A book of her life and work is planned, based partly on an unfinished autobiography and papers found after her death.

From *The Times*, January 28th, 1983

J. H. writes:

Your admirable obituary of Christabelle Lang omits to mention the charm and buoyancy of her nature, which at times could exasperate as well as please and was the product of a remarkable resilience, which took her forward when other lesser mortals would have floundered. Those of us who remembered her as a shy and far from formidable orphan in youth, marvelled at the driving force behind the more mature woman, which, while undoubtedly complicating her life in some directions, helped her to survive its personal tragedies, at least until 1962 when she left London for good.

Her wit and cynicism were tempered by an innate warmth for those who cared to seek it. Her friendship once given was lifelong.

Nobody and *has-been* were terms she often applied to

herself in moments of rare bitterness or wry humour. Yet, in the eighteen years since her retreat to the Cotswolds, a reassessment of her contemporaries has inevitably led to the rediscovery of her own work, which was forecast by the indefatigable Patrick Guggenheim who still handles her pictures. This might, in a small way, have compensated for the neglect of her work in the 1950s, which culminated in the modest one-man show organised by her friend, Dr. Oliver King, who sadly did not live to see it, at which not a single sale was made – a disturbing comment on the judgment of critics and collectors alike. How sad it is that she did not live long enough to know of the Tate's acquisition, made ironically on the day of her death, of the painting she once described as "The peasants' path to heaven".

ALLISON & BUSBY FICTION

Simon Beckett
Fine Lines
Animals

Philip Callow
The Magnolia
The Painter's Confessions

Hella S. Haasse
Threshold of Fire

Catherine Heath
Lady on the Burning Deck
Behaving Badly

Chester Himes
Cast the First Stone
Collected Stories
The End of a Primitive
Pink Toes
Run Man Run

Tom Holland
Attis

R. C. Hutchinson
A Child Possessed
Johanna at Daybreak
Recollection of a Journey

Dan Jacobson
The Evidence of Love

Robert F. Jones
Tie My Bones to Her Back

Francis King
Act of Darkness
Ash on an old man's sleeve
The One and Only
The Widow

Colin MacInnes
Absolute Beginners
City of Spades
Mr Love and Justice
The Colin MacInnes Omnibus

Indira Mahindra
The End Play

Susanna Mitchell
The Colour of His Hair

Bill Naughton
Alfie

Matthew Parkhill
And I Loved Them Madly

Alison Prince
The Witching Tree

Ishmael Reed
Japanese by Spring
Reckless Eyeballing
The Terrible Threes
The Terrible Twos
The Free-Lance Pallbearers
Yellow Back Radio Broke-Down

Françoise Sagan
Engagements of the Heart
Evasion
Incidental Music
The Leash
The Unmade Bed

Budd Schulberg
The Disenchanted
The Harder They Fall
Love, Action, Laughter and
  Other Sad Stories
On the Waterfront
What Makes Sammy Run?

Debbie Taylor
The Children Who Sleep
  by the River

B. Traven
Government
The Carreta
March to the Monteriá
Trozas
The Rebellion of the Hanged

Etienne Van Heerden
Ancestral Voices
Mad Dog and Other Stories

Tom Wakefield
War Paint